SEE FRIENDSHIP

A Novel

Jeremy Gordon

NEW YORK • LONDON • TORONTO • SYDNEY • NEW DELHI • AUCKLAND

HARPER PERENNIAL

FIRST EDITION

Designed by Jamie Lynn Kerner

Library of Congress Cataloging-in-Publication Data

Names: Gordon, Jeremy, 1988- author.
Title: See friendship : a novel / Jeremy Gordon.
Description: New York : Harper Perennial, 2025.
Identifiers: LCCN 2024026566 (print) | LCCN 2024026567 (ebook) | ISBN 9780063375093 (trade paperback) | ISBN 9780063375109 (ebook)
Subjects: LCGFT: Bildungsromans. | Humorous fiction. | Novels.
Classification: LCC PS3607.O593735 S44 2025 (print) | LCC PS3607.O593735 (ebook) | DDC 813/.6--dc23/eng/20240715
LC record available at https://lccn.loc.gov/2024026566
LC ebook record available at https://lccn.loc.gov/2024026567

ISBN 978-0-06-337509-3 (pbk.)

24 25 26 27 28 LBC 5 4 3 2 1

You forget whole years, and not necessarily the least important ones.

—JAVIER MARÍAS

Part I

AMERICA WAS ON ITS WAY OUT, THE STRANGER INSISTED. THIS much was clear. He wrote history books nobody read, and taught classes nobody revered, and composed tweets nobody shared—a path he didn't regret, because his work was vital and had led him to conclude, at odds with the forgivable naïveté of his undergraduates and the unforgivable naïveté of his peers, that the signs were dismal. Fucked, even. The student loan bubble? Tensions with China? The hollowing of rural America? The collapse of the reasonable center? Medical debt, race relations? My God, the climate crisis, and on top of all that the looming threat of another four years, which, all liberal hysteria aside, our enemies in the Kremlin were probably planning right this moment? It added up, and it added up, and it added up until one actually could not believe how much it was adding up.

"For sure," I said, stretching to see if the bartender was back with my gin and tonic.

"It's ironic," the stranger said, leaning into the bar, "because the Russians are only doing what we've done to however many other democracies around the world. In a way you could say we're getting our just deserts. Actually I'll say it exactly like that: We're getting our just deserts."

He apologized for getting bent out of shape, he knew it made him no fun at staff meetings or baby showers, but if you looked at the world with unblinking clarity—the way one must if they wanted to fall asleep every night with a clean conscience and clear heart—it was the only possible takeaway, and if it meant he was "drinking by himself on a weeknight" instead of "spending time with his kids," well, that was a tolerable trade-off. There were worse fates, such as obliviousness or unearned arrogance, he said, along with something else I didn't catch in the ambient noise before I nodded several times and walked away.

I was not interested in feeling nihilistic about the state of the world. I was more interested in the bar, as part of my ongoing taxonomy of Los Angeles nightlife. The walls were painted pitch black and lined with taped-up cushions. The jukebox didn't follow any logic beyond "music for people to kiss to," skipping from Lynyrd Skynyrd to Travis Scott to Sade. The room was blanketed in an ominous red light, except for the cheap, fluorescent glow of the beer fridges behind the bar. Overall, it had the vibe of an Amsterdam sex dungeon. But it was no more bizarre a place to meet Kelsey than anywhere else in Los Angeles, because I hadn't been anywhere else in Los Angeles. When she suggested it, I didn't possess the knowledge to confidently counterpoint with *No, not there, how about here*, as I might have in New York. I was just along for the ride.

In fact I'd agreed so enthusiastically that I hadn't considered how unusual it was to be meeting her at all, until I walked into the bar. Five more days until my medical leave ended and I flew home, which meant five more opportunities to hunt down the night in this alien city, and I was using one of them to maybe awkwardly hang out with a professional acquaintance, or whatever you called those tertiary friends from way back you followed on social media without ever thoughtfully interacting with them. I knew what Kelsey looked like now because I'd seen photos of her on Instagram and received her press releases in my inbox, but I didn't know how she talked. I didn't even remember how she'd talked when we'd actually known each other, because it wasn't like we'd been close in the first place. She'd mostly been a girl from high school, until the unfortunate sequence of events during the summer after high school when I tried to make her my girlfriend, which not coincidentally was the last time we'd hung out. I hadn't really thought about all that in at least a decade, but it pushed its way to the front the instant we recognized each other in the bar, and after the requisite hug and burst of hellos I sat down hoping she didn't remember, or at least that she hadn't held it against me.

It had been a cloudless, perfect Chicago day. We were sprawled atop Navy Pier's verdant lawns, near the cubist water fountain at the center of the park. Tandem bicycles rolled along the sidewalk; the sound of children's laughter skipped through the air as they chased the perfect cylinders of water erupting from the ground. Navy Pier was infested with tourists and suburbanites, but it had always been one of my favorite places to sit, not spend money, and ponder a bold life move, like bleaching my hair or getting into country music or telling Kelsey she was the dreamiest girl alive, and that was just swell. I would've been happy lying there forever, fixating on her blond punk bangs and her bright red lipstick, searching for the tender look hinting she wanted me to divulge all the infinite mysteries of my heart and mind.

Anthony had said my plan wouldn't work but I'd insisted on proceeding, and I listened patiently as Kelsey rambled about the wonders of home-studio technology while leaving no room to hear my confession of undying affection, which was really just a limp, unexamined crush. That's why I'd invited her out after hearing she'd broken up with her boyfriend at the end of senior year, though we'd talked for an hour and I hadn't made my move.

"With the right plug-ins, your laptop is just as good as a real studio," she said. "Still, I'm going to major in music tech just so I can get that formal experience."

"That's fascinating," I said. "Hey, did you know how potatoes are a perfect expression of love?"

I'd read the whole spiel on a message board after Googling "things to say to girls," and it had struck me as romantically absurd in a way that Kelsey, the punkest girl in our graduating class who didn't hate me, would surely appreciate. Potatoes could survive in any climate. They were ugly, but nutritious. Stick one in a jar of water and it would sprout branches against the glass, growing with and within its surroundings in perfect symbiosis. You could even turn them into a working battery, sort of. Potatoes were durable, hearty, adaptable—everything found in true love, I said, mustering my most earnest voice.

It's hard to believe I was ever such a fucking idiot. Even then, I had enough intuition for faces to tell Kelsey was deeply put off by what I'd just said, though she spared me her thoughts and graciously maneuvered the conversation back to laptops.

Another half hour went by, Anthony happened not to show up, and when Kelsey continued asking where he was, I made a big show of texting to find out. "I'm confused," I told her. "He's usually so punctual." A few minutes later he replied with the exact phrase: *I can't make it, my mom says I have to clean the bathroom*, just like we'd talked about. "He can't make it, his mom said he has to clean the bathroom," I said, showing her my phone.

The truth was he'd never planned to be there in the first place, because I had a desperate crush on Kelsey but high school was over so I couldn't exactly ask her out in the hallways after AP Calculus, and because she and Anthony were real friends a group hang was the perfect pretense for me to see if she might be into me asking her out, and if Anthony happened not to show up I could just skip the middleman and find out for myself. But as soon as I confirmed his absence, Kelsey said she should get going, because she had work in a few hours. I asked if she was sure, and the way she said *yes.* with a period at the end indicated I shouldn't offer to walk her to the train, or force the issue of my undying affection, or even go for a hug. I was eighteen years old, I'd kissed one girl in my life—an unimpressed classmate named Natalia, who'd given me the boot not long after—my favorite movie was *Reservoir Dogs*, and I'd never been published outside the high school newspaper. I didn't yet know how to bring a conversation around to where I wanted, how to subtly gesture at an idea until it emerged through its own momentum. When I looked at Kelsey then, all I saw was a dead end I could do nothing about, except smile and say, "Okay, see you around."

A few days later, Anthony and I went by the Italian ice window where Kelsey worked. We were transcendently stoned and giggled constantly while requesting a half dozen samples, but despite our obnoxiousness Kelsey was warm and talkative in a way that surpassed her professional obligation to the customer. Exchanging jokes under the outdoor lights, the summer heat thick on our foreheads, I could almost believe we'd be real pals from here on out.

"That went well," Anthony said as we walked away. "Not at all what I'd expected." He told me Kelsey had texted him right after she'd left Navy Pier to say how deranged the whole ordeal had been, and how if he ever participated in something like that again, she wouldn't talk to him for the rest of our lives. "She saw right through your trick, dumbass. I told you it wouldn't work."

"What? Shut up." I tried to brush him off, but I obsessed over what had happened for days, devastated by Kelsey's powers of observation, by my total romantic hopelessness, by the unquestionable truth of Anthony's judgment. I *was* a dumbass, and enough of a misguided romantic to think Kelsey could be convinced by my passionate declarations, though she'd never so much as flirted with me, only smiled—something young men confuse for flirtation when so psychotically horny and lovesick the sudden memory of a close hug is enough to sustain them for months at a time. Though I'd eventually learn how to tell the difference between mutual interest and basic courtesy, whatever I believed back then was only enough to make me act like a fool.

Right now, Kelsey looked incredible. Her red lipstick was the same, but she'd grown out her bangs into some wavy mermaid veil, and her punk fashion had evolved into whatever you called the way women looked in French New Wave movies. As for myself, I'd finally learned how to dress, or at least avoid color clashing. My hair was grayer, and I was definitely fatter, but I was still cute and desirably tall, or so I'd been told on second dates. We were drunk, and I felt attractive enough, and if we'd been sitting side by side on the cushions I might've seen it as an electric opportunity to make out, thousands of miles away from where I lived, thirteen years out from that disastrous day at Navy Pier, and ninety-six hours after I had spent the equivalent of my combined utility bill on a purple chore coat that looked unquestionably sharp in the bar's red lights because I was in Los Angeles, and that was what you did here when you finally had a bit of money.

Kelsey had become a somewhat successful musician, and I'd become a somewhat successful writer, and we'd both matured into the type of sociable and interesting adults who could have a conversation more involved than "So . . . what's up?" We still followed each other on Instagram, giving me the satisfaction of informing my postcollege friends, "That's my high school friend," whenever one of her new songs was released to increased acclaim. We'd stopped interacting somewhere in the Obama years, but when I realized I hadn't made any real plans in Los Angeles, I trawled social media until I remembered she existed, thought "Why not," and shot her a message saying I was in town, and did she want to catch up. She responded surprisingly fast, and on my sixth day we were happily drunk and talking like the lifelong confidants we weren't.

We'd gone through current events and career moves and future plans and started on relationship history before she asked if she could get a serious answer about something. "I know it's going to sound crazy, but I have to bring this up," she said. Soon we were dissecting the entire Navy Pier afternoon as though it had happened yesterday.

To my surprise, she didn't seem to remember it with disgust. Like me, she recalled the weather, and the novelty of lingering in a space hated by most people we knew. She made a touching comment about how I was "such a cutie," confirming her complete lack of sexual interest. "Yeah, ha-ha, a cutie," I said, instinctively running my hand through my hair, glad she couldn't see how gray I'd gone.

Most revelatory, however, was the admission she hadn't just relied on my emotionally stunted body language to recognize the construction of the entire charade, because Anthony had spoiled my plan the night before. She paraphrased his heads-up: *Jacob has a crush on you but he's too nervous to say it, so what's going to happen is I'm going to not show up, and then he'll ask you out or try to kiss you or I don't know, he's sort of a retard about this type of thing.* Just like that, with no pretense.

So what I'd correctly recognized as Kelsey's hesitancy following my moronic potato spiel was in fact a more complex web of reactions encompassing her annoyance about the whole scheme, and the secondhand embarrassment of realizing that this had been my big shot, that I'd really thought about this, for real, and could do no better. "I always did attract the tragically awkward types," she said. "No offense." (I nodded sagely, to communicate I had transcended offense.) It was all that experience with the strangeness of boys that allowed her to intuit afterward that Anthony also had a crush on her. In the end she delicately brushed off his feeble attempts as well, easier to do when he never formally announced his intentions beyond a few feints at "chilling."

They'd drifted apart during college, and she had no idea what he was up to. Neither did I, but everyone had a digital paper trail. Kelsey and I took out our phones to discover that he now operated a yak farm in Delaware with his husband. "No way," we said simultaneously.

The people from your youth were rarely doing exactly what you'd expected of them—I knew that, and could process Anthony's unexpected traversal with the all-obliterating logic of "that's just how it is." What was actually unexpected, even thrilling, was learning about how that period of time hadn't transpired as I'd perceived it in the moment—about the secrets churning under the surface. Kelsey and I may have been professional acquaintances, but we'd independently traveled along parallel arcs toward becoming fully considered and reflective human beings, which was why we could soberly—even though we were drinking—break down the interpersonal dynamics of that disastrous afternoon, recalling the emotional valences with the neutrality of a psychologist.

I had the distinct feeling this was an unfamiliar conversation, that we weren't trying to impress each other, that there was no end point in mind. I wasn't trying to go home with her. We weren't going to be best friends the next day, and this wasn't some burning issue we needed to resolve in order to move on to a new phase of our lives. It was just the kind of thing that came up when you had history with someone, history you'd never considered because it didn't matter that much, until suddenly it did.

I WORKED AS A WRITER FOR A MODERATELY RESPECTED WEBsite. It wasn't *The New Yorker*, but it was the last place I wanted to work before *The New Yorker*. My beat was "culture," informally defined as the music, movies, television, books, video games, memes, food, and designer drugs worth thinking about, but more formally understood as the phenomena most likely to be read about by the college-educated eighteen-to-thirty-four-year-olds whose attentions were desperately craved by our advertisers. I inhaled these products seven days a week, and wrote medium-length essays on how readers should think and feel about them. Sometimes my pieces contained original reporting, which if I was lucky meant talking to a celebrity in the lobby of a ritzy Manhattan hotel. Occasionally I was allowed to cover a more obscure happening, like a retrospective at Film Forum or an exhibition at the Whitney, pieces that were read far less but that suggested we were not totally shackled by the abyssal demands of the market, and more importantly identified me as a writer who could reject the industry-wide directives straitjacketing my peers into incoherence and expound at length on "the historical dialectic of the sublime and the bizarre in Hilma af Klint's work," or something like that.

I was a senior writer, allowing me first crack at every subject, much to the annoyance of the junior coworkers who thought people over thirty shouldn't be allowed to write about people under thirty. But I'd labored, in theory, and my aggregate body of work now identified me as "a leading expert on the intersection of modern cultural industries," according to my bio at the college conference where I lectured a room of undergrads on how they, too, could be paid to write about Pixar movies. In nearly three years, I'd survived three rounds of layoffs, my traffic high enough to avoid the vampiric accounting firms responsible for trimming financial waste across departments, which invariably meant firing the writers and editors. I had more than twenty thousand Twitter followers. I went viral every once in a while, sometimes for my writing. Media was dying, "journalist" was a slur in half the country, and many of our competitors had been snapped up by hedge funds who didn't give a fuck about anything, but on the bright side I felt upward of 50 percent confident that I wouldn't be let go before the end of the calendar year. I also knew that relative job security was contingent upon publishing at least once a week, ideally more, the tradeoffs in rhetorical quality made acceptable by the tidy amount that appeared in my bank account every two weeks.

While I cherished the consistency of that tidy amount, those accounting firms and hedge funds couldn't be avoided forever. Not a day passed when I didn't register their presence in the distance, just waiting to expel me from my ergonomic office chair. I didn't only need to justify my value within this precarious landscape, I had to expand it, embrace synergies and growth opportunities, remodel myself into a name included on the pitch decks presented to potential investors. My coworkers felt the same way. We'd become digital men and women of letters for all the typical romantic reasons—we believed we had something to say, we thought public discourse needed correcting, the sight of one's published byline provided a dopamine rush that might last upward of twenty seconds. But under these conditions, everyone quietly understood that if you weren't going up, you were going down. Nobody wanted to go down.

That's why our company had started producing podcasts. The podcast industry was flush with advertising dollars, and the bosses did not want to pass up the opportunity to cash in. Over the last year, our audio division had rapidly grown, and now encompassed a series of podcasts where the more convincingly charismatic and cool writers hung out and talked about whatever. *Shallot of Love* was a weekly series in which our food writers, Hannah and Joyce, cooked their way through buzzy cookbooks and discussed how this coincided with their uninspiring dating lives. *Bro, Dog* was a sports chat panel meant to be a parody of sports chat panels, though my colleagues Bill and Simon seemed to sincerely relish calling each other "pussy." I appeared on these podcasts, and my appearances were mostly fun, but I recognized the limits of relying on my personality to generate highly consumable content. I was a writer, not a talker, and I took pride in the distinction. I understood the value of specifying exactly what was on your mind, without qualifying it with the verbal tics of someone who's "just saying." I did not want to become a character, a collection of familiar jokes and reactions for listeners to project onto, and shuddered at the way my otherwise pleasant coworkers discussed the social expectations foisted upon their increasingly well-defined personal brands.

If we wanted to create a real future for ourselves, the move was to come up with a narrative podcast. Something with a story, structure, characters, themes, moral takeaways, life lessons—a saga with real stakes, ideally even rooted in the personal journey that had brought us to work at a moderately respected website. "Hedgehog content," a gray-streaked man named Karl—my boss Sadie's boss's boss—told us in a morning meeting, where he almost never appeared except when there was an opportunity to make money. A concept for the audience to burrow into week after week, their satisfaction increasing with each installment until they realized they were waiting on edge to see where the story went next and couldn't spend a day without our voices. A concept so magnificent, so idiot-proof, that we could produce season after season, organized around the same loose premise—like the one about the murdered girl that had morphed into the one about the captured soldier that had morphed into the one about criminal justice.

"To be honest with you," Karl said, "I did not listen to those. But I understand they were tremendously popular."

At first I'd resisted. Still, the success of my podcasting peers at the company bred some envy, especially when they received raises. Lately I'd felt a creeping suspicion that Sadie and her bosses were beginning to see me as tolerable deadweight—someone who'd stuck around long enough to become a trusty hand, but who wasn't pushing himself into the profitable future. Besides, what was I really resisting? Surely I could leapfrog the shallow standard set by *Shallot of Love* and *Bro, Dog.* There was no reason why I shouldn't be able to come up with something uniquely monetizable, propelling my income and reputation into the stratosphere. "That's a *great* idea," Sadie told me when I raised the possibility during our weekly check-in. "I've been waiting for you to go for it."

One night, after skimming the pieces I'd written in the last three years for inspiration, I mood boarded a list of potential topics:

- military-oriented superheroes
- cancel culture
- Asian pop-culture representation
- antihero superheroes
- canceled superheroes
- once-beloved books that had lost their sheen in the intervening years
- 9/11
- music inspired by 9/11
- movies not literally inspired by 9/11, but if you read closely they were
- canceled Asian people
- millennial murders
- millennial superheroes
- things canceled by 9/11
- the cultural decline of rock music
- the cultural decline of rock music . . . among millennials?
- the impact of 9/11 on millennials
- the impact of 9/11 on millennials in grade school and high school, at the time
- millennials in grade school and high school
- the impact of grade school and high school on millennials (possibly Asian?)

I continued mood boarding until my list stretched past a dozen pages, before whittling the themes into a cloud of partially conceived pitches and staring at them until the best idea descended through inertia: an investigative series looking at the works of art whose trajectory had been irreparably altered by the September 11 attacks. For example, the makers of *Forrest Gump* had started developing a sequel based on *Gump &*

Co., the literary follow-up to the original novel, but after 9/11, screenwriter Eric Roth had criticized the script as "meaningless." So for this launch installment I'd track down Roth and director Robert Zemeckis, and perhaps even Tom Hanks—pending availability—along with several of the principals to interview them and then talk about how *Gump & Co.* would've most likely arrived in the middle of the psychically fallow Bush years, when the filmmakers might not have been up to the task of inspiring a nation to believe once again that, yes, one man could make a difference. On the other hand, maybe they could've pulled it off. Who could say for sure—except me, backed up by reams of research, hours of interviews, and considered conjecture? At the very least we could probably gin up a lot of aggregate traffic from entertainment websites. The potential headlines materialized before me, as if revealed by prophecy: "Zemeckis Says Forrest Gump Talking About the Iraq War Would've Been 'Too Weird.'"

I thought this was a winning formula and decided to sleep on it. Unfortunately, the next morning it seemed likely that I'd never had an interesting thought in my life. I needed to reject the instinct to make yet another podcast about a *thing*. My coworker Jarrod was developing a series about the history of the Black Panther, the first Black superhero, after which he planned to highlight another Black superhero, and then another, and keep going for at least three or four years until he switched races. "Maybe the Asians," he said, "if I have your blessing." He did, but staking his creative and professional future on what was essentially a series of detailed Wikipedia pages felt immeasurably depressing.

That night, I returned to my mood board. Maybe the move here was to venture inward, as Karl had suggested—find something fantastically unique in my backstory to excavate and interrogate. Seduced by my buttery and authoritative voice, it wouldn't matter to the audience whether I'd dumbed myself down to achieve accessibility, losing the nuances of tone and syntax found in good prose. But how inward? What was unique about my life or the way I saw the world? Why should anyone pay attention to what I had to say?

You're being so dramatic, Ruth texted me, after I gave her my spiel about all this. You're Chinese, or at least half. Your dad is dead. That's more unique than like 80% of the people I know. Ruth had been my high school running mate, a spiky truthteller with dyed green hair and merciless eye rolls ripped right from the pages of a comic book about teenagers who hate everything, except she was also good at homework. She'd been up front about the Navy Pier scheme: "You have got to be *fucking* kidding me," I remembered her saying, a warning I'd brushed off as Ruth being Ruth, the lack of romance in her heart an obvious byproduct of having academics for parents. But I relished being the sweethearted yokel to her acid-tongued contrarian, and I knew she felt the same way. We'd tried dating the summer after our freshman year of college, a disastrous decision. Not all high school best friends were destined to end up together; sometimes they weren't even destined to have good sex. She'd only stopped holding it against me after three years of talking but not really talking, during which time she'd started sleeping with women and I'd learned how to perform cunnilingus, both of which had vaulted us into adulthood.

Once college was over we'd rekindled our friendship following a powerfully drunk, cathartic make-out session, where she choked me out, just a little, on my mother's couch before declaring we needed to keep things platonic. She was one of the few people from high school I still talked to, and certainly the person I talked to most. The advancing years had repealed most of her teenage intensity: She currently lived in Washington, DC, with her fiancé, Donald, who worked for a Democratic congressman, and it had been years since she'd attended a party where they played rap. But she remained an emotional realist, and because we no longer had anything to prove, our text relationship mostly consisted of us bitching about the minor indignations of our lives.

I am not going to make a podcast about my dead dad,
I wrote back. Too cliched.

What about a dead friend? That's maybe less cliche.

Depends on the dead friend.

Just pick one from high school. What about Caroline Blanchard? Josh Richardson ate it in a bike accident a few years ago. But I guess you guys were never close. Jenny Collins—you had that big crush on her, right? That's a podcast. Or Seth Terry, even.

Her logic was callous, but understandable. Whenever Ruth and I got to talking, invariably we ended up discussing our dead classmates, and how strange it was to have so many dead classmates at an age when most people's parents were still alive, as the mortality rate of our graduating class was strikingly high. Our high school was small; even if you didn't know someone personally you knew who they were, so every time someone died you had a new and specific type of relationship to a dead person.

For example, Caroline Blanchard, who'd died of lymphoma our freshman year, was "dead girl from the Gay-Straight Alliance I got poetry recommendations from" to Ruth, and "dead girl from the Gay-Straight Alliance whose lymphoma freaked the shit out of me" to me. Her death was commemorated with a public memorial, where our classmates lit candles and held hands as one of the school ska bands played "Amazing Grace." Jenny Collins, who was T-boned by a drunk driver, was "dead girl from homeroom who seemed nice" to Ruth, and "dead first overwhelming high school crush" to me. But the only dead person who meant the same to both of us, which was "dead best friend," was Seth Terry, who'd died suddenly, in his sleep, the year after we graduated high school.

Seth was in the class above Ruth and me. I'd met him at a meeting for the literary magazine, which I'd joined during my second week of freshman year, and watched in a daze as this cherubic wisp of indeterminate racial origin with floppy hair and skinny jeans explained the group's structure and goals in a bravura monologue about truth, beauty, justice, the ideas we needed to pursue lest we cave into baser feelings like fear and spite, and while the magazine didn't look away from uncomfortable subjects, if you were only here to prove how smart you were, the Libertarian Club met on Thursdays. "But just remember," he said in a singsong voice, "they hate faggots, so that's the type of company you'll be courting." I was fourteen years old, and it was 2002: I'd never known anyone who talked so boldly, who seemed so confident, who was already out of the closet at an age when "you're a big homo" was still an insult of devastating magnitude. He wasn't even the editor of the literary magazine, he'd just taken it upon himself to set the tone for all the newcomers.

Right away I figured out Seth had ascended to that rare status of universally beloved, despite being only a sophomore. He radiated friendliness and exuberance, and was quick to introduce himself and make you feel like you were on the inside of a joke only the two of you understood, even if it was just quoting some lines from *Family Guy*. We were at that age when we thought graphic T-shirts were acceptable, but Seth really did own the best graphic T-shirts, covered with funny puns about communism and dinosaurs. He knew everything about Harry Potter, but in a way that wasn't annoying. That Halloween he wore a ballerina skirt to school, and when the security guards grumbled that it didn't adhere to the dress code, he shouted at them to stop queer bashing and threatened to call GLAAD if they took him to the principal's office. Scripted for a modern teen comedy, that kind of thing would be framed as empowering and norm busting, but to us it was just hilarious, the pigheaded defiance of our friend to tie up his Tuesday fending off attempts to make him wear pants, even though nobody else was in costume.

During the next four years Seth and I were constantly around each other, slowly evolving from school friends to group-hang friends to actual one-on-one friends. We lived fifteen minutes away from each other, so whenever there wasn't anything going on I'd think, *What's Seth up to*, and before long we would be headed to the movies, the bookstore, another friend's house. Those afternoons were the entry point to so many things I'd never thought about before Seth brought them up. He was curious about everything, whether it was classic movies (he showed me *Citizen Kane*) or contemporary literature (he loaned me *The Fortress of Solitude*) or even biraciality, which I'd never thought about for one single second until Seth asked me what it was like to be Jewish and Chinese, he was Black and Brazilian, and from what he could infer about our lives the differences were vast but the experience of being confused for one thing when you were really another thing or in fact two or three things (since he was gay, he reminded me) might be similar, to which I said that I would have to get back to him. He pushed me to be interested in everything around me, not because it would get me into a better college or help me pick a future career or impress my grandmother or be recruited by the FBI or prove some asshole wrong, but because it made life more enjoyable.

Despite our closeness, there was plenty I didn't know about him, or at least never thought to ask. He had some sort of stomach problem and was constantly missing school; he had to stay for a fifth year, which nobody thought twice about because it was great to have him around, whatever the reason. He always made the honor roll, but he told us he was taking a gap year instead of going right to college. His parents were hardcore Catholics who didn't "approve" of his "lifestyle," which mattered only because they said they wouldn't pay for his degree unless it was medicine or law, or unless he married a woman. Seth was definitely 1000 percent a gay man, and he had never thought about medicine or law in his life, so he said he'd just save up money, maybe spend a year or two at community college, and transfer once he had some savings. It seemed unimaginably stressful, but whenever I asked him about it, he said, *It's fine, it's fine.* I was busy starting college myself, so I took him at his word, and a year later he was dead from what his parents had said was a severely perforated ulcer, an ending so tragic and banal for someone so lively that it had stayed on my mind for years, certainly every time I had indigestion.

The gist of all this, I typed to Sadie the morning after texting with Ruth, was a podcast about my dead classmates, beginning with Seth. It beggared belief that someone as vibrant as him had just flickered out of life—but there was also a broader story to be told about, I don't know, digital afterlives, growing up gay in the early aughts when marriage wasn't legal and teens still said "fag" semi-ironically but in the cities it was inhumane not to be for gay rights, communal grief, the mutability of memory under social media, the friends we made along the way, etc. Format-wise, maybe this could be an oral history in which dozens of voices were stitched together to tell the story of a person who'd meant a lot, but also, pause for dramatic effect, meant so much more. I might chime in with some broader reflections about society and so forth, but the insights about our classmates could be shared by all of us—the veterans of Gale Sayers Preparatory High School, who'd suffered through so many deaths and surely felt a way about it.

Before I could start typing up a primer on Jenny Collins, Sadie cut me off. Hmmm, she typed. I'm sorry about your friend, but I think this would be a lot of work to sustain past a few episodes, without a focused narrative. The goal is to come up with something that would come out on a weekly basis for at least 8 weeks. All of these people just died and now you're sad about them, right? No offense.

Sadie was a few years older than me. She'd been a senior writer, too, before graduating into a decision-maker, someone with the authority to encourage or quash any of the ideas I sent her on a daily basis. I'd become overly sensitive to her moods and how they informed our relationship, the days when we could goof around and the days when a bad first date the night before made her feedback a little crueler. She was like an older sister, except she wasn't, and sometimes I resented the way she mistook our daily proximity for insight into my fundamental character. Often her criticism fell along the same lines: I was thinking too much, I was complicating something that wasn't that deep, I should stop clearing my throat and get to the point. But wasn't the point to find something to get lost in, since the audience would presumably follow our curiosity if it was, I don't know, curious enough? This felt like a concept I could really run with.

Frankly, no, she typed. It's a crowded market, and it doesn't seem realistic; I don't want you to chase the carrot until you run off a cliff. I mean, forget the number of interviews you'd have to do—can you imagine how the sales team would pitch it? Just keep at it, there's no point in moving so fast you end up wasting everyone's time, not just yours.

AFTER SORTING OUT THE NAVY PIER DEBACLE, KELSEY AND I ORdered new drinks and moved onto our dating lives (she'd dated seven straight losers and was now experimenting with voluntary celibacy; I was occasionally having sex I enjoyed, but echoed her out of solidarity), movies we'd seen (too few for her, too many for me), celebrity gossip (she had it all, I had none). I told her I was staying with William—William from, you know, math class?—which she received politely. Then we went back to talking about our careers. Lately, she'd started to think it was time to pursue a different track. Music was great—"I, like, *love* music," she declared, with an overdramatic air of whimsy—but critical acclaim did not pay the bills, and neither did streaming. More than that, she felt this pressing need to expand her worldview, to do something different for the sake of it. She was thirty-one years old, it was time to get over herself. She was . . . possibly . . . maybe thinking about taking some improv classes, and she was learning not to be embarrassed about admitting this out loud. "But what about you?"

"First of all, I will never tell anyone that you took an improv class," I said. "I'm trying to come up with a podcast, because my company is so horny for them right now. I sort of think I might be fucked if I can't come up with something in the next few months."

"Why, have they said so?"

"No, but it's in the air. It's always in the air: *You're going to be fucked if you don't come up with something.* My first idea was about high school, but my boss turned me down—so it's back to the drawing board."

"A podcast about high school, huh?" She leaned forward in her seat and gave me a flirtatious grin I understood was not serious. "Something about the girls you tried to ask out at Navy Pier, to no avail?"

"Ha-ha," I said. "No, it was sort of about our dead classmates—I was freeballing ideas and Ruth, who I guess I'm still pretty friendly with, pointed me in that direction. I thought it wasn't bad . . . but I guess not."

"Our dead classmates?"

"You remember how many kids died at our high school: Caroline Blanchard, Jenny Collins, Josh Richardson, Seth Terry? I'm sure there were more. I was really interested in probing the sum effect of that, what it's like for all of us to have had so many dead classmates at this relatively early stage of our lives. You know, like we're supposed to have these common ties, but those common ties fray a lot earlier than any of us could've expected, and then what? So I thought maybe we'd start out by looking at Seth's life, combined with something about legacy, relationships, the lives we lead, digital afterlives—like when someone dies and their Facebook wall is just weeks and weeks of people saying nice things about them, and then you look at their Twitter a while later and realize you're reading the long-ago thoughts of a dead person and you're just like, *What the fuck* . . . that sort of thing. And then I'd move to another dead classmate, and another dead classmate after that until we ran through a season. We could probably do it for three or four seasons? I mean, we had a lot of dead classmates."

"Well . . . Jesus Christ, Jacob," she said, with a small laugh. "Not really the sunniest topic in the world."

"Yeah, but every podcast is about death. True crime, right? And those podcasts are just salacious. This is legitimately tragic."

"Uh-huh, uh-huh." I couldn't tell if her face was playful or dismissive. "Jenny Collins," she said softly, as though she were testing the name for structural leaks. "I haven't thought about her in years. What about Jenny Collins?" Well, I hadn't worked that out so much because, honestly, there wasn't much to circle back to—no cool memories of arms brushed under our desks, no grainy photographs capturing our tragic aughts fashion and tragic aughts haircuts. The only evidence whatsoever that we'd known each other was an unacknowledged comment I'd left on her Facebook wall the year before her death, wishing her a happy birthday.

"But Jenny is a *little* meaningful. First real crush, that's not nothing. And somewhere in there is a thread about . . . I don't know, the lives we lead, like I said, or the impact we have on each other, in all these crisscrossing variable ways that are deep but also not, and it takes a while to figure out what's what." This sounded very drunk as I said it out loud, and I felt the need to qualify. "Or that was the idea, at least. Shit, maybe Sadie was right."

"That's interesting," Kelsey said. "But I suppose I know what you mean. You know I was close with Josh, right?" I did not know this, and adjusted myself so that I was more clearly facing her. Josh Richardson was this do-gooder type who loved hardcore punk and went to every single antiwar protest. That's how he and Kelsey had gotten to know each other, and how they'd become close. In our junior year his mother was diagnosed with cancer, but he continued protesting even in the months of her decline, approaching her impending death with a calmness Kelsey found disproportionate to the looming tragedy. They'd also drifted after high school, but she never forgot how angry Josh sounded talking about things that were so far away compared with how serene he felt about his own life, a centering of perspective that still felt instructive today.

"A bike accident," I murmured. "Jesus."

"I sometimes think about if we might have reconnected, had he lived. You ever think about that with Jenny?"

"Not in the same way," I said, embarrassed to have brought her up in the first place. "With us, it just wasn't that deep." For me, it was less about what could've been. I fixated on a more encompassing void—the idea that a future was swallowed entirely by nothingness, denying any closure or narrative advancement. It didn't matter exactly what hadn't happened, only that none of it had happened, or ever would.

But the reality was that most of the deaths we were talking about hadn't impacted me all that much. I hadn't really known Caroline, or Josh, and barely Jenny; I couldn't completely perceive what had been lost.

"I guess the only one I'd feel comfortable talking about on the record is Seth," I said. "Just because we were so close."

Kelsey's face went gentle, and the space around us seemed to thicken. "We were close too," she said. "God, Seth. That's the one that really sticks with me. Josh . . . that was freakish. But what happened with Seth was tragic on a different level. That's why you wanted to do a podcast on him, right?" I nodded, though I didn't exactly know what she meant. "How did you learn he'd died?"

"The first night of sophomore year," I said, "when all of my friends were busy drinking and playing *Guitar Hero*." I shook my head at how stupid it was. I'd ignored Ruth's texts to call her, because I assumed she wanted to talk about our just-concluded relationship. When she told me, in a shuddering and unfamiliar voice, that Seth had died, I didn't understand what she meant. Even after we continued talking, during which I learned he'd died in his sleep, and that nobody knew the exact cause but everyone said it was probably something with his stomach, I couldn't completely process the words coming out of her mouth, beaming hundreds of miles through the phone, and landing right in my ear. It was totally unimaginable. After returning to my dorm room, I told my roommate that one of my best friends had apparently died, and I just had to say it out loud because it felt completely crazy.

"Damn," he said. "Come hang out if you're in the mood?"

Sophomore year of college was bad for other reasons. My father had died in the winter from a surprise heart attack, which some days felt like the world running its course, other days like something I would never overcome. My mother thought she might lose the house. My classwork was unexceptional; the professors who knew what I was going through kept their distance, and I gave them no reason to collapse it. The weeks passed without anything to distinguish them, and so Seth's death was another tragedy to consider when I closed my eyes. I spent more than a few parties blinking back tears at the most inopportune moments, like right before I was about to flirt or take a shot. It wasn't that I was afraid to look weak or cry; if people asked me what was wrong, I'd tell the truth or something close to it. But I just didn't want to take up anyone's time with something that everybody eventually went through. On some level, it felt like talking about puberty. Death was normal, grief was normal, there were millions of people who had it worse than me, and my pain didn't matter so much even if it was the pain of Seth, the pain of my father, the pain of my grandmother and my cousin Ricky and my childhood neighbor

Sandy and even Jenny, in her own small way, all stacked and cemented into some kind of misery monument lodged in my frontal lobe, demanding to be worshipped even as I said, *It's fine, it's fine,* whenever someone asked.

But years had passed, so the monument only merited a knowing nod whenever I remembered it was still standing. Most of the people in my life today didn't know that Seth had even existed, and why bother filling them in? He lived only in the past, and I lived only in the present. At the same time, I'd passively absorbed thousands of details about people I didn't give a shit about because they'd continued to be online in a way that Seth hadn't, filling up Facebook and Twitter and Instagram with their thoughts and facial expressions, generating an encyclopedic recording of their existence for everyone to internalize. I could recap my old colleague Meredith's postelection slide into radical ecofascism, just based on her posts, but I couldn't tell you Seth's favorite color. Many things about technology depressed me these days, but that really cut to the core.

And this was everything I wanted to unpack in the podcast, I realized as I said it out loud. "But I guess our sales team couldn't sell fucking whiskey ads against it, or whatever."

"Yeah," Kelsey said. We didn't talk for a moment. I worried I'd said too much, which always happened when I drank—I convinced myself we were in the proper physical state to share intimate secrets and assert potential truths, forgetting that because my tolerance was so awful I often reached that state before my drinking partner did, so that even if I felt dizzy and voluble and ready to dispense all my thoughts, it was just as possible that Kelsey was far more sober, that she was currently thinking about what a turn this night had taken, listening to this acquaintance she still remembered as the sweet dipshit who'd once tried to con his way into a tight hug when they were teens give a monologue about death and college and fucking podcasts.

"I'm just thinking about the funeral," she said after a moment. I told her I didn't remember much, just that it was miserable and never-ending. It was held at a massive church on the South Side, with pews that went back at least thirty rows, surrounded by ornate wreaths of purple and yellow flowers. Unlike the other funerals I'd attend, there were no collaged photographic displays—just a single and garishly large portrait of Seth in a gray suit, smiling demurely, propped on a tripod next to the coffin. It looked at least three years out of date.

I sat all the way at the back with Ruth, who'd flown in on short notice. The priest wasn't using a microphone, so it was impossible to hear most of what he was saying. None of his friends spoke, which seemed insane given how many friends he had. The parents didn't say anything either; after the priest was done talking, they lined up at the entrance to receive everyone with penitent faces. I remembered blubbering some kind of stock condolence: "I'm so sorry for your loss," "I can't believe it." This was probably the last time I'd ever talk to them again, I realized as I looked at them, the permanence of the circumstances beginning to harden.

The only thing I'd learned about going to funerals was how they forced you to acknowledge what a person had actually meant to you and how you felt about it, as you looked over their body in the coffin. If you weren't close to the deceased, you couldn't fake it—you'd experience the whole ceremony from a place of detachment, paying more attention to the feelings around you than your own. Or if the dead person was at the end of their life, you might accept the oft-recited bromides about death as a journey, life running its course, "she's in a better place now." The abyss, however terrifying, was no worse than a drug-induced unconsciousness spent on a hard hospital bed. But with Seth all I'd done was sob, which I hadn't even done at my own father's funeral. Much of the day floated away into the ether, a blur of depressive thoughts and wispy generalities.

I didn't recall seeing Kelsey but it made sense, as I knew she had remained in the city for college. "I saw you there," she said, reading my mind. "I think. I'm not really sure." She shook her head. "It was a bad day. There was just too much drama."

"What do you mean?" I hadn't stayed long after the ceremony ended, just long enough to wordlessly exchange hugs with some people and promise Ruth that I'd call her when she returned to Mount Holyoke, before taking the train back to campus. I'd even gone to my afternoon lecture on Chekhov.

Kelsey's face was completely neutral as she looked past my shoulder at something in the distance. "Well, because the guy who sold Seth the heroin he accidentally overdosed on showed up, and was trying to sell to someone else before Patrick and a bunch of Seth's friends chased him off."

I heard her, but I thought I must have gotten it wrong. "Say that again?"

She turned her face back to me, and leaned in closer. "Lee, who sold Seth the heroin he overdosed on, showed up and was trying to sell to someone else, before a bunch of Seth's friends chased him off." I asked her to repeat herself again, which she did, and then again, until I could really understand what she was saying.

OUR HIGH SCHOOL'S COOLEST BAND WAS MILPOOL, AN EMO-punk six piece with a singer, two guitar players, a keyboardist, a bassist, and a drummer. They were absolutely, completely just all right. One guitarist wanted to be teenage Jack White, and the other wanted to be teenage Richard Hell; the singer mumbled through all his lyrics like Julian Casablancas, which helped disguise the fact he could not sing; they were the coolest band because they were good-looking, not because they wrote memorable songs. When I was a junior the Richard Hell wannabe quit because he didn't want to play "in a shitty Strokes tribute act"—his words, circulated in an instantly iconic Xanga post.

Lee had entered high school from an advantageous position: pouty lips, dreamy hair, crystalline blue eyes, perfect punk-rock fashion. In every movie and show about high school there's always a devil-may-care loner type who coasts on hotness and charisma, but the stereotype is true; every high school really does have at least one and Lee was ours. To his credit, he committed fully. While his bandmates were firming up their extracurriculars for their future college applications, Lee knifed anarchist patterns into his locker door and regularly clashed with the security guards. It was unclear why. He didn't come from a bad family, or live in a food desert, or have any sort of structural deficiency in his life. I myself had never invested in punk rock because I didn't think I had much to rebel against, given the sturdiness of my existence. But Lee, for whatever reason, had come not to give a fuck within our privileged magnet school environment. He wasn't that tall, thank God, or else he would've humped his way through the entire high school, not just the girls who wore purple eyeshadow.

Not long after Lee quit his band, he was abruptly expelled. The reasons why ranged from the mundane to the cinematic. One account claimed that upon having his backpack selected for a random search, he bolted to the bathroom and flushed his stash just before they broke down the stall door. Another said he'd just flunked out, having come to the end of what a 1.5 GPA could do for you. The stories were contradictory but altogether seemed more or less true, considering his reputation and his hasty disappearance.

A couple of years after his expulsion he was leading a new group of his own, Black Lodge. That period was a renaissance for Chicago music; there were dozens of exciting artists breaking out of the local topography into national consciousness, and Lee's band received attention alongside Cool Kids, Flosstradamus, Lupe Fiasco, Kid Sister, the Hood Internet, Smith Westerns, Salem, Anon, Good Nurse . . . names I summoned instinctively, despite how much time had passed, because of how exciting it felt to be from a city at the center of so much cultural attention. Lee's band had been one of those bands, absolutely, though I didn't remember much about them.

At any rate I hadn't seen Lee in person since high school, and aside from his band's brief flare of activity I couldn't say I'd ever thought about him until more than a decade later, when Kelsey told me he'd sold Seth the heroin that had inadvertently killed him.

I began bombarding her with questions. Why had Seth bought the heroin? How often was he taking it? Was Lee a dealer? Did they hang out? What did Lee do afterward? Did he know the heroin was tainted? Did Seth's parents know? Did they know about Lee? Did Lee's parents know about Lee? To which she answered I don't know, I don't know, I'm not sure, I think so, I don't know, I don't know, I think so, I don't think so, I don't know, her voice hesitant and her hand curling tighter around her glass, until I became aware that my mania had flipped in a different direction, that despite the morose tones of my sad bastard monologue it was maybe worse to be talking the way I was now.

I apologized, and tried to change the subject, but she waved off my transparent pivot. "It's not that I don't want to talk about it," she said. "But I just forgot that everybody didn't already know this, and it's taking me a moment to remember the details. It's ancient history, you know?"

If we were starting from the beginning, Kelsey said, then we should start halfway through senior year, after she'd transferred to a high school in the suburbs because her father had gotten a new job. (I hadn't remembered her transferring, but when I thought about it I had no specific memories of her that year, besides my ambition to ask her out.) But the security guards at Sayers still let her in; they weren't paid enough to differentiate between current and former students, not unless they'd committed some expulsive crime. Lee, for example, would've been tackled on sight.

If it seemed silly that she'd drive an hour from Winnetka to Old Town on a Tuesday afternoon just to have something to do—well, yes. One afternoon, she was wandering the halls, looking for someone at photography club or art club or the Gay-Straight Alliance, when she started to feel a little ridiculous. Thinking about it, she couldn't believe she had kept showing up to her old school, expecting for some plan of action to spontaneously cohere upon running into someone, anyone. She and Samson, her high school boyfriend, had broken up before she moved to the suburbs, and he was already seeing someone new. The teachers politely registered her presence, but they were confused to see her now that she was no longer enrolled.

She remembered sitting in the cold on the stone benches outside Sayers, feeling like a dumbass who'd overstepped her comfort zone. "I wasn't used to not getting what I wanted," she said. "I was cool, I'm not afraid to say it. But I was there with no friends, and nowhere to go."

Ben was a beautiful biracial punk who'd played in a band called the Spit Lickers, graduated two years before us, and steered right toward the ditch. As Kelsey was contemplating all the cruel mysteries of the universe on those stone benches, he was waiting outside to pick up Rafael, a friend of his, for their usual routine of getting sky high and establishing squatter's rights at Taco Bell. I had rarely interacted with Ben during our overlapping years—like Lee, I was wary of his beauty, his punkness, the sly energy he weaponized into charming half our classmates and some of the teachers. But Kelsey was disarmed by the familiarity with which he greeted her, as well as the soft curl of his eyelashes, his coy smile, his confident laugh. After talking for an hour (Rafael was in detention, having disrupted class), they exchanged numbers.

Before long it was graduation, and then the summer, which included our detour at Navy Pier and several other near flings with boyish doofuses, and before much longer Kelsey was learning about dynamic microphones and compressed mixes and the many other tricks of the trade. She lived downtown in the dorms, and surrounded by the attention of near strangers she nonetheless counted as friends, she slowly felt her personality recover to where it had been before Winnetka. "I didn't feel like a loser anymore," she said.

So when Ben sauntered back into her life, she was in a place to better receive him. There he was, stupidly charming in the corner of an art student get-together, which he'd come to because he had nothing going on except for undergraduate parties at colleges he didn't even attend. Kelsey's personal style was already turning away from punk, but Ben still wore it well, and she was just drunk enough to respond positively to that smile, that laugh, that coy expression and confident approach. When they went home together that night she remembered thinking to herself that she was in control. It was college, she was young, there was no future with the beautiful punk, but there could be this fraction of a moment and perhaps a series of fractions after that.

And for a while, it had gone how she'd wanted—they saw each other once or twice a week, they rarely hung out before the sun went down, they didn't talk about exclusivity, she didn't invite him out with her friends, and he didn't seem to mind. But then he brought her to the Joy House.

The name, she eventually learned, wasn't meant to be sarcastic. Nor did it seem like such a bad place when he invited her over one night, several weeks into their courtship. Rafael would be there, he explained, as well as some other people she probably remembered from Sayers, like Lee. At the mention of his name, I involuntarily tensed up.

From the front it was a sedate-looking Logan Square bungalow. They even had a welcome mat. Rafael and this other guy, Dominic, were technically on the lease, but Ben told her that multiple people stayed there and contributed to costs as necessary. He made it seem like some kind of forward-thinking commune, instead of what it was: a bunch of gross punks in a small house, growing moss together.

But in the beginning it was mostly a space to get drunk, which they did on the ash-stained leather couch they'd inherited from Rafael's uncle. The rooms smelled of semen and cigarettes. Dominic had brought over his younger brother's PlayStation 2 so they could watch movies, and Hector had donated his older brother's college mini fridge so they could keep cold beer in the same room, and Rafael had stolen a record player from some other punks, so they could blast *Rocket to Russia* when they weren't screening *Alien* for the hundredth time.

Though they'd all graduated not that long ago, high school was like an entirely separate part of their life, permanently walled off in the past. In Joy House the only memories that mattered were the ones they made there together. "You remember the band Lee started, Black Lodge?" Kelsey asked. I nodded too quickly. Joy House had a basement where Ben had set up some music equipment—he was always trying to get the Spit Lickers going again, a project that was cursed to fail because they weren't any good. But the first iteration of what would become Black Lodge had taken root in that basement, where Lee would practice by himself. "I remember he'd come over and go downstairs, and we wouldn't see him for hours, only hear the vibrations coming through the floor." They never really talked—she was with Ben, and she sensed Lee didn't have any interest in women he couldn't fuck. One time she told him the music sounded good and he didn't even nod, just went right back down to the basement. It might have bothered her if there wasn't always something else going on, something requiring her attention more than Lee.

Mostly, that meant people getting fucked up in increasingly permissive variations. That was why she allowed Ben to all but finger her on the couch in front of everyone, not that anyone cared, because they were too busy trying to all but finger a girl of their own. She didn't blink twice whenever she stepped over a prone body passed out next to a patch of vomit, and she didn't press too hard the first time she saw Lee pass a small plastic bag of something brown to Hector, who disappeared into his room with a very thin former classmate whose name she couldn't remember now. *Don't worry about it,* Ben had said when she asked. Worry had been such an evergreen constant of her life—over her high school social life, her major, her parents' relationship and her sister's rotten boyfriend, and the future of her music. A handsome guy was giving her license to push all that aside, and she took it.

Don't worry about it became a constant refrain, though after the next few times she witnessed this type of transaction in different permutations among Joy House's rotating cast of characters, Kelsey could pretty well hypothesize what they were up to, especially when she watched Lee pull out a knife and threaten a stranger he'd welcomed into Hector's room just a few minutes before. Somehow, that hadn't offended her middle-class sensibilities. It was dangerous, sure, but in a way that seemed appropriate given the milieu. It was relaxing not to care, to mimic Ben's *fuck-it-all* attitude while she was still young, and besides, she was never in the same room whenever anything was consumed. Ben, for all his dirtbag tendencies, was at least sensitive enough to discern her actual boundaries, not the ones that could be provocatively tested. She would've dumped him, were that not the case.

"Was Ben using?" I asked. That, she knew the answer to: yes, he was.

It was difficult to rationalize today, she said, but she felt comfortable enough to look past the fact that several of the people with whom she spent an incrementally large amount of time, as well as her maybe-boyfriend, were all casually using a drug that parents and high school health classes and government literature and VH1 specials and *Rolling Stone* articles had repeatedly stressed as one of the worst things possible, a drug whose abuse would lead to a future of arm sores, poverty, rehab, early death. Most of them had been using since Sayers and had welcomed whatever else came with it. One night, she and Ben had come back to find Lee gleefully recounting his experience tagging along with his dealer to rig a rival's Jeep with a homemade gas bomb, and accidentally setting off a chain reaction of exploding cars down the block. By that point Black Lodge had released a couple of songs and were attracting a mild buzz, but he was jeopardizing all of that for some bullshit. Yet it all had only registered as a curious detail of her social life. It would've seemed the same if everyone had been into battle rapping, or antiques road shows. To be honest, she said, it was more frustrating that Lee was being so cavalier about his music career, the thing she wanted most but had yet to attain.

Kelsey spoke in a casual manner, but as she talked her face grew soft and melancholy. She wasn't a performer in desperate search of an audience, transparently pausing to solicit my reaction or emphasize a narrative beat. This was just something she was sharing with me because it had happened to come up, and I'd happened to ask for more details, and it happened to still matter. Throughout her story I'd nodded, and nodded some more, and occasionally contorted my mouth and eyes in sympathetic and surprised configurations, but what I was thinking underneath, and had to constantly resist from saying in order to avoid disrupting her cadence, was "What the fuck . . ." and "How the hell . . ." and dozens of other alarmed exhortations.

For the most part I remembered high school like one remembered sports games: it had happened, and I was occasionally happy. I had few regrets, I needed no do-overs, and when some alternate understanding did unspool before me, like when Kelsey had told me of Anthony's deception at Navy Pier, it registered as a novel reading, something that expanded and enlivened my interpretation of the past. What she was saying now felt vastly different, the unveiling of a shadow history that made it impossible to believe I'd ever understood anything at all. Instead of the self-aware, sharp teenager I'd considered myself to be at the time, or even the goofy well-meaning sweetheart I considered myself to be in hindsight, I had instead been some kind of oblivious Pollyanna, surrounded by people and events he not only misunderstood but whose existence was occluded entirely, meandering in a perpetual state of unknown unknowns.

Anyway, Kelsey said, she and Ben stayed together for only a few more months. There were a thousand reasons why—he flirted with other girls; she was encountering new guys in college; there was no possible chance he'd ever meet her parents; to be frank, he didn't go down on her and she was old enough to know that was a problem—but what formally initiated their relationship's end was the night Lee brought Seth over.

It would have been the spring, she said. They were lounging around, trading beers and joints as usual, when the front door eased open. Nobody ever looked up to see who it was, but this time Kelsey did, and as she watched Lee walk in her neutral feeling warped into shock when Seth materialized behind him.

It was the first time she'd seen him in over a year. They'd once been close; she'd been in the Gay-Straight Alliance, as I might have remembered. Beyond that Seth had encouraged her music when she was still mapping the outline of her ambitions, and hadn't yet realized she wanted to perform instead of producing for others. They hadn't talked in a long time, but there were a lot of close friends she hadn't talked to since graduation. That was just how it went. So she was thrown off by his hollowed-out frame, how his chipper voice had ebbed to a nervous burble when she tried to strike up a conversation, before she realized what he was there for. The moment of recognition made her as profoundly uncomfortable as she felt now, remembering it. She didn't care so much about the regular cast of Joy House, but Seth was a real person, and his appearance forced a violent reappraisal of what she was involved with.

"What's Seth doing here?" she remembered asking Ben. He gave her a look, like she had to be an idiot. Or no, that wasn't fair, Ben had never been so nakedly condescending—his look communicated that he thought she knew, because how could she not know, hanging out all the time at a place like that?

When Seth slipped into Hector's room along with Lee, she told Ben she was leaving and not coming back. Not tonight, not ever. Ben laughed and said she must be kidding, and only when she was out the door did he take her seriously. On the sidewalk he tried to convince her nothing was wrong, it wasn't anything to worry about, but she didn't budge.

"All right," he said, his voice newly cutting. "If you want to be some kind of stuck-up bitch, go ahead." What surprised her was how unmoved she was by his vitriol. Her affections had shifted immediately, casting him and this scene as entirely disposable. It was followed by a soul-coring shame that it had taken this long, and in the following days she got in touch with Seth over text. At first he was receptive, and even sympathetic—yes, it was weird to have seen her at Joy House, he didn't mean to alarm her, it was just a bit of this and that he was up to these days. It's really okay, he insisted, and she believed him. Their correspondence quickly tailed off, and though he stayed on her mind, she soon returned to her usual routine of school, parties, studio sessions.

It never occurred to her that he was at any serious risk. It really didn't. At that age, who was? Even if they were using heroin.

The funeral had gone very differently for her.

She arrived early, and up close she heard every word the priest said, a ceaseless procession of platitudes that emphasized Seth's role in the church (he never went, she thought) and his status as a devoted son (his parents rejected him, she thought), and the longer he talked the angrier she became.

It was insulting, this pretense of civility and ceremony. They were all behaving as though he'd passed peacefully in old age, but Kelsey had been on a fact-finding mission, working the Joy House denizens she was still friendly with to construct a partial timeline of events. In her mind, there was no hesitation about what had actually happened. Samson had scoffed at first, and scoffed again when she'd repeated herself over the phone, but then took her seriously as she continued to insist. Eventually, though, he told her to stop. Seth had made his decisions. It wasn't what she wanted to hear but it was the truth, and if there's anything he'd learned it was that you had to allow people their mistakes.

"That's the stupidest fucking thing I've ever heard in my life," she spat. Their friend was dead. That's the mistake they'd let happen.

But they were together at the funeral, and she concentrated on squeezing his hand as she tried not to let the priest's words get to her, holding tight the feeling of rage and sadness thrumming her skin. In order to distract herself, she turned around to see who'd shown up. Never before had she sat in a packed church; she'd been raised with no religious affiliation and rejected the concept even more as a teenage atheist. It was quite something to look at. She skimmed the curve of the ceiling as she looked up from the ground, taking in the friezes and brass work and golden crosses.

Her eyeline trailed down to the pews, where she looked at the rows stretching all the way back to the entrance, trying to figure out who she recognized. Mr. Bortz, who taught Algebra 2. Rose, who worked on the yearbook. Ben, *yuck*. And Lee, who was sitting next to Ben and Hector, and reaching into his coat pocket.

He was wearing a ratty top hat, a stained black-velvet jacket, and an uncinched necktie over a T-shirt of his own band, an outfit she recognized from when they were just hanging out and now instantly loathed. Hector kept glancing to the side, hoping to sniff out anyone who might be surveilling him, but Lee looked glazed over, like someone had wheeled him to his seat. He pulled something out and attempted to hand whatever it was to Hector, an action she'd witnessed a thousand times at Joy House, but lost his grip. She watched Hector scramble to pick it up from the floor as Lee sat there, his mouth pulling into a small grin as he made a *whoopsy-daisy* face. She was too far away to catch Ben's eye, but could see him start to laugh.

Whatever sadness she'd been feeling convulsed in another direction. She felt her vision cloud over, and heard Samson suck in his teeth as her nails dug into his palm. "What's the matter with you?" he whispered, softening when he registered the furious look in her eyes. But she was too upset to speak. All she could do was shake her head, until she realized the priest had stopped talking, and it was time for something else to happen.

I ASKED SEVERAL MORE QUESTIONS, CONSCIOUS NOT TO OVERstep any boundaries or make her feel as though I were holding her accountable for events she'd barely been a part of. But Kelsey was eager to answer, she held nothing back, and said "I don't know" when she didn't know. At the exact moment I worried I had pressed for too long she anticipated my thoughts and said something like *It's good to talk about this, it's been a very long time, I just don't know anybody who cares these days.* Then we'd circled back to discussing work, until it was suddenly midnight and time to go.

Outside it was very still except for the occasional car rattling down Sunset, and the wafting chatter of the drunk and tired passing us on the street. Our conversation lapsed into small talk, we went over our plans for the next few days and how the weather had been, making loose gestures about seeing each other the next time someone happened to be in town. An idea had come to me as we'd talked inside, and it returned to me now. "I might go back to my boss with all of this," I blurted, careful to notice how she reacted. "It might be the hook we need to get the ball rolling . . . and if she's into it, I'd like to formally interview you."

Her smile glitched, just for a second. "I was afraid of that," she said. "Jacob, you know . . . it happened so long ago, and I don't know the use of dragging it back up."

"But you did tell me," I said.

"I know, I know." Under the white glare of the street lights, she suddenly looked and sounded very exhausted. "I suppose it's very easy to tell you things. But listen: Can't you just hear something, and leave it at that? It's your job, I get it, I don't want to discourage you from doing what you need to do. But I don't know if I can promise anything."

I couldn't ask for more, so I nodded. When my rideshare was close, I asked if she wanted to hop in, I'd have the driver stop at her place first and she didn't need to worry about splitting the cost. But she said it was okay, she was only ten minutes away and she liked the walk.

"Even when it's dark?" I asked.

"Yes, even when it's dark." We hugged, holding our embrace for a few seconds before she pulled away, turned toward the hills, and disappeared into the night.

I grew drowsy in the car. When it came to a stop, and the driver told me we were at my destination, it took a moment to recognize my surroundings. Now I stumbled up the driveway to William's house, mindful of the incline's stress on my ankles. His golden retrievers met me at the unlocked gate leading into the house, barking until I addressed them firmly by name and pointed my finger at their heads. Instead of following them inside I walked over to the lawn, which offered a reclined view of a distant skyline localized within a tight circle, surrounded by the city's sprawl. I stumbled onto a striped lounge chair on the grass, my brain emulsifying from the momentum, and took out the crushed remnant of a joint I'd bought the day before.

As I thought about it—and it was hard to think about it, because odds were strong I should prepare to throw up—I couldn't believe I'd so quickly accepted the circumstances surrounding Seth's death. Sure, maybe there was something wrong with his stomach, but nobody just died in their sleep at home, in their own bed, at the age of twenty. We'd seen each other less than a month before he died, and he'd seemed happy, normal—like Seth, like he always did. Beyond that I'd never seriously pursued an answer, and to my knowledge neither had anyone else. What were we going to do: Demand answers from his parents? Bribe the coroner? Dig up the corpse, run our own tests? Plane tickets were expensive, classes and tests were difficult to miss, and in the end most people had enjoyed Seth's company but likely hadn't talked to him in months, or even years. I don't know what I would've done had I not been at college just a few miles north, capable of hopping the train to his funeral. Did I love him enough to spend five hundred dollars on plane tickets? Eight hundred dollars? Twelve hundred dollars?

This was the type of thing I'd wanted to work out in the dead classmates podcasts, before Sadie had shot it down—the ties binding us upon closer examination, the market forces and marginal differences that subtly affected our feelings about each other. Now I had new motivation to return to the scene of the crime, especially since it might actually be a crime scene. The issue to sort through, I thought as I moved inside to retrieve what was left of a burrito I'd clawed apart earlier that week, was how to combine these new thoughts with my initial idea. The fact that Seth had died from an accidental heroin overdose, enabled by the apparently thriving heroin ring at our high school, spearheaded by the former scion of a buzzing indie-rock scene, unsettled the entirety of the original premise. In fact, it revived and transformed that initial premise into something dynamic, exciting, titillating—something Sadie couldn't deny, once I brought it to her attention. Surely the sales team could do something with drugs and rock 'n' roll, and the sex that would probably pop up once I started my research.

I found the couch, burrito in hand. First, I needed a source list. Kelsey knew a little, and the members of Joy House—Ben, Hector, Rafael, the girls she'd mentioned—knew a little more, but twelve years ago, while not an untraversable stretch of time, wasn't just an airport layover. I wasn't afraid of looking for answers, but I did not live in Chicago, I barely talked to anyone from high school, I didn't check Facebook. And it wasn't just the Joy House members I needed to pin down. They'd only seen Seth in a very specific context toward what had been the end, and if I was trying to understand how he'd arrived at that point I'd probably have to start much further back and cast a wider net among all of the people who'd known him, not just the people he'd done drugs with. So maybe it didn't even matter that the former group, like me, had received an incomplete picture of his death; they had their own feelings and memories of his life, and that he had apparently lived a very different life beneath the surface didn't necessarily render those feelings and memories moot or misguided. In theory, at least. I wouldn't know until it all shook out. And his parents—no wonder he'd been taking drugs, given his home life. Hadn't they ever wondered what their son had been into? Or did they just want to bury it for good, along with everything else they didn't like about him? I needed to talk to them, I needed to figure out what they knew and didn't know.

The golden retrievers agitated for a scrap of meat, and I tried to shoo them off. I caught a glimpse of myself in the reflection of the television, lit up by my computer screen, wad of burrito in my hand. My hair had lost its shape; the top buttons of my shirt had come undone at some point, and about half of my chest was showing. I laughed at how fried I looked, before another, incredibly obvious thought struck me: I needed to hear from Lee. Why had Seth bought the heroin? How often was he taking it? Was Lee a dealer? Did he know the heroin was bad? Did they hang out regularly? What did Lee do afterward? Did his parents know? Did they know about Lee? How could Lee be in a buzz band while he was enabling his friend's overdose? Was Lee's buzz band even that good? Were they even that buzzy? These were mostly just the same questions I'd asked Kelsey, I realized, but she hadn't known and I still wanted to know.

After hunting down my Facebook password, I logged in and clicked the button in the upper-right corner to clear my sixty-two notifications, most of which were spam. My abandonment of the platform was only the natural end point of a slow decline in usage throughout my twenties, coinciding with the ongoing reports about how a tool meant to facilitate hot sex between single coeds had somehow caused the downfall of American democracy. Most of my "friends" were from high school and college, which is why my first search for "Lee" immediately returned a profile for "Lee Finch," with whom I had forty-five friends in common, and whose profile photo was recognizable as the adult version of the person I'd known as a teenager.

Before I clicked further, I opened a new window and Googled "Lee Finch," combined with every social network and noun I could think of. I also opened another window to separately search for Black Lodge band, Black Lodge Chicago band, Black Lodge streaming, Black Lodge review, Black Lodge Pitchfork, Black Lodge the Fader, and several other phrases that might return any receipt of their existence.

All I could find were a couple of press clips dating back to 2008 and 2009—small write-ups in the local alt-weekly, a couple of track reviews in defunct music blogs. "I'm mostly just hanging out and trying to survive," Lee had told a writer at

Drowned in Sound, in response to a question about his goals. Their music wasn't streaming on Spotify or Apple Music, but a couple of tracks had survived on YouTube. I plugged in my headphones and listened to a gauzy garage rock song called "Dreaming" and a druggy Joy Division–type thing called "In the Final Run." It wasn't amazing, but there was something there . . . I couldn't remember exactly why I hadn't paid more attention, but most likely I'd brushed off the concept of "Lee Finch's band" altogether. Lee had just been some high school hotshot in my peripheral vision—there was no reason to believe he was capable of anything special. But now, I had to admit it wasn't bad.

Information about his personal life was harder to find. He didn't have a Twitter, at least not under his real name. He didn't have a LinkedIn. His Instagram was private. Nothing else looked promising, so I clicked back to Facebook. The initial rush I'd felt downgraded into disappointment: his photo was the only public asset, as everything else was hidden by the privacy settings. I couldn't see how many people had "Liked" his profile photo, but I could zoom in to examine the details. His sideburns were long; his face was wider; he wore sunglasses; he was also holding an acoustic guitar.

I ran a few more Google searches, none of which came up with anything interesting, and went back to Facebook. There was nothing more to look at, so I clicked the "Add Friend" button at the top of his profile and stared at it for a few minutes, as though he might respond this instant.

When it became clear that wasn't the case I went downstairs to the guest room. Before shutting the lights off, I opened up an email to Sadie and tweaked it until I was comfortable sending it off at this late hour. Then I got in bed, where I slept for ten hours, and didn't dream.

I WOKE UP TO A TEXT MESSAGE FROM HAMILTON, ASKING IF WE were still on for lunch. After showering, I checked Facebook to see if Lee had approved the friend request. He hadn't, and I tried to not think about it, which only made me think about it more.

The bedroom door opened, and a ball of foil smacked me in the chest. "I'm not your maid, bitch," William said from the hallway. "And the dogs have no object permanence—they do not register the coffee table as forbidden territory, and will scavenge whatever remains of your disgusting burrito."

"Sorry about that," I said, lobbing the foil toward the trash can and missing badly. "It was . . . a late night."

"Yeah, I heard you stumbling around. At least you didn't bring a girl over."

"Don't remind me. And I know you're not my maid, but please, sir—perchance would you have any breakfast on hand? A smidge of breakfast for an old friend, down on his luck?" He flipped the bird, but gestured for me to follow as he turned to walk upstairs.

Besides Ruth, William was the other person I kept up with from high school. Though we had some of the same friends, we had been only a little chummy back then. He was somewhat of a snob, and I always suspected he considered me obnoxious, confirmed whenever we accidentally found ourselves alone together and he'd take a close interest in the wallpaper.

Things were different on our first day of college, when we—the only two people from Sayers—were assigned to the same orientation group. While most of our peers were idling around, he'd beelined toward me and drawled, "Well, well, well," like an old-timey detective. Some evolutionary process had taken place in the summer after graduation, and withholding William now looked like the modern version of an old Hollywood star: hair gelled into a suave pompadour, puckish glint in his eyes, skin dewy and smoothed over by anti-acne medication. He was wearing a light jacket, even though it was seventy degrees outside. It was like some postscript to a movie sequence in which a nerd takes off his glasses and suddenly has cheekbones, and I was flattered by the directness of his approach.

We exchanged amiable and inconsequential small talk as we crossed the campus, and eventually fell in with a larger group of students, one of whom asked for his last name so that they could add him on Facebook. I watched him hesitate for a split second before answering: Smith. "You heard that right," I said, failing to be cool about it. Somehow, we'd grown much, much closer than we'd been in high school. (He did, one drunken night, confirm that he'd found me obnoxious.) When my father unexpectedly died at the start of winter term, he came to the funeral—and when his own father unexpectedly died at the start of spring term, I returned the favor. I only missed a week of school, but William was gone for nearly a month. Most of our friends struggled with what to say because even the intelligent ones didn't know or understand anything about anything, but I thought about what would help and settled on a short email reading something like: *Sorry, that sucks. It sucks for me, and I think it's just going to suck for a while.*

The experience had further bonded us once he came back, and even though we'd moved to opposite coasts after college, we'd remained close. When I texted him that I was taking a break from work and that I was thinking about going to Los Angeles, he offered to put me up for my entire stay. When I said I'd be happy to take an Uber to his place, he showed up at the LAX terminal in last year's Lexus, as handsome and svelte as he'd been in college. I pointed this out, and he said he had a personal trainer. "Five sessions a week," he said as he hoisted my suitcase into the back of his car.

"Jesus, why don't you read a book sometimes?"

William hit me with his most sweetly dismissive look and slammed the trunk shut. "I'm a gay man in Los Angeles, I have a reputation to maintain."

Within a few minutes of leaving the airport we'd assumed the jocular and performative conversational rhythms of our college years, now undergirded by a maturer understanding of where our lives had led. Unlike the childhood friendships tinged deeply with nostalgia for the tiny people we'd been, and the fully adult friendships inflected with pragmatic considerations like "Can this person help me get a job?" and "Are we too old to snort—what's this called, Vyvanse?" William and I had bonded as semiformed young people still piecing together our desired identities. Our lives had been radically and thoroughly reconstituted by death, and we'd watched each other figure it out through this mutual annealing, which is partly why we remained fond of each other even as we'd taken different paths. In some regards we were still near strangers trying to feel each other out on the first day of orientation, now that he was a financial adviser and objectively rich, and I was a writer and subjectively rich by the standards of my writer friends, but objectively not rich at all.

We stopped at the In-N-Out just outside the airport. After parking, we convened on the grass outside to eat. I'd picked Los Angeles because it was the farthest and, most importantly, sunniest place away from New York where I had friends, but it had always seemed like a frivolous city. New York was the epicenter of relevance and culture, an all-night paradise where you closed the bars at four and grabbed a bodega sandwich at five, a bastion of staunch realism in a world peddling artifice and falseness at every turn. Where else could you live?

I'd invested all of my twenties into becoming a "New York person" but I still felt like more of a "Chicago person," except for when I was visiting home. Relatively speaking there wasn't much difference between the two, except New Yorkers were snobs and Chicagoans were almost proudly anti-intellectual. But whichever way you broke it down, the reality was I'd spent my entire life in cold-weather cities where everyone was locked in a mutual race to appear more grimly honest, because they thought it made them interesting. In New York it was increasingly unbearable being surrounded by so many twenty- and thirtysomethings who pathologized each new experience as some ironclad proof of reality, when they were just anxious and sexually confused like anyone else. Finality was always in the air; everyone needed to be the greatest in order to avoid falling behind and being declared out of date by the next generation of narcissistic strivers who, too, would have a mental breakdown the moment they realized their existence was built on quicksand.

"Huh," William said, not unsympathetically, as he crumpled his burger wrapper. "All right, we should probably get going before traffic hits."

As we drove toward his apartment in Silver Lake, which I understood was the L.A. equivalent to the stereotype aroused by the idea of Williamsburg, a neighborhood I avoided in

New York, William told me he was also rethinking things. He worked at a big firm, though every time he explained his work beyond "I help rich people get richer," my brain emptied out. "Isn't the money good?" I said. His expression didn't change as he confirmed the salary was phenomenal, as were the semiannual bonuses, and the office freebies like Dodgers tickets and personal electric scooters. He had no student loans, no spouse, no real medical problems besides an occasionally invented need for Adderall. At some point the money began stacking up, and even with the charitable donations, the spontaneous vacations to Cabo and Milan, the 401(k) contributions and car lease agreements and personal trainer expenditures, there was more of it than he knew what to do with.

I thought about joking that he could give some of his money to me, except it wouldn't have been a joke. Instead, I said: *Uh-huh, uh-huh,* my expression thoughtful and concentrated. I was good at listening—friends had complimented it as a particular skill, as had ex-girlfriends. William wasn't one to brag about money, and during my previous trips—always for work, never for pleasure—I'd figured out that in Los Angeles it was gauche to ask people what they did for work, unlike in New York, when it was the second or third thing that came out of anyone's mouth. Here you had to discern what people did behind their back, and the soft and hard power they wielded, so that you could have a conversation where all the stakes were intuitively sketched out without anyone having to clarify them out loud. I understood all of that, but I also wanted to hear him say, "I make four hundred thousand plus benefits," which he eventually did once I asked.

We pulled through some neighborhood whose name he said, but which I didn't recognize and forgot right away. For the first time I could observe buildings that rose high above house level, how the street widened into several lanes. We passed a bail bondsman with a sparkling neon sign in front, a couple of coastal chain restaurants. His office was nearby, which was part of the reason he wanted to leave—no matter where he was coming from he always had to pass through this area to get home, which always made him think about work and how he no longer cared about it.

"So what are you going to do next?" I asked. He was thinking about getting back into writing, he said as he made a right turn.

It was easy to forget that William and I had both majored in journalism, now that he was a wealthy man. He'd been our peer group's most talented stylist, but as graduation approached he revealed he was studying for the LSAT. Carving out a worthwhile writing career would take too much time, and he didn't want to slum it in New York. I'd teased him about being a quitter roughly a hundred thousand times, but after I was slumming it in New York and William was posting photos from Cabo, I'd summoned the decency to declare it a draw.

But earlier this year, he'd swung by his mother's house, where she'd moved in her widowed retirement, to pick up an unused blender. He'd ended up sidetracked in the spare room she still kept for him, riffling through boxes from college that had survived the trip from Chicago. Among them were a few copies of the school newspaper and some of the essays he'd written for class, and he spent several hours combing through his old writing, retracing his evaporated thought process and admiring the clarity with which his younger self had diagrammed the world—a clarity that seemed absent in his current life. From the future, the reasons why he'd abandoned writing felt small and unfortunate, and he once again felt the itch of self-expression.

He'd started with nothing serious, closer to journaling than anything else. But he'd kept at it and slowly erected the outlines of a memoir about his father. "I know writing about your dad isn't the most original thing, but I really feel like I have something worth sharing," he said, as sincerely as I'd ever heard him. It was difficult to think about one's life that way, until you came to the end of a story and realized it might be yours to tell.

BREAKFAST WAS A HALF-FULL CUP OF GREEN-GRAY PROTEIN sludge, which William had prepared every morning. So far the smoothies had mostly bored a hole through the impacted toxins and preservatives lining my colon and pressed me to abandon his kitchen for the bathroom, where I'd spend a humiliating stretch of time expunging my bowels. Nonetheless I'd continued to drink them, motivated by the belief they were doing something for my system, even if that meant accelerating its total collapse. I wanted to be healthy in Los Angeles; the sun and the beautiful people and their haircuts were a powerfully motivating factor.

William was about to meet his trainer, so we took our sludge standing up. "Where are you going? What did you get up to last night, actually?" I had told him I was meeting Kelsey, but he'd declined to join. Besides me, William had lost touch with his high school friends. He hadn't known Kelsey all that well and felt no need to go through the motions of reconnecting.

"We just got some drinks . . . too many drinks, and too much conversation, it's why I went burrito mode. But I'll tell you later—I do have to get out of the house."

Apparently everyone I knew in Los Angeles lived on the

east side, whether it was Silver Lake, Los Feliz, Echo Park, East Hollywood, Atwater Village, and now Highland Park, where I was meeting Hamilton. Every city had its constellation of young, hip people congregating around the coffee shops, bookstores, and cool restaurants that propelled salaried and/or trust-funded urban life, and I was stitching together the vision of Los Angeles that matched my vision of New York, where the circumference of a place narrowed to a needle point and you could confidently broadcast an idea of "what the city's like" based on a few recurring locations and routines. No doubt I'd live over there, too, were I ever to change cities.

I'd first become aware of Hamilton in high school, when I started noticing his byline on the music magazine articles I liked reading. Toward the end of college I'd followed him on Twitter and was blown away when he followed back, only to find he spent most of his time dryly posting about meals he'd eaten. We had a few public exchanges, carving out a loose acquaintanceship that would've dazzled both my fifteen-year-old self and Seth, who'd also loved Hamilton's work.

From my first days using the internet it had always felt normal to first interact with someone through a message board or personal blog, and after months of glacially advanced contact, tentatively tunnel through to an authentic in-person friendship. Twitter paid off after I moved to the city and attended a record label holiday party for the free drinks only to find myself greeted by Hamilton, who somehow recognized me almost immediately. As we talked, I realized he worked for this label, that he'd been working for them for a few years, that I couldn't remember the last time he'd written something. The transition had occurred seamlessly and invisibly, away from the internet.

Hamilton and I continued to stay in touch, mostly over email. He'd hopped around and was now doing A&R for one of the majors, working mostly with the types of bands who would've once scanned as "alternative" but were now anxious to make money. We hadn't talked in a few years, and he'd switched coasts at some point, but when I'd posted a photo of my In-N-Out burger to Instagram—ironically or sincerely, I couldn't really tell—he messaged me saying that we should meet up for lunch.

My rideshare stopped at the base of William's driveway, and I quickly hurried out the door. My driver drove a new Corolla and had the considered look—slicked-back hair, leather jacket, carefully trimmed beard—of someone who was clearly trying to be somebody in the city, though maybe he was just good-looking and earnest. The sky was uncontroversial and radiant, and as we wound our way down the hill and onto the highway, my driver, whose name was Adam, asked me where I was from. Without thinking about it I said New York, but before I could correct myself, he launched into the story of his life. He was from Oklahoma, and had been living in Los Angeles for three months. He was trying to be an actor, he said, and working part time. Driving for Uber wasn't so bad, you read stories about high fees and crazy passengers, but the money was totally solid and the people were actually nice, and it was easy to do in between auditions and gigs, and you were your own boss, a feeling he relished. He hadn't found much success thus far, but he was looking into joining an improv team at the Upright Citizens Brigade because that's where all the stars had been discovered. He lived in Santa Monica, in an apartment on the beach with three other actors he'd met on Craigslist. Los Angeles was so much different from Oklahoma, which, duh, it was Los Angeles and Oklahoma was Oklahoma, but even so he'd been shocked by the culture clash; there was a happier vibe you couldn't manufacture in a dark place like Tulsa. He and his friends had been the happiest people they knew, but it didn't matter, there was too much baggage and residual depression from, when he thought about it, the actual Great Depression. He'd been the only one of his friends to make it out here after high school, because his parents had given him his dad's second car but also because most of his friends would probably top out at community theater. He wasn't going to judge that, but you know, it was, *you know,* community theater, not to judge. He was twenty years old. His favorite movie was *The Dark Knight.* He hadn't spent a lot of time in Silver Lake, though he knew it was where all the cool people were. Most of the parties he attended were in West Hollywood. He hadn't experienced anything too crazy, though he'd heard all the stories about casting couches and cocaine and prepared for the worst. Not that he was ready to pimp himself out, he said, with an overeager laugh, just that you had to be ready for whatever it took, though he really hoped that didn't mean pimping himself out.

While he talked, I didn't say a word beyond an occasionally affirmative *uh-huh*. The drivers here were friendly, that was a difference I'd noticed—back home it was all grunts and frustrations, the occasional outburst at a bicyclist. I didn't mind listening to Adam, but his monologue evoked a combination of sympathy and embarrassment. For all he knew I was the person who could elevate him to the next tier of Hollywood society—a rich and mysterious color-coordinated someone with spotless shoes and a better jacket, who lived in a ritzy house like this one, who might respond to this flurry of self-promotion with an invitation to audition for some upcoming studio picture. But I didn't want to correct him, so I said all of that sounded nice, and I was rooting for him, as I excused myself to fake a call to Hamilton and pronounce loudly that I was just a few minutes away, which although not true at all produced its desired effect: silence.

THOUGH MANY OF MY FRIENDS HAD PERFORMED IN THE SCHOOL plays, not one of them had pursued acting in the long run. Even if they indulged the pleasures of makeup, costuming, a spotlight, and the knobby fondling of your costars, acting wasn't practical unless you had some kind of generational talent, and thankfully Mr. Stewart, who ran the drama club, was kind enough not to lie.

Understanding they were only motivated amateurs had freed up the drama club from the anxiety of expectation, and as a result Mr. Stewart drew deeply from the student body whenever he was casting. Kelsey, for example, had donned a wig over her punk bangs and done a nice job as Marianne Dashwood. Ruth nabbed a few supporting roles; the members of Milpool guested with the house band; even William had a bit part, at some point. Seth had performed many times, though I could only recall his leading role in a Chekhov play, during my junior year.

In the car, I blocked out the sound of Adam's dashboard drumming and concentrated on summoning the memory. On Wednesdays, when we both had a double lunch period, Seth and I would find each other to eat off campus, and on the day *The Cherry Orchard* opened, Seth asked if I wanted Einstein's. Neither of us had jobs, but for just a few dollars you could purchase a warm bagel luxuriously garnished with butter, all the sustenance we needed at that age.

A couple blocks from school, we walked by the sex shop remaining defiantly open amid Old Town's ongoing gentrification, where a neon cutout of a naked woman in the window threw off pink light, even in the sun. "It's time," I said, nudging Seth with my shoulder as I usually did whenever we passed it, and he humored me by chuckling as he usually did whenever we passed it.

I could still appreciate these uncomplicated moments, the bits and gags we continually reenacted because we had no real imagination, no external force inducing us to behave more maturely or take ourselves more seriously, and could thus crack about a hundred million jokes about someone finally wanting to buy an ass dildo as though it were organically funny, which at that age we thought it was. We passed the Panda Express just beyond the sex store, and Seth pointed to the window. "Want to say hi to ancestor?" he asked, in a bad Asian accent. I looked, as I always did, at the anonymous Chinese person working the food line and shook my head. It was a sign of our closeness that we could make these uncreative offensive remarks to each other but never in front of other people—a trust we both intuited even as we were teenagers and could barely describe the dynamic.

Seth was in a jittery mood. He wasn't sure whether he had all his lines down, if he knew his cues, if all his costars were locked in. "I'm still not sure if I completely understand the character," he said, as we neared Einstein's. "I haven't figured out if I'm going to do my accent."

Even considering his usual confidence, this was something else. "You have an accent for this?"

"I mean, you know my accents. *I have faults enough, but they are not, I hope, of understanding.*"

"That is straight-up fucking Mr. Darcy, idiot."

"Yeah duh, *idiot*—I'm saying I have accents. But I just don't think I can use it tonight, it's too complicated, and if I whiff because I'm thinking about the Russian way to pronounce *windmill*, Mr. Stewart is going to throw me in the gulag. Like, for real."

We ordered our bagels. When I put my backpack down at the foot of our table, I turned around to see Seth was still at the register, talking to the cashier. They were laughing, though I couldn't hear the conversation. I waited for a moment, and then waited some more, before he came back with two soda cups in hand. "Yours," he said, jostling a cup at me.

"You did not pay for that," I said. "What did you say?"

He tsked, then shook a finger. "One day you will learn to talk to strangers. I truly believe it's possible."

I wasn't more reclusive or awkward than anyone else; I had plenty of friends. But Seth was just preternaturally friendly to everyone, with no particular motivating intent. In retrospect it was clear I'd aspired to arrange my social life into a glamorous shape, or at least glamorous by the standards of a teenager who wore cargo pants and liked Weezer. I wanted to be surrounded by people who I thought were cool and smart and funny and beautiful; I succeeded through what at the time I believed were the invisible forces pulling me toward these types of people because it was meant to be, instead of what I now accepted was a sly, self-selecting impulse toward massaging my connections to find the most personally desirable friendships. On the one hand it was ridiculous I'd attempted this in high school, since it wasn't like I possessed any special cachet or knew anyone with special cachet, but this amateurish reorganization of my social circumstances had repeated throughout college, and now my adult life. I was about to meet Hamilton for lunch, though we had no particular connection besides the fact that I'd once looked up to him, and even aspired to be him.

Seth, on the other hand, was a membrane; he allowed everything and everyone to pass through, and allowed himself to flow out toward everything and everyone, making and sustaining connections with no pretensions. Nobody disliked him, and this was a period of time where the clichés do apply and everybody is hated by someone: the jocks are hated by the losers, the losers are hated by the jocks, the prom queens are hated by the virgins, and so on, and so forth. But never Seth. For him it was as basic as asking people how they were doing, and from there eventually finding out about their problems with their parents. There wasn't a single person at our high school he didn't get along with, and he could expand this invitational aura to include anyone, such as an Einstein's cashier.

It's just the walk I remember, along with the fragment of conversation and the free soda cups. All of a sudden we're in the school auditorium, waiting for the play to start. The program says Seth is playing Lopakhin, which at the moment means nothing to me. I'm sitting in the third row with Ruth and Anthony, who's come to support Seth but also partly because he wants to ogle the cute sophomore playing Anya, the landowner's daughter, a role that requires her to enter in a nineteenth-century nightie, which some other drama teacher might have recognized as unnecessary but not Mr. Stewart, who will sleep with at least two students after they graduate.

We don't spend much time in this auditorium. Every now and then an assembly is called for some special occasion: a visit by Jonathan Safran Foer, a town hall meeting on racism after a classmate is caught posting slurs to her LiveJournal. Mostly it's plays, and from our third-row seats, the room is unrecognizable. The back of the stage is overlaid with a painted tapestry simulating the Russian countryside. The sky is a hazy gray, occluding a smear of sun that hangs above a clotting of thick trees, their narrow base centering a bundle of leafy branches containing the titular cherries, dotted precisely within the leaves. In front the students have constructed a facsimile of a modest Russian estate—a rickety wooden table topped with silver cups, a dining-room table draped in a lacy cloth, a pair of opposing armchairs, a couple of velvet curtains suspended midair.

The lights go out. When they return, Seth is sitting in one of the armchairs, book in his hand, fast asleep. The saga of the cherry orchard unfolds as the student-actors buzz about onstage, trying their best. The performances are energetic and memorized, but the accents range from nonexistent to truly intolerable, and I can't blame Seth for deciding to forgo his. Anthony whispers something lewd about the cute sophomore, until Jenny Collins turns around, a smile on her face (because Anthony is regarded as a charming pervert, I don't understand anything about this but it's true), and tells him to relax, she's trying to pay attention.

It won't be until I study *The Cherry Orchard*, just weeks after Seth's funeral, that I'm able to contextualize the nuances of his performance. At the time, I'm bewildered by how subtly he's playing the role, how completely he's muzzled his personality. His Lopakhin is a coiled murmur, at times barely audible even in the third row. He'll move hesitantly, as though outfitted with a corset restricting his motions, always on the verge of human contact before pulling back at the last moment.

Lopakhin is the rich merchant, born to a serf, whose lack

of education and social mores are denigrated by the Ranevskys and the Gayevs, all of whom clearly consider themselves to be his better. In the end, he secretly purchases the orchard they've spent the whole play trying to preserve, and proclaims his intent to chop it down against their protestations. He's supposed to be their friend, he's supposed to know his place, but Russia is changing and Lopakhin with it. The supremacy of the bourgeoisie is no longer inevitable; Lopakhin worked his way up, and can spend ninety thousand rubles to raze the cherry orchard just to prove a point.

Stagings of *The Cherry Orchard* often locate Lopakhin as morally neutral, too deceitful to be a hero but somewhat sympathetic by nature of his upbringing. Today, it's easy to find a more strident interpretation that views the Ranevskys and Gayevs as spoiled monarchs unaware that their privileges and luxuries will soon be reclaimed by an insurgent underclass ready to remap Russia, and Lopakhin as the righteous executor of this proletarian will. That's what I was half expecting, even if I couldn't articulate it—some kind of hysterical parable about greed and justice delivered from a soapbox, the type of strident and dramatic moral scenario exclusive to Russian literature (which I understood completely, of course, because I'd just read *Crime and Punishment*).

But Lopakhin isn't a hero, even if you move the moral goalposts. Regardless of his upbringing he's become content to weaponize his wealth for revenge and invert a power structure he has no interest in dismantling, only mastering. So there's another way to play it, with Lopakhin a barely concealed villain, whose disgust for his rich cohort is palpable in his sneers and gestures, whose betrayal comes as no shock to the audience. That's also what I was half expecting, with Seth getting a chance to flash his messy-bitch chops like a toothless Dracula seeking vengeance.

Now I've read Chekhov, I've thought about Russia, I'm thinking about Seth from the back of the car as we speed toward Hamilton in Highland Park. I'm a junior, and he's a senior. It's spring, so he must know he isn't going to graduate with the rest of his class. He hasn't told any of us because he's too proud, though eventually we'll find out because that kind of secret isn't even a secret, only a fact destined to be revealed by the linear progression of time. I don't suspect anything; as far as I know we've had bagels as usual, and his nerves are exclusively related to the play. But he's thinking about the future, how he isn't quite sure what'll happen when you have a bad stomach, and your test scores are good but not spectacular, and your parents don't understand you, and it would be otherwise so boring to have to deal with that stereotype of the confused father and mother who just want their sweet son to stop thinking about kissing boys, but when you've got a bad stomach and good but not spectacular test scores, your future depends on their capacity for largesse.

He's thinking about where he is in life, the work it'll take to move past what's hopefully just a blip, and here he understands something about Lopakhin, which is that even if you've transcended your station, earned your money, and thrown off the yoke of serfdom, you'll always remember where you came from. This is nineteenth-century Russia—there are no therapists or SSRIs, and that feeling only burns inside you. It's something you've got to live with.

I remember the next day, when Anthony asks out the cute sophomore outside of the lunch room and she responds,

"Weren't you the guy who couldn't stop talking about my tits?" In order to stem his minor humiliation, Seth and I take him out to eat. Anthony's feelings blow over right away, so Seth spends the entire meal talking about how he performed too quietly, and how he'll consciously amp it up in the future. That sounds great to me, because at the time I'm confused. I don't understand subtlety, I don't understand hesitation. I'm sixteen years old, I will not kiss Natalia for several more months, and my favorite movie is still *Reservoir Dogs.* Russian literature is supposed to be blustery and emphatic, at least according to the one Russian novel I've read. I don't understand what Seth is doing at all.

"I want to be someone who smiles as he readies the hidden blade," he tells us. We nod like we understand. By all accounts—specifically Ruth's, since she returns for the show's second night, ever ready to support her friend—this emotional relocation turns out very well. Maybe it means he might have ended up as an actor, in another life. But I'm pretty sure he never acted again.

I'D ASKED FOR A TOUR WITHOUT THINKING, AND HAMILTON rolled out the full treatment as we moved throughout his office, which was not the anodyne corporate satellite I'd half imagined but in fact a multichamber complex from which one could wait out the apocalypse among piles of fancy microphones and tangled-up audio cables. He'd greeted me at the front door like we were old friends, yanking me into a hug and immediately starting on about how great it was to hang out after all this time. Hamilton had always been "handsome for a music writer," but in Los Angeles the last traces of boyishness had been excised and now he was just good-looking. He wore a wine-colored bomber jacket and expensive-looking jeans; his light brown hair was cut neatly around his head except for an asymmetrical tuft of curls hanging just about his eyeline. He looked like what he was: a label owner, a person whose responsibilities had extended past the identification of talent to the projection and creation of success.

I followed him through the building, nodding at the appropriate intervals during his explanatory monologue. The bands he signed tended to be rock acts currently making dance music, a stylistic misdirection that had been en vogue at the start of the millennium, but was now swinging back around as the culture tilted increasingly toward pop and rap. Hamilton's grand innovation was to work with women and minorities, a demographic excluded from the previous excursion by nature of the scene's natural biases, now easily bypassed, as he could find any number of potentially dazzling talents by lurking on social media.

Now he was genuinely inserting himself into mainstream culture, opposed to just commenting on it, and the label's music was found regularly on streaming playlists and television shows. It was hard to remember the type of relatively uncommercial music he used to champion, and though his former peers groused online about how he'd abandoned his roots, there was no denying how well this had turned out.

"It's a busy time," Hamilton said, as he led me around a corner. "The release schedule is already crammed, but there's also television and film opportunities that we've got to pounce on if we want to get out there."

"That's awesome," I said. "I'm glad to hear it. This neighborhood seems awesome too." I didn't know what I was talking about, but it seemed like the right thing to say. "Where did you say we were going to eat?"

"I made a reservation at this great café, but I wanted to show you one last thing before we head over." He gestured for me to enter another room, where a man was reclining on a leather couch. Another sat at a desk, pushing around a mouse with a guitar cradled in his lap. They were younger than everyone I'd met so far, clearly in their early twenties. The man with the guitar was white, and sported a nearly shaved head, except for a crown of fringe bangs, like some kind of hipster monk. The other, who was Black, wore a long-sleeve white shirt with text reading LIFE IS A FUCK down each of the arms, and ruby-red circular sunglasses that covered half his face.

"This is Connor," Hamilton said, pointing to the man with

the guitar, "and Jayson. They're called Boy Brigade, and we've been working with them for a few months. We're getting ready to launch their debut single."

"That's cool," I said. "How long have you guys been together?"

Connor swiveled around to face me. "Just a few months, actually."

"It's a funny story," Hamilton said. "I met Connor last year at a Grammys party, and we'd talked about working together. Then Jayson emailed me some demos, and I thought they might sound great together, so I ended up bringing him out from Wyoming." He sounded like a proud father, though they didn't seem to notice: Connor had already returned to the computer, while Jayson was buried in his phone.

I looked around the room, which didn't quite resemble any of the others; there were stacks of amps and piled-up synthesizers, but also a Nintendo Wii, a mini fridge, and a Ping-Pong table. "This space is for . . . what, exactly?"

"It's for hanging," Hamilton said, in a satisfied way. "You know, we just relax and try to make something happen—find an unconventional solution to a conventional problem. Have you ever tried to sing while lying down?"

"No, but I have blogged in bed," I said.

Hamilton laughed unreasonably hard and slapped me on the shoulder. "See, you get it. Hold on, check this out." He snapped his fingers, and Connor spun around in his chair while Jayson looked up from his phone. "Hey guys, we're about to run out, but I can just"—he moved over to the computer, as Connor slid out of the way, and tapped a few keys—"queue up the backing music."

"What about the reservation?" I said.

"It'll only be a minute." I looked at Connor, who was plugging his guitar into an amp, and at Jayson, who was massaging his throat. "It's good practice, to perform on the fly, and I think you'll really enjoy them." Hamilton pointed at the couch, and like a trained animal I took my seat.

Connor plucked out a few aqueous chords, his guitar tone rippling inside the room as Jayson ran through a series of vocal runs. Hamilton watched them with his arms crossed, smiling. I wasn't sure what to do; I was hungry and William's health sludge wasn't sitting right. When Connor and Jayson's warm-ups had reached a perfunctory quality, Hamilton cut them off with his hand. "Let's get started," he said, turning back to the computer and dialing up a slowly alternating kick-drum and snare, undergirded by a sensuous bass line.

Now Connor's freeform playing congealed into an elliptical and hazy melody, followed by Jayson's vibrantly androgynous voice. *If you were on my mind*, he sang, *I'd think of what I'd tell you / I'd think of how I'd hold you / If I ever had the time*. Leonard Cohen this was not, but uplifted by Jayson's mournful energy and buttressed by Connor's murky guitar tone, the lyric sounded almost profound. I began nodding along, first to give the impression I was enjoying it, then because I basically was. Hamilton was nodding, too, his face focused in deep concentration. As Jayson launched into the second verse, he held up his hand.

The music stopped. "Connor, you're a half measure behind the melody—we want slow, but we don't want *slow*," Hamilton said. "It's supposed to feel like you're floating down a river, not like you snagged a branch along the way." Connor nodded and, for the first time, seemed to be paying attention. "Okay, let's try that again."

Hamilton hit the keyboard, and the drum-and-bass instrumental started from the beginning. The same elliptical, hazy melody sprung from Connor's guitar, now almost imperceptibly upbeat. Jayson began singing again, and I lay back on the couch, already ready for this to be over.

FOR THE LONGEST TIME I HAD ACCEPTED "KEEPING AT IT" AS necessary if I wanted to achieve my goals, such as publishing a book or working for *The New Yorker*. There was no other option, really, given how keeping at it had allowed me to slowly carve out an accomplished lifestyle. I lived by myself in a brownstone owned by Miss Dolores, a Haitian woman who'd lived in Clinton Hill since before the word "gentrification" had been invented and never raised the rent I paid in cash every month. I had two plants I forgot to water. I owned a PlayStation 4 and was looking forward to the PlayStation 5. I'd reached my thirties without any major psychological events besides the usual bouts of mild depression and lethargy, the late nights spent thinking about my mother getting old, the women I hadn't slept with, the script I hadn't made any progress on, the book proposal I hadn't made any progress on, the projects and goals I sensed bobbing off into the distance like buoys on a restless sea.

Still, I was mostly at peace with the recurrent nature of my life, or so I thought until one evening the week after Sadie had initially passed on my dead classmates idea, when as I was waiting for my dinner to finish cooking, I found my armpits pooling with cold sweat, my hairline creasing with heat, my face stupefying and ossifying, and my breath quickening until it felt as if a three-hundred-pound weight was pinned against my chest, before I located the cool surface of my bed, lowered myself like a lame animal, and lay there breathing and not breathing.

One of the most famous singers in the world had surprise-released a new song at midnight, her first in three years, which I learned about on my phone within twenty seconds of waking up. Motherhood was a great pleasure, she wrote in an accompanying note, and so was working on the soundtrack for the live-action *Pocahontas,* but her solo artistry afforded her an unparalleled creative freedom. I didn't need to check with Sadie to know this was my assignment for the morning. As I listened several times, first on my headphones and then on my speakers, the song split apart, revealing several disparate elements to consider—the musical arrangement, the lyrical content, the clear evolution from A—'s previous material, the contemporary artists who'd been influenced by her, how this new song acknowledged said influence by softly updating her aural touchpoints in a way that felt artistically true, and the single art, in which a regal A— posed in a fur-lined coat on top of an ornate silver throne carved with potentially Arthurian sigils—before curdling into what was clearly the outline of a thesis. An hour later I had about nine hundred original words comprising context about A—, analysis of the song structure, a couple of wry one-liners, and a broad gesture at why anyone should care in the first place. "A—'s return comes at a moment when big-budget pop is less of a commodity than ever before, thanks to the rise of a new generation of bedroom auteurs less interested in global domination than in protecting their fiercely curated post-Tumblr aesthetic," I concluded. Sadie passed it back to me ten minutes later with a thumbs-up emoji. After the piece appeared on our home page, I tweeted it out and stopped thinking about it altogether.

Later that night, right before I was about to eat dinner, I received a push alert on my phone informing me that A— had announced a brand new album, which would be released at midnight. I was making some kind of fancy pasta dish, the type I'd made dozens of times over the years. I'd smoked some marijuana. A movie from my watchlist was loaded up on my television, as it usually was. While I cooked, I'd scrolled my phone, logging dozens of fresh data points to inform my understanding of the world I was responsible for understanding—and now this new album, out in a few hours.

I'd first heard A— in college, when I'd written about her debut album for a campus website. We were the same age, and since then she'd ascended the pantheon of global celebrity, selling millions of records, winning dozens of awards, giving birth to one child, and becoming a shorthand for recession-proof pop success. Meanwhile, I was once again writing about her new record for a website I worked at. I was, as I thought about it, always writing about A—'s new record for a website I worked at, on which my entire professional and personal existence rested, because if I wanted to pay for my apartment and my PlayStation 4 and my underwatered plants and my drinks with serotonin-deficient women I needed a job, and this was the one I had now, and would possibly have forever.

When I was stoned, I could sometimes feel a revelation materialize like a cruel and horrible sun, suspended low in the air and blazing with alien light. I could look away, and I could dither, and I could close my eyes and whisper "Mm-mm, no thank you, not now," but acknowledging it was inevitable no matter where I turned. It was happening now, and I felt my thoughts vibrating with expansive force: beyond the brute numbers of *stuff to pay attention to* were the thousands upon thousands of corresponding and intersecting interpretations also standing in direct opposition to one another. I was just trying to keep up, performing infinite fieldwork toward an unclear resolution, when there was no real way to reconcile all the myriad dynamics, considerations, symbols, phenomena, themes, moral takeaways, and life lessons that every possible other writer might tease out. It was, frankly, insane that I thought I might have something firm to declare about any of this. The enormity of it hit me all at once, the contradictions and intrusive thoughts I'd waved away under the guise of "that's just how it is" colliding and multiplying until my chest constricted and I found my bed a moment later, lying there and hyperventilating as the pain crested and receded and crested again.

For a moment I thought I might throw up, but the nausea did not surge beyond a handful of violent throbs. Slowly I became aware that my breathing was returning to a normal place, that my eyesight was no longer a canvas of static. When I managed to sit up, I thought I might keel over again from sheer exhaustion; it felt as if hours had passed, but when I looked at the clock on my nightstand, the entire episode had lasted barely ten minutes.

After texting Sadie that one of the junior writers could handle it, I went to bed early. In the morning, I felt fine, and thought I was in the clear—except it happened again the next night, and then two nights after that.

My insurance-approved therapist pointed out the connection between my job and these anxieties. "You've made your living by trying to understand the world around you," she suggested, "and now you're wondering if you've understood it all wrong." I'd never thought about it like that, I really hadn't. I'd automatically privileged the mission of interpretation throughout my life—the belief that all sorts of things were lying underneath the surface, waiting to be dredged up by my unique thoughtfulness. But possibly there was nothing unique about my life, as I'd suggested to Ruth, and thus nothing unique worth saying.

The therapist suggested I reorient by engaging with something outside my usual routine, so after a cluster of meetings with Sadie and Sadie's boss (but not Karl, who preferred not to hear about such things), it was agreed I'd go on medical leave for six weeks. I'd spend some time out of New York—something I hadn't done in a very long time.

Now I waited for Boy Brigade to finish their song in the confines of the hang room, looking at them looking at Hamilton looking at me, trying desperately to remove myself from this hopeless equation. The awkwardness of the staged scene seeped further into my thoughts as I felt my throat tightening, my breath quickening, my skin itching, and my vision dizzying over. That Hamilton had sprung this filled me with doubt about why he'd even wanted to get lunch in the first place, because maybe he thought I was just some kiss-ass eager to please anyone who'd been nice to him, and maybe he wasn't wrong, because here I was nodding along when all I wanted to do was Google the song they were playing and figure out when it was going to end.

I tilted my head forward to close my eyes and take a series of deep breaths, hoping that if anyone noticed they would think I was just vibing to the groove. My phone buzzed, and instead of being polite I took it out.

I can't believe you're working, Sadie had texted. But okay, I floated it to the audio team. The new producer loves your new idea, but he has some other thoughts about the direction. I don't know if it's breaking HR guidelines about boundaries or whatever, but can you talk tomorrow morning?

Whatever simmering panic I'd felt suddenly cooled, and as I started typing a response, the band stopped playing. "That's good for now," Hamilton said. "What did you think?" Before I could say anything, he raised his hand to stop himself. "Sorry, I'm being rude. We can chat about it at lunch."

DID I LIKE MY JOB? DID I LIKE LOS ANGELES? WAS I GETTING around okay? Did I miss New York, in spite of the West Coast's sunny charms? Was I thinking about moving here? Had I been to Erewhon? I tried to match Hamilton's enthusiasm in responding, and he nodded vigorously through all of my answers. "That's awesome," he said when I mentioned I'd eaten in Koreatown the other night, as though I had really indulged myself.

"Yeah, I'm having a great time," I said. We were sitting in a booth at a nearby restaurant called Seed and Tunnel, and poking at our respective fennel salads. "I know everyone says they love Los Angeles, but it does feel meaningfully different from the last time I was out here. Maybe it's just because I have more money, ha-ha."

"That's awesome," he repeated. "I can't emphasize how good it is to get out of New York, when you're sick of the rat race. You just needed a vacation?"

I hesitated before answering. Talking openly about your mental health wasn't a taboo for my generation, but I didn't want to sound like I needed a sympathetic ear, not in this context. Instead, I said that I'd been looking for a new project out here. "I just can't write about another fucking record," I said.

He laughed a little too hard, and flashed that world-class industry smile. "I *definitely* get that."

"Last night I was talking to a friend from high school, and she mentioned this band that a classmate of ours was in, after we graduated. I realized, *I don't really remember this band at all*—and I knew this guy! Not well, but I knew him. I think there's just way too many bands."

"Who was that?" His phone buzzed, and he briefly fiddled with the screen. "Sorry about that—business calls, sometimes."

"You remember Black Lodge? From that whole scuzzy late aughts Chicago thing?" He shook his head, so I took out my phone and played the first thirty seconds of "Dreaming" on YouTube.

Hamilton listened intently before making an expression I couldn't quite parse, somewhere between surprise and amusement. "Oh, sure. *Sure*. That rings a bell."

"Yeah?" This was a normal thing to say, but Hamilton's eyes were now wide open, the telltale sign of a man with a secret. "I can't tell if you're messing with me."

"No, I mean." He smiled, and took a drink of water. "You never heard what happened with those guys?"

It was weird to think of our overlapping social circles—that while I'd been clueless in Chicago about people I'd actually known, Hamilton, from half a country away, was privy to "what happened with those guys," natural information for someone in his line of work. "I didn't . . . I really didn't know him like that, we'd just gone to high school together."

"Well," he said, gripping the edge of the table as if to say *Brace yourself*. "I was still in the game then, and I saw plenty of bands from the quote-unquote 'scene.' Like you said, those guys were part of that Chicago garage wave . . ."

". . . right, Smith Westerns, Caw! Caw!, White Mystery, bands like that . . ."

". . . and they came to New York to play one of those obnoxious industry functions where everybody jacks off to the idea of the next big buzz band. It might have been 2008, or 2009? Some shit went down."

The way he remembered it, Black Lodge had played pretty well. "Or whatever 'pretty well' meant at the time—they were sexy and moody and everyone knew they were going to make some money." The music was loud, the drinks were comped, it was just another free-flowing night in a city organized around free-flowing nights. "Brooklyn indie rock was tilting away from that kind of shaggy-dog leather daddy downtown thing, but it seemed rawer coming from the Midwest. The city of big shoulders, right?"

I nodded as though this made perfect intuitive sense—these instantaneous recollections of granular scene dynamics were just how a lot of people I knew talked. I had the nagging thought my recorder should be on the table, but didn't want to interrupt him. I'd acquired the habit of packing it whenever I left town, because I never wanted to be caught off guard in a chance scenario. Now here I was, caught off guard in a chance scenario.

Anyway, Hamilton continued, they—meaning he, his peers, the band, and the loose retinue of relevant industry figures surrounding his peers and the band—ended up at an unofficial after-party at a nearby bar. And he remembered this very well, actually, because it still seemed crazy: At the back of the bar, in a circular seating booth, he saw the lead guitarist start shooting up, right there. He sort of did it under the table, out of sight . . . but nobody there was a pure idiot, obviously this guy was doing some drugs. "Was that the guy you were talking about?"

"He started shooting up right there in the bar?" I was growing sick of how often I was repeating myself, but even by my received wisdom of how drug use manifested in people who didn't give a fuck about anything, this was fairly surprising.

"Yes, right in the bar. You know, he had his needle and rope and bag of smack or whatever. I think we were all pretty taken aback, me and whoever I was with. Rock 'n' roll, you know, but a little *too* rock 'n' roll. The story definitely got around; I mean, I talked about it. Maybe that's not what buried them, but it didn't help, and I don't think they ever made a record. And, not to diss your friend, that made them just like every other buzz band that went nowhere in New York, so I think we all moved on."

Once again he laughed a little too hard as he picked up a piece of fennel with his fingers and popped it into his mouth. I was annoyed by the breezy way he talked, and especially by the fact I'd never heard about any of this. Lee and his stupid band were notoriously shooting up at hip New York parties, and it was just some story passed around by a bunch of assholes who worked for websites?

"Do you mind if I take my recorder out? This sounds actually pretty relevant to this new project I'm thinking about."

He drank from his water bottle, and shook his head. "Sorry, but I have to keep it casual here. You're too sharp for me to go on the record." I tried not to be flattered: my defenses fell whenever praise came from someone I admired, even if Hamilton hadn't written anything in years. "We're just jawing here, right? Happy to jaw about something else."

We sat there in silence, the first time we'd stopped talking since I'd met him at the studio. Maybe I'd erred, because Hamilton had entered a transactional line of work, and I had nothing to offer. I didn't want to promise to write about fucking Boy Crush, or whatever, just so that he'd participate in some podcast that wasn't even real yet.

I tried to assume my most neutral journalist voice. "I'm just curious, really. You saw a lot of these types of bands, back in the day. A lot of them seemed focused on 'making it.' But here's a guy who, as you tell it, behaves like it doesn't matter. Do you see a lot of guys like that?"

Hamilton leaned forward and laughed. "I cannot tell you how many guys I see like that. It's every cliché story in the book: the fuckups who just can't get out of their own way. But this guy was different, I think."

Lee just sounded like a regular type of asshole, but I didn't need to let that on. "How do you mean? We didn't know each other very well in high school, he wasn't my friend."

"You just have to know that type of thing is going to be off-putting, even among the most craven exploitative types. So maybe he wanted us to fuck off. I'm not pretending like we were all noble actors. It was my job to find the next big thing, and when something's your job, you can't help but think about the dollars and cents. Which is, you know, the entire opposite of how you first started thinking, when you were reading magazines as a dopey little teenager. It's why I moved over to the label side: eventually, I just had to be honest about what my work actually was."

Hamilton's phone buzzed again, and this time he apologized and excused himself, he really needed to take the call. As he walked outside, I thought about what he'd just said. All day, I'd been trying to retrieve my specific memories of Lee; we'd taken some classes together, but I couldn't recall a single conversation we'd had, or a time when we'd ended up hanging out together after school, or a time when we'd sat at the same lunch table, or any of the other hundreds of spins on "high school interaction." Lots of people from the past were categorized this way, not just in high school or college; we'd shared the same space for a few years without anything lasting to show for it beyond a passing thought of "Oh, *that* guy" when they somehow came up in conversation. I knew Lee was a troublemaker, and that girls liked him, and that he played in a band I'd seen a few times, but that was literally it, hardly something to confidently spin into a story like Hamilton's.

Yet I did remember something just now, triggered by what Hamilton had said. It was a slight memory, maybe just a scrap, but . . . Seth and I, sitting in the school library, poring over a magazine, maybe it's *Rolling Stone* or *Entertainment Weekly*, both of which are circulated in the school library, we're passing it between us, we're talking about some article, it must be *Rolling Stone* because who cares about the articles in *Entertainment Weekly*, we're looking at some photo, maybe it's the Yeah Yeah Yeahs, Seth is attracted to their guitarist, Nick Zinner, because of his hair, I'm attracted to the singer Karen O because she's Karen O, rumors abound they're working on a new album, perhaps I'm making this up, could we really have been passing a magazine back and forth in the library, but it must have happened because there's Lee, who appears from nowhere and snatches the magazine off the table, he ignores me entirely, he's talking to Seth directly, and what he says is "The Yeah Yeah Yeahs? The fucking *Yeah Yeah Yeahs*?" Seth just looks at him, completely unamused, his face has been sucked of all joy, his emotions are set to *zero*, he sticks his hand out and gestures like *come on*, he doesn't say anything, I'm not saying anything either, just looking at Seth looking at Lee looking back at Seth with that rude smile on his face, until Lee rips the magazine right in half, throws it at him, laughs, and walks away, I start to protest but Seth tells me to forget about it, *He can't help himself*, Seth says, *You'd have better luck convincing a dog to stop licking shit*, and that's Lee in my mind, a dog licking shit, a guy who ignores you and starts trouble because he's bored, and who will end up being the end of my friend.

My thoughts were interrupted by the sound of Hamilton bumping the table, as he slid back into the booth. "Anyway," he said, "guys like that either become art superstars or kick it early, I've tended to find out. You know what happened to him?"

It took me a second to collect myself, as Lee's afterimage faded from my mind. "It's neither of those," I said. "He's around, but I don't know more than that. He's not dead, I know that. He lucked out."

"I guess that's not surprising." Hamilton started to pick at the remaining part of his salad, but then thought better of it. "There are some things you can't come back from, but most of the time you can just move on. The years go by and the past barely matters, I'm telling you. You can do whatever you want, if you want."

AFTER I FIRST MOVED TO NEW YORK, I QUICKLY GREW USED TO the reality of having no dough in a city that demanded you have money to burn and picked up the shortcuts to cheap living: the third-rate grocery chains selling just-expired frozen pizzas for fifty cents a pop, the subway turnstiles you could hop with no oversight, the way to time an ATM overdraft so you'd only get slapped with one penalty. But above everything else, I walked. When the weather was nice I'd hump the twenty or forty or sometimes even seventy blocks from one place to the next, the sound of the city commingling with the music thrumming through my headphones.

Soaked with sweat, and itchy in all the wrong places, I made connections that my conscious brain could never have anticipated, taking note of how *this* bass line echoed *that* underfoot rumble of the A train, how *this* chorus sunflowered right as the summer sky broke right through the topiary of Manhattan skyscrapers and landmarks that, despite my own upbringing in an urban environment, never failed to fill me with some kind of mawkish awe. Never mind that these connections were obviously personal: I was addicted to the potential of a world whose depth was conditional on what streets I wandered down, what happened to be lurking around the corner, what song might be shuffled into some profound juxtaposition if I was paying close enough attention.

That I now made more money did not prevent me from embarking on these long walks, soundtracked by the yawning blob of some 11,273 songs I'd saved to a playlist titled "Walking Around." This was partly why I'd never taken to podcasting: out in the world, the rhythm of listening to two or three people talk, whether they were talking at each other or about some subject, was never quite right. A car would roar by and I'd miss some humorous conjecture, a key detail from the unfurling narrative, some word or clause or sound whose absence would render the following words or clauses or sounds entirely meaningless, and by the time I'd pull my phone out to rewind, I'd have walked further and retained absolutely nothing. Then I'd feel annoyed that I was trying to learn about the dissolution of the Ottoman Empire or whatever, and tab back to the Walking Around playlist, happily humming along to the wisps of melody and instrumentation popping out from underneath the city's messy soundscape.

This reticence to fully engage with podcasting had informed my thinking about the podcast I was proposing, I told Reggie, my company's new producer, as he patiently listened through the other side of the screen. There was a clear story to be told and a clear investigation to be conducted, but maybe we could approach this podcast in a way that anticipated what I was talking about—the myriad distractions that made any devoted listening experience somewhat difficult for people like me—and structure the storytelling in a more disparate, ethereal way. I wanted to center the tragedy of Seth Terry's death from an accidental overdose, and the role of once-buzzy indie rock guitarist Lee Finch in providing the fatal batch of heroin, and outline how a beloved honors student had wandered down such a ruinous path. But in my head I also heard a series of overlapping voices, not even necessarily identifiable as specific people, an oral history summoning the deceased from the void to tell the full truth of who Seth had been in life and death, as well as who they themselves had been, in order to explore the ramifications of a tragedy within a community in ways that resonated beyond "I was sad" or "I was scared" or "I thought about death," because every death made someone think about death, and I wasn't trying to hit the nail on the head but uproot the nail altogether, in order to make people ponder the heavy stuff in a way they'd never pondered before.

I hoped I didn't sound insane. My call with Reggie was only meant to get us on the same page, not serve as a formal ribbon cutting. But I was infected with the potential of what this project might be, if it came to fruition, and with every spare moment to linger on what I'd learned I became further possessed with learning more. I was empowered by my free time and drifting attentions; I could wander between moments like a director in the editing room, comparing footage and stitching my reel together until something finally made sense.

Part of it was the pot, and the number of ways I'd consumed it in the city—popping low THC gummies between meals, nursing infused seltzers, openly lighting joints on the street because someone had told me it was legal, though it wasn't. My medical leave was really a vacation, and vacation was about relaxation, and the ease of walking into a legal dispensary and purchasing the maximum allowable limit of THC had, within hours, reverted me to my collegiate levels of consumption. Perhaps I was indulging, but I wasn't exclusively indulgent. I'd used the marijuana time as a means of expanding and organizing my thoughts as they webbed together, tugging one revelatory strand after another until I chased down what felt impossibly true.

After Hamilton and I parted ways, I was killing time at William's by petting his dogs and hoping for a text back when he'd subtly asked me if I had anywhere to go in the next hour, because a potential sex friend was coming over, and while he didn't mind if I hung around he assumed there were other things I'd rather overhear on the tail end of my trip. I didn't want to be an ungrateful guest, and was happy to scramble even if it meant sitting by myself at an unfamiliar bar, scrolling my phone. I took an edible, and as I waited for some friends to show up I started thinking about this and that, and before long was tunneling toward a series of conclusions about what type of person Lee must have been to expedite something so terrible, nearly trembling over how terrible I felt about it. High school was about discovering yourself, sure, but some of us hadn't ended up enabling the deaths of our classmates during that fact-finding process. I wanted to hear some kind of explanation for his behavior, how he'd pulled Seth into his orbit and encouraged his habit.

More startling was how immediately my existing memories of Seth had shifted following my night with Kelsey. In the years since his death, the specific impressions I retained of him had faded into a more general recollection. But Kelsey's revelation had displaced those general recollections, filling me with overriding dread that I'd completely misunderstood him in the first place. There were whole swaths of his existence I wasn't privy to, things he'd never shared with me. Perhaps we hadn't been so close at all, difficult as that was to accept, though who's to say my existing memories weren't a postscript invention, though who's to say postscript inventions weren't the default texture of our subconscious, considering the impossibility of creating a truly objective record of our lived experience, but regardless we shared some responsibility toward fidelity because life was too indelible to actively lie to ourselves about what had been. Whatever it was, I could no longer trust my memories of Seth, because there was too much I didn't know or understand. Even after the pot wore off, I returned to the same conclusion: I needed to piece together what had happened so I might resettle some of this disturbed terrain.

I'd texted Ruth about what I'd learned, but even if it was difficult to communicate tone over text message I'd expected more than a bloodless *That's crazy.* Not even *That's crazy!!!!!* or *That's CRAZY.* I needed someone else to acknowledge how completely destabilizing it was. It wasn't solely the drugs, because come on, we weren't completely naïve about drugs even if it was heroin, but the fact that it was Seth, our Seth, wrapped up in something he'd kept entirely hidden from his most loved ones, something that had ended up marking the end of his life.

When I said something like this, she replied that she and Donald were currently organizing their future honeymoon, her energy was all over the place, and I shouldn't read too much into a text. *Of course that's fucking crazy,* she texted. *I'm just having a hard time processing it right now. It's not like there's anything we can do about it.* I said that I could try to get in touch with some of our other mutual friends from high school, and take it from there.

That's a good idea, she said. *Let me know what happens.*

Before that, I had to get on the same page as Reggie. I apologized that I was sitting on William's guest bed rather than somewhere more professional, but he told me not to worry about it. "Frankly, I'm amazed we're having this talk while you're still out of town," he said.

"Just ask Sadie about it," I said. "I'm sure she'll tell you all about my problematic work habits."

Reggie wore short dreadlocks and a scratchy mustache that

did not threaten to become a beard. He'd just started at our company and told me about himself: he was from Queens, he'd worked in theater and produced pieces for public radio, and my company had hired him because they thought he could bring a more sensitive, inquisitive perspective to their storytelling.

"Podcasting is a very white industry," he said. "Mostly it's guys talking over one another, and at one another. I'm not really interested in the banter-banter-banter format."

I nodded furiously, to communicate that I agreed. "That's great, I feel the same way. It's like—you're just a guy saying stuff, who gives a shit?"

Reggie smiled thinly and nodded. "So you've done a couple of interviews—how have you been recording them?"

"No interviews, actually, but—I've got a handheld Zoom recorder, I forget the model but it has three microphones, it's very high tech."

His eye was fixed on a corner of his computer screen, and I could see his hands moving around the keyboard. "That'll work for now, but I'm going to order a more formal podcasting kit that'll be waiting for you back at the office. I assume most of the voice-overs will get done in New York, but if you like thinking about work, it's not a bad idea to get in that mindset while you're still out in Los Angeles. But we're nowhere near the voice-over stage, to say nothing of a script. I'll send you a few pitches for reference, so you can get an idea of how these things work."

I appreciated his go-getter directness, but didn't quite understand everything he'd just said. "Voice-over?"

"It's not enough to just cut up everyone's interviews, right? The audience needs a way into this story."

"Oh, sure, like why this is happening at all. Of course, I think I know how to make it interesting, I have some ideas."

"Have you thought about how involved your presence should be? Like, do you want to take the audience the entire way, from beginning to end? Do you want to paint your own conclusions about what happened, or do you want to leave them thinking about it? You know, what's your role here as we try to invest people in your friend's journey?"

Well, I started to say, but he kept talking: Moreover he had a more basic series of questions that he liked to ask all the talent, though he quickly corrected to "host," he didn't like to say "talent" because it gave the "talent" an inflated ego about their importance, when with all due respect "host" was just more accurate. But the questions: Why this story? Why me? Why *audio*?

I think it's like, I started to say, before veering into a neat recap of my friendship with Seth, and what he'd meant to me, and how he'd returned to my thoughts over the years despite the essential mystery of his death, or more accurately *because* of the essential mystery of his death, and because I'd gone so long thinking one thing about his life when it was really the other, I thought there was some space to delve into these thoughts not only as they'd come to me, but to the people around him. There was a very direct story here about Seth and Lee, and how their relationship had led to Seth's dying at a young age, which I was ready to report out. But that story might also be folded into the broader idea I'd pitched to Sadie in the first place, about the lives we lead and digital afterlives and that sort of thing, all of which still felt valid to me regardless of her doubts about the sales team. If I was being honest, my position at the company also meant that I was looking for inspiration wherever I could find it, and I felt this story had the narrative and emotional stakes to propel me toward a satisfying conclusion, rather than the banter-banter-

banter format that seemed to spin out once it ran too long. As for audio, writing felt like too small a medium to contain Seth. While I understood the necessity of my perspective, I didn't want to center myself exclusively, because so much of Seth's life and death now hovered on the margins of my conscious memory; I couldn't easily transcribe a beautiful story about a day we'd spent together but I might, with some prompting, dictate a series of recollections that might later be edited into a fitting and generous tribute, which coupled with the fitting and generous tributes of our peers felt like a more appropriate approach, this collective storytelling from all of his loved ones about the person who he'd been, even if it wasn't exactly who they thought he was, which the bulk of my reporting would eventually reflect. For example, my friend Ruth, who I'd dated after college—that was a long story, I didn't need to get into it—wasn't a writer, but an audio project would allow her to meaningfully contribute because apart from the words she might say, there was her tone of voice, a tone that might communicate something deep and earnest in a way that text, flat on the page, could not. And given that, it just seemed like audio was the best way in. It also introduced some interesting possibilities for the structure: we could begin with some nice recollections, before transitioning into a more serious rumination about his death, and then kind of swoop back to the beginning, and then bing-bang-boom, some of the reporting about the heroin would eventually make its way in, or something like that. Maybe this sounded abstract, but I wanted to play around because podcasting had never quite been my thing, and I started to explain why, walking him through my experience with the city and music and sound and why I thought this kind of format might work instead, hoping that he'd agree that it was a good idea and that I wasn't entirely insane.

What felt like entire eons passed before Reggie cleared his throat. "I just have a couple of thoughts," he said. What I'd just said wasn't necessarily a bad idea. He empathized with the desire for experimentation, the desire for flouting the rules, the desire for taking a form and inverting the form and making everyone say, *Goddamn, what happened to the form?* But there were limitations to what I was describing. Foremost that he'd been hired to do a very specific job, and that Sadie had found it appropriate to assign him to this particular project suggested that she was allowing him to get his feet wet at this new company, which in his experience meant doing a more traditional thing. Not that a more traditional thing was even a bad idea, contrary to what I might have assumed about—he swept his hands through the air—all of those *other podcasts* taking up space. Convention wasn't just a copout, there were benefits to adapting a model that the listener could immediately recognize, because from what he'd learned through his own experience, a lot of people consumed podcasts the way I'd purported to avoid—casually, without much concern for picking up every single sound through all the distractions of modern life. It wasn't like anywhere on Earth offered a complete respite from extraneous sound, even in your car you were subject to honks, barking dogs, squealing brakes, strangers in other cars screaming at strangers on the street, and so forth. The euphoric music experience I'd described wasn't immune to that, either, surely I didn't pick up every detail of every song as I trod through the city.

Because this wasn't a casual undertaking, he stressed. We'd probably be working on this for the next six months, at minimum. There were the logistical challenges of tracking down all of these interviews, and the emotional challenge of sustaining my interest. There were possibly legal concerns, which a lawyer would be better suited to answer. And there were Seth's parents, who couldn't sue the podcast out of existence but could make my life hell if I didn't at least give them a good faith heads-up about what we were looking into. "Just imagine these weepy Catholics going on about how some New York motherfucker exploited their boy for content.

"I know you're invested because this was your friend, but we can't take any shortcuts or waste time on any wishy-washy roundabout digressions because we don't have any answers," he continued. "I understand your need to hear from everyone who knew him, and maybe there's a place for that, but don't get confused: This is a podcast about a person who died, unnecessarily, and this hotshot who had an outsize role in that. Who, what, where, why, when—the fundamentals still matter. What you said about this atmosphere of death, and the way everyone around you felt—that may be the case, but it's not the only high school in America with some shit going on. I grew up in Queens in the nineties."

I understood what he was saying, but I bristled at the idea I was maybe in over my head. "Maybe *you* should host a podcast," I said.

Fortunately, this made him laugh. "One day," he said. "But it's worth thinking about those questions. You know, your answers should be righteous and pure and all of that shit. You should be an arrow, not a shotgun—something pointed right at the heart of the matter, not spraying all over the place. If only so that when someone asks you what this is about, you don't just fall on your ass."

Sadie had never talked like this, and hearing it made me feel like I'd chugged seven Red Bulls. Who didn't want to be an arrow pointed right at the heart of the matter? I wanted to get this right, so that Reggie would understand my motivations were true and good, that I wasn't just pursuing this to get a raise and a promotion. "These are good questions," I said, to break the silence. "I just don't have any answers right now that wouldn't sound made up."

"I understand," he said. "Listen, you're out of town, we don't have to get into all of it right now. It's only when you get back to New York that we can't have any doubts about what we're doing here."

AFTER MY CALL WITH REGGIE ENDED, I WENT UPSTAIRS TO TELL William what I'd learned about Seth. I found him on the couch, where he was giving one of the dogs a neck massage. But as I talked, he focused more on brushing the dander off his hands, and when I was finished all he managed was a tepid "Oh, wow." I was used to William playing it cool, but the reaction surprised me. I knew he and Seth had never been all that close, but come on, wasn't that an unbelievable story? Everyone always wanted to know "the big event" at your high school, and possibly this was ours.

This did not appear to convince him. "The big event at Sayers is when Devin Jones got caught fucking his girlfriend in Ms. Krystal's office," he said. "Or when Sonya Devers beat the hell out of that pregnant girl . . . Why am I even debating this? What you're talking about didn't even take place at school. Anyway, I know everyone loved Seth, but he was everyone else's best friend, not mine. And Lee, I *hated* Lee."

"You hated Lee?" I didn't like that much of what I knew of him, but would've never said something so strong.

William had a way of talking that could make everything he said sound like it was part of some dramatic and sexy banter, but right now he was completely serious. "He was just such a cretin. He always treated me like I was a joke—like there was something he knew about me that I couldn't see for myself."

"That's kind of intense, no?"

"Some things you take personally, and you never forget. I hold grudges."

William didn't need to remind me how shy he was back in high school, but listening to cool music granted casual friendship with other people who listened to cool music. One time, he had ended up in a blob of Sayers people at a concert—he couldn't remember the band—that included Lee, for whatever reason. Lee didn't seem interested in socializing with him, but that was fine, it was loud inside the Metro, you didn't need to talk. After the show ended everyone ended up migrating to Clark's, which still existed then, in order to dawdle over a plate of fries.

He smiled now, thinking of it—it wasn't anything special, only the typical bullshitting of bored teenagers who believe they're the most interesting people in the world. That's why William was having such a good time, because this wasn't his usual attitude, and it felt nice to be with other people even if they weren't exactly friends.

"I remember we were all packed into these booths, and Lee—not only was he not really including me, but he was staring at me whenever he wasn't talking to someone else. Just staring, without saying anything. Finally when I worked up the courage to ask what was going on, he only laughed." He gritted his teeth, and braced his arm against the doorway to his kitchen. "I don't know what his deal was. It's like he knew he could make me uncomfortable, and he got a kick out of it. Not a nice person, fundamentally. It doesn't make me happy to learn he was even more of a piece of shit. It just makes me think, *He was a piece of shit.*" William seemed authentically bent out of shape talking about this. I didn't want to press, so I changed the subject.

Since logging back into Facebook to find Lee I'd spent more time surfing my timeline and clicking between profiles, compiling a list of potential interview subjects who were apparently living in Los Angeles. Mostly they were acquaintances I'd lost touch with immediately after graduation. There was also Natalia. Though she'd never been my girlfriend, she was technically my ex, as we'd dated for five and a half weeks the summer after our junior year. It began innocent and mostly chaste: we kissed a few awkward times and held hands in public, before graduating to a handful of tempestuous make-out sessions when my parents were at work. So when she announced she was having a nice time but we should just be friends, I reacted like a colossal loser: I told her I loved her, I said she was doing unbelievable things to my heart, I lay in bed thinking *Why me* and listening to the same Neil Young songs on repeat. But Natalia, who'd emigrated from Ukraine at a young age, was immune to tormented boys who didn't know what to do with their hands. She ignored all my texts, didn't talk to me for the first month of the school year, and only remitted when she started dating another guy, since by that point in my woe-is-me depression quest I wasn't anywhere recognizable as a threat.

We'd fallen out of touch after high school, but last year she'd followed me on Instagram. She'd moved to Los Angeles to work in an administrative capacity at the Broad, a contemporary art museum where her best friend, Anna, was a curator. Both of them were still friends with Audrey, the third girl in their group, who now designed airplanes at Raytheon—a job I could not believe anyone our age did, much less a former punk.

After thinking about it for two seconds, I messaged her to see what she was up to—I was in L.A. for a few more days and wouldn't mind seeing her if she was around, after all this time, and in fact if she wanted to invite Audrey and Anna, that might be a nice idea. To my faint surprise, she replied immediately saying yes, she'd float the idea right this moment.

As we hiked up to the Griffith Observatory, which Audrey had suggested might be fun, the sun was scorning me personally as I slipped off my jacket and folded it into my tote bag. Sweat aside, I had to admit it did feel good to walk along this trail, adjusting my stride to account for the crumbled rock underfoot my now-dusty new Jordans, surveying the different groups making their way up and down the path, and pausing as we approached a ridge in order to look out at the city.

"Where's that?" I said, pointing to a patch of buildings in the distance.

"I have no idea," Natalia said curtly. In high school she'd been standoffish and blunt, and I appreciated that these qualities had not ebbed with time.

"You know where that is, it's downtown," Anna said. She untied and redid her long black hair into a ponytail. "We work there." Anna was also Ukrainian, but she'd been born in Chicago, and the difference was she did not appear to regard America and American life as permanently stupid. She and Natalia made a funny pair in high school, wearing identical eyeshadow and studded bracelets and torn band shirts, but Anna was fundamentally approachable and Natalia was fundamentally not.

Audrey was just as friendly as Anna, but less idealistic—immediately after high school she'd let go of her flirtation with the counterculture and joined a sorority. At the start of our walk I'd casually asked about her job, halfway expecting a self-conscious response about how she'd never expected to work for *Raytheon*, but instead she happily walked me through a typical day, a narrative that included the sentence "During our afternoon meeting, sometimes I'll have to talk to one of the retired generals on our board." It was difficult to connect the words coming out of her mouth to the spindly girl I remembered walking into school with bandaged arms. I respected her lack of defensiveness, but also I was having a hard time hearing any of this, so I unconsciously let myself drift toward Natalia while Audrey and Anna wound their way ahead of us.

Now we were pacing our way up the trail and resuming a conversation about movies we'd recently seen. During my first day in town, I'd found myself walking down Sunset toward no one in particular, when it started raining. I didn't want to be caught outside without an umbrella, so I slipped into the movie theater I'd spotted just as the weather turned, and bought a ticket to the only movie that was about to start: a largely improvised melodrama about a British college student's doomed romance with a pretentious addict. The plot was hard to follow and every character seemed desperately unlikable, and I was drifting in and out, but at least when it was over the rain had stopped. Still, I'd been shocked to learn the movie had received rave reviews, most of which praised its "lived-in dialogue" and "meticulous set design" without mentioning it was "boring as shit," and not in the "I am learning something" way of other art-house cinema, where maybe you also fell asleep in the theater but at least walked out feeling like you'd gleaned something about the secret heart of life.

"All of that sounds terrible," Natalia said.

"I saw the live-action *Aladdin*," Audrey offered. "Also not very good."

I pulled a wad of Kleenex from my tote and wiped my forehead. "I think it's possible that every movie is bad. At least the ones in the theater."

"That can't be true," Audrey said, taking me literally.

"Oh, I wasn't being literal, it's just—"

"Look at that." Anna cut me off and pointed in the distance, where the summit had materialized. I looked around, but only saw groups of people taking photos of one another.

"Weren't we walking toward the observatory?"

"You don't always walk up to the observatory, this path is much better," Anna said. She directed me to turn around, where I saw the Griffith floating in the distance. "We can walk there, but it'll probably take another hour, and then we'll have to walk farther to get back to the car."

"Never mind," I said. "Hey, let's get to that summit." We made for the clearing and found a spot along the incline, where we resumed our panoramic appraisal of the skyline. I slowly turned my head to take in the city as a whole, no closer to competently deciphering which parts were the ones I'd visited, but nonetheless feeling like I was accomplishing something. Nature! The outdoors! Los Angeles! We'd made it up here without any real fuss, and I felt a resurgent warmth at how seamlessly we were reconnecting, even if I hadn't found a way to bring up the podcast just yet.

As we stood around, I attempted to recall the roots of our initial bond. I hadn't interacted with Anna or Audrey whatsoever since high school, and unlike someone like Ruth or William, it was difficult to remember why we'd ever been friends in the first place. They, along with Natalia, were three cool, charismatic punk girls. What had I ever offered? But I knew I had to stop myself from obsessing over every which way I might have initially misinterpreted our friendship, unless they gave me a reason. It was a luxury to sift through the detritus of the past until I pulled out something that mattered; unless people went to therapy or were about to die it wasn't what occupied their time, not with all the forces marshaling one's focus.

There was nothing suggesting that my presence should be natural, and yet it was. We'd skipped past "getting to know each other again" and right into "passively comfortable with doing nothing" as we stood here, silently turning from left to right to left to right and around again, walking in small circles around the edge of the summit and staring at the ground—well, that was just me, the girls were frozen in place, but they weren't talking either.

Natalia looked at me, and I looked back. We'd kissed each other half a lifetime ago, an incident that had permanently swung my taste in women toward the contemptuous and unsympathetic. She would probably stop talking to me if I ever said this out loud, and in fact I wondered if I could stop talking to myself for having even thought it to begin with, but it was still true. The air around us felt perfumed with meaning, though I conceded it was possibly the endorphins, or the mild edible I'd taken before we'd started hiking.

I was on the cusp of saying something profoundly corny, but before I could embarrass myself, Audrey suggested we take a selfie. She nestled closer to Anna and Natalia, and I took my place at their side. "No, let's turn around, I don't want the background to be fucking rocks," she said. After a couple of attempts, she showed us the finished product. The women looked wonderful, the sun hitting their faces just right and their hair blowing ever so in the wind. I was smiling with an earnestness I did not often recognize on my face, and told her to send it to me.

"All right," I said, and thought about what to say next. I took another look at the skyline, and, feeling satisfied, turned back to the trail. "How does everyone feel about getting drunk?"

THE BACKYARD OF THE BAR IN HIGHLAND PARK WAS INDEED SPAcious and convivial, just as Anna had promised. We'd planted our flag in a sizable corner, which was now seeded with many faces I recognized as I looked around.

Right now that was Audrey, who was telling me something very serious. "Here's the thing," she said. Raytheon had been praised for its gender equity, and she agreed there was something nice about how many women sat on the board, but at the end of the day they were defense contractors, and there's no such thing as an egalitarian defense contractor. So every day she wore the same bland outfit, and ordered the same bland salad in the cafeteria, and spent her day making bland technical adjustments to blueprints of machines she would never see in person, because they were built at one of her company's rural manufacturing hubs, whereas in Los Angeles they got to do the glamorous work. "I mean, it's not glamorous at all. But it's not Iowa."

The trade-off for this flattening of her identity was a tremendous amount of money, but also a profound separation from the people in her life. Not socially, she stressed. Socially, she always did stuff like drink in the backyard of a cool Highland Park bar, and besides, I remembered her in high school, she never had a problem getting along even when she was depressed. But even though nobody here talked too much about work, whenever she went to parties she always noticed how different everyone else carried themselves. They were in film, or television, or modeling, or public relations, or cannabis, or waitstaffing at the cool restaurants, or entertainment law, or entertainment agencies, or in the case of her two best friends, at the Broad—at this Natalia, who was sitting one table over, made a face I instantly identified as "disdain"—or any other number of hip industries whose work, more than conferring any real hipness, empowered them with an unconscious entitlement about how life was meant to go. Like, duh, of course, let's just pick up some prerolleds at Med Men, and wait for a table at Night Market Song, and drink on some roof. We'll look handsome and beautiful, we'll make the right references and wear the right clothes, we'll kiss a stranger and feel satisfied with our decisions whenever we collapse into bed.

She wasn't bitter about this, or judgmental—she liked all of those things as well, and did them herself. But it was a conscious lifestyle for her, not something she took for granted. She was choosing how to move through the world, rather than assuming she could. The release, for her, was in the intentionality—of knowing she wasn't falling into a pattern of behavior because her social climate demanded it. She wasn't saying this well because she was slightly drunk, and she was in a good mood—*I haven't seen some of these people in so long,* she said, dramatically sweeping her arm across our backyard cluster—but what she was trying to describe was the buzz of knowing she wasn't lying to herself. She didn't believe she was contributing to some kind of cause like the people who'd accrued the sheen of righteousness as though what they didn't do was model, or public relations, or write shitty TV shows nobody watched. She went to sleep knowing she wasn't beholden to any asinine fictions about herself or her place in the world.

She spun her head around the backyard with avian self-awareness, to make sure nobody was listening in. (Natalia, I noticed, had stopped looking at us.) "I'm saying it's fucked up to sit in meetings with retired generals, but not much more than trying to develop a convincing brand for a hotel."

"Ha-ha . . ." I tried to think about what to say to this. "I mean, brands are not good, but . . . what?"

She made a *yap-yap-yap* gesture with her hands, and finished her cocktail. "Oh, you know what I'm saying."

"I'm trying, but Raytheon . . . like, *Raytheon* Raytheon?" I concentrated all of my energies on not laughing. "I think I just need to hear more about what you do."

Her eyes squinted with something I recognized as deliberation, now that she'd picked up on what I really wanted to talk about. "I am not paid enough to tell you. I'm just not. But on that note, I'm going to get another drink. Do you need anything?"

I'd take another, I said. I really couldn't believe how many people had shown up to the bar—that Audrey and Anna and even Natalia had apparently sent a series of crisscrossing texts within their social network of former Sayers students now living in Los Angeles about spontaneously getting together on this shiny day and that several people had not just said *maybe* or *sounds interesting*, but headed over on short notice to drink with us. (William, unsurprisingly, had been a gracious pass when I texted him.) Some of them I'd been friendly with—Joe H. and I used to talk about comic books, and Zoe had been my chemistry partner once, and Esteban was on the school newspaper, but others I remembered nearly nothing about.

Had we ever hung out together outside school, even in a group? It was possible, but I hadn't talked to Joe K. or Serena since then, and certainly not that much in the first place, and as for Joe H. and Zoe and Esteban and—Jesus, was that fucking Chris Larkin walking over, dressed like some bloated DJ? "Goddamn," Chris Larkin said, passively raising his fist for me to bump. "Look at the motherfucking homie." Chris Larkin was the genuine kind of idiot you first and sometimes only met in high school, but seeing him now conjured a not-false wave of sentimentality, ebbing instantly when he said I was fat now.

But even this was the reason why I'd suggested that the girls invite all these people, in order to recall the general environment of high school, and from there broach the question of Seth and Lee and their secret lives among those who possibly remembered them too. I'd meant to subtly tease this out once we were all chemically comfortable with each other, but it was becoming harder to find the moment. When we'd all returned to Natalia's apartment, Audrey and Anna split up into their separate cars. When we showed up at the bar, we started drinking. When we started drinking, we went back to talking about what else I wanted to do before flying back to New York, and while I appreciated the interest, what I really wanted to do was dramatically put my glass down and say *Hey, I'd like to bring something up.* My courage kept approaching as the conversation went on, but it still never felt right, and not much later we were into our second drinks, and then our third and fourth drinks, and as more people showed up dropping what might have been a past-altering bombshell among this happy group of old friends who only wanted to get drunk on a lovely summer Saturday seemed akin to a war crime, the type Audrey enabled every single day, which was crazy as hell the more I thought about it.

I am in a hilarious and weird situation, I texted Ruth, who didn't respond. Come to the bar bro, I texted William, who immediately replied: No. I tried to concentrate on mingling, cycling through the dialogue I'd repeated several times since arriving in town—my life was going like this, New York was going like that, I'd done such and such and was looking forward to doing such and such more, the tone of my voice pitching toward something I recognized as false cheer, as though I were auditioning to sing Christmas carols.

After hearing this spiel, Chris Larkin passed me a rolled cigarette. I accepted without asking him what was in it, before taking another drink from Anna as she made her way back to Natalia, who was looking at me with an amused expression. *I'm trying to be nice,* I tried to say with my face. She nodded back. What I wanted to do was get rid of this crowd and attempt to guide this afternoon back toward a fact-finding mission, not suffer through Chris Larkin's appraisal of my life. "I read your shit," he said. "That interview with Vince Staples? Fucking killer, man. That's real hip-hop . . . not that fake bling-bling and bitches crap. What's he like?"

Adjusting Chris Larkin's racial framework was not my responsibility, at least not right now. "He's nice. Normal," I said. "More normal than you'd think."

"That's tight as fuck." He inhaled the joint down to a stub, before smashing it out. "What are you working on now?"

"Actually, let me run something by you." I didn't know where I was going with this, but: "You remember Seth Terry? He died under some shitty circumstances that I just learned about, and I'm staging an investigation. We're thinking"—I made my hands attempt to replicate a flashing marquee—"podcast."

I did not know Chris Larkin well enough to read whether he was interested or stoned. "Why Seth Terry?"

"Well . . . the circumstances were really shitty, I'm not kidding. You'll have to listen to find out the rest."

"Uh-huh," he said, seemingly unconvinced. "I don't remember him that well but you should look into what happened to Josh Richardson. Unsafe bike lanes are a fucking conspiracy, dude. But who benefits? *That's* what the fuck is going on in every city." He shook his head, and as I was thinking about what to say he pulled out another joint. I raised my hands to excuse myself and pointed at my full drink as though I needed a refill, before walking away.

I was definitely losing the thread. I wanted to hear my friends talk about themselves, but sometimes they couldn't be trusted—nothing Audrey said had made any kind of sense, she claimed she wasn't lying to herself, but clearly that was a defense mechanism against coming to terms with what her life had turned into. Or maybe she really believed what she said, and so even as it seemed obviously deluded to me, she was the one who'd just bought a house in the hills with her husband, and had booked tickets to Burning Man in the fall, and was living the secure existence of a willing participant in the American empire. *American empire*, Jesus—I was thinking like a fucking asshole is what I was doing, instead of just going with the flow, letting Audrey and Chris Larkin and Joe H. go on just as I had gone on, our small talk papier-mâché-ing over any interesting topic. Such as: When's the last time you thought about death? Or your mother? Wow, I really couldn't help myself, nestled within this familiar and unfamiliar scene, completely wired and desperate to stick out even though I had nothing to prove.

My timeline for leaving the bar sped up from "in a few hours" to "right now," and I swung by Natalia, who was somehow sitting by herself within this mass of acquaintances. "How's it going?" I said casually.

"It's fine," she said, signaling nothing of her true feelings.

"That's cool. Listen"—I put my drink down—"I need to get the fuck out of here." Without saying anything, she picked up her purse and stood. Anna was the only person who noticed, and they exchanged looks I couldn't decipher—something like *Good luck* or maybe *Oh, brother*. "Anna," I said, turning to her, "if anyone asks where we went, just say I wasn't feeling well and had to peace out. Okay? I'm giving you formal permission to say I couldn't handle my shit."

"Don't worry," she said, pulling in for a hug. "Your reputation is safe with me."

AUDREY HAD MENTIONED ANOTHER PLACE, I SAID, AND WHILE IT was probably a ridiculous idea given that most hotel rooftops invoked the sleazy, monied atmosphere native to date rapists and cokeheads, it might be halfway all right. If she was open to it. *Sure*, Natalia said, the *sure* of the mostly apathetic, a response I would've taken as spite were it coming from anyone else. That was the problem, wasn't it? Natalia was sort of a jerk, and while this brusqueness won you many points in high school and college, it lost its cachet as we rocketed into our early and soon-to-be-mid and even late thirties. Still, she was sitting in the backseat of the Uber with me as we sped toward the Freehand, looking at her phone but not being rude about it. I told the driver he could drop us off in front but he said he'd been here before, it was better to stop across the street so we wouldn't interfere with the valets. "I'll make sure you're not near any homeless people," he said, and I did not know how to reply. Immediately I felt embarrassed—me, the tourist with on-demand access to a good time, and the driver, who'd repeated this process a thousand times.

We did not see any homeless people when we stepped out. We didn't speak inside the elevator. A part of me was energized by the setting; in another world, two people like us might have a single drink before retreating downstairs into a room we'd rented for the night. Natalia looked gorgeous, though I tried not to look at her too obviously. I was still getting used to her face, after all this time apart. She no longer wore heavy eyeliner or thrift-store buttons, and her platinum dye had faded to its natural brunette, but the cumulative effect of these adult changes was annoyingly hot. Why couldn't she just have looked slightly worse, like everyone did after hitting their thirties? But I knew better than to try anything, even if I may have wanted to in a world where we had no obligations to anyone, no history beyond the moment, no fear of consequences or ramifications for one's bad actions. I could accept we didn't live in that world, much in the same way we didn't have world peace or universal health care. But also, I wanted to know if she was looking at me. *You need to dial it the fuck back,* I very wisely told myself.

The roof was about half full with other well-dressed twenty- and thirtysomethings. We found a table along the edge, underneath a pink umbrella and some string lights. Frank Ocean was playing in the background. I went to get us drinks, and when I came back Natalia didn't appear to have moved; she wasn't even looking at her phone. I couldn't shake the feeling she hated being here, even though she'd agreed to be here, and jokingly attempted to float this theory. "Don't be an idiot," she said. "I thought we left so we didn't have to talk to anyone."

"Yeah, you were very visibly not into Audrey's shit."

"She's like a hologram of what a person should be. I know we go back, and that's not nothing, but sometimes when she talks I think to myself, *You are such a fucking dumb bitch I'm going to kill myself.*"

"Well, we can talk to each other," I said. "But thank you for being rude about it, to confirm I'm insane."

"You are insane. You're the same as you were fifteen years ago."

"No I'm not," I attempted to say in a cool way.

"'No I'm not.' Yes, you are. Don't make me explain why."

"What if I want you to explain why?" Despite all the mental guard rails I'd thrown up in the elevator, maybe I was trying to flirt.

Her laugh was a harsh, clipped thing. "Do you really want me to?"

"No . . . I was joking, please don't." Suddenly the moment I'd been waiting for materialized before me, as I became aware we were very alone. I took a long sip of my drink and felt this new infusion of alcohol bloom through my system. "I had something else I wanted to bring up though."

I began with Kelsey and how we'd met for drinks a few days before. I hadn't been expecting anything other than a hopefully not-boring night with an old friend, because it's nice to see everyone from time to time. "Even Chris Larkin," I said. Her face said *I don't know about that*, but I continued talking: For a while it had gone fine, we went over how I'd embarrassed myself at Navy Pier (I'll explain that in a second, I added) and some other things, but Kelsey had casually revealed this insane thing about Seth, how he'd died from a heroin overdose enabled by Lee, you remember him, dynamiting all of my ideas about the podcast idea I was knocking around (I'll also explain that in a second, I added) but more importantly dynamiting all my ideas about Seth, because what the fuck? Right?

"Hold on," Natalia said, her expression broadcasting something I hadn't seen from her in a long time, maybe not ever: confusion. "Seth, like *Seth*?"

Natalia had worked on the literary magazine too. "Yes, our Seth." I condensed what Kelsey had told me about Joy House and the funeral, then what I'd gleaned from Googling Lee and from talking to Ruth. Which brought me back to the podcast.

As much as I hated talking about my work, talking about *talking* felt even stupider, though I was hopeful that some of this made sense as I rounded toward my crescendo. "I think all of this can be roped into sort of an experimental narrative about memory and truth at this formative moment in our lives—the teen years when all our ideas about ourselves are getting worked out, even though as that's happening there's so much else happening outside the margins, stuff we may never have been privy to even as it had an immense impact on the lives of others. I mean, my producer wants there to be a straight investigation into Lee's role, and I definitely want to pin that down, but there's something more beautiful and tragic here, right?"

"Slow down a second," she said. Over the day I'd grown reacquainted with Natalia's default passivity, and I was surprised how engaged she now seemed—how much she, too, wanted to get the details straight. "I'm still getting over the idea there was a heroin ring at school?"

"Yes," I said. "Isn't that insane? It's crazy that there were people doing heroin at high school. Heroin? At our school? It's crazy that Seth was buying heroin from a guy we knew. I don't want to exploit it, it would have to be done sensitively, but isn't that crazy? Also, do you mind if I record this?"

"I just . . . I never saw any of that," she said, as I made sure the recorder was picking up her voice. "I was such a goody-two-shoes. Hold on, don't fucking record this."

I feigned indignity and clicked it off. "You were not a goody-two-shoes. You were a nightmare."

Natalia raised her hand like *Stop*. "I was a goody-two-shoes pretending to be a nightmare. I came from strong, Ukrainian values; I didn't know anything about heroin. Lee was dealing heroin? Did Seth's parents know about this? Obviously they knew what happened, they must've kept it to themselves." She downed the rest of her drink and shook her head. "You're really going to interview Lee about all this?"

Natalia was providing the staggered reaction I'd been waiting for, not the absentmindedness of Ruth or the apathy of William. "I don't know, I hope so. He didn't add me back on Facebook. A lot depends on how he seems. I never really knew Lee. I don't know what to expect."

"I knew Lee," she said. She started to speak, then paused. "He was a total shit."

I shifted my weight in my chair. "Yeah?"

"The type of pervert who wants to charm you into giving him a hand job because he thinks it'll be the greatest."

"My God," I said. "Nothing happened though?"

"Of course not, he was disgusting. But he was good-looking, I'm not blind."

"Did you ever see his band play?"

"No, I wasn't living in Chicago, it didn't matter to me. Anyway, what are you hoping to get out of this?"

Ever since my talk with Reggie, I'd thought about this. Natalia wasn't my coworker, though, and with her I might recite some appeal to truth and emotion, the clarification of the passage of time and the gradations of nostalgia, the slow chiseling of reality to reveal the grime underneath, like in David Lynch movies. Beyond that, it was fucked up to admit, but a part of me just wanted to look Lee right in the eye and mortify him into feeling the most intense feelings of shame and guilt, as though I were the pope.

But all of that seemed too messy for the moment, so what I said was: "I'm still figuring it out."

She seemed to accept this, and asked how it was going so far. So-so, I said. I was still on leave, and I didn't exactly know who I should talk to—so far I'd marked down Lee and Ben, but no one else. I'd spent the last few days wondering if I should get up with anyone else in Los Angeles before I returned to New York, though given the party we'd just left it was clear my focus was divided. "I'll regroup when I get home," I said. "Try to assume the role of the neutral journalist, as the work demands. I can always come back out here if I need to."

"That sounds like a plan," she said.

"Would you want to talk about Seth? Maybe even right now?" I nudged the recorder, which I'd left on our table, and tried to smile in a playful way.

"Hmmm." Her face broadcast another unfamiliar emotion: authentic contemplation. "I don't know. I was very sad when Seth died, but it's been a long time. I'd just need a minute to think about it. To see if I have anything to add. Or remember."

That was fair enough, so I decided it was time to change the subject. She was far more interested in circling back to my retelling of the day at Navy Pier and forced me to repeat every part of it in slow, unblinking detail, especially the speech about the potatoes. I even looked it up on my phone for her.

"That's what I remember about you," she said, after she was finished laughing. "You were so earnest even when it was clear you had no idea what you were doing."

"Thank God that's no longer the case," I said, and changed the subject before her expression could correct me.

AROUND MIDNIGHT, NATALIA SAID SHE WAS FALLING ASLEEP. The conversation had dwindled; our drinks were empty; I felt the pleasant stillness of nonintrusive company, the absence of expectation or forward momentum. Not-talking was its own reward, after the amount of time we'd known each other. When she offered to reimburse me for the drinks I'd bought I told her not to worry, it was my treat, I appreciated the opportunity to fuck off in private.

"It wasn't so bad," she said, conceding a small smile.

"Even so, what a world. Could you ever have imagined," I said, the words coming out a little too quickly, "that your old high school boyfriend might be okay for an all right time?"

Natalia's face was very bemused, as though she couldn't quite believe what I'd said. I couldn't quite believe it either. "You were never my boyfriend," she said. "But yes, it's been an all right time." She stood up, and I mimicked her. "My car is coming, so I'd better get downstairs. You're sure I can't Venmo you?" I shook my head; I was already embarrassed enough.

I walked her to the elevator, and we stood there in silence as we waited. "This thing with Seth . . ." she said as the doors opened, her voice suddenly small. "Please let me know what happens. *I want to know what happened.*" We hugged, and she even pecked me on the cheek. I said I'd text her if I got up to anything else while I was still in town, knowing that it was unlikely.

As I opened my phone I found a half-dozen messages with apologies from my friends, they were stuck in Santa Monica or Mid-Wilshire or Pasadena, their boyfriends or girlfriends had dragged them to a party they couldn't get out of, the screening had run late, they were battling a stomach thing, they were fading fast and just couldn't make it out, they were sorry about that, but they'd see me the next time I was in Los Angeles, or the next time they were in New York. I hadn't told any of them that I'd left the bar to drink with Natalia, but it had worked out of its own accord. I typed out a half-dozen messages absolving them of their responsibilities and ordered a final drink at the bar. I never drank to excess, but it felt good to cut loose in an unfamiliar environment, embrace unfamiliar surroundings. And now it was time to go home.

My driver didn't say anything, and it was a short ride from downtown to William's. The golden retrievers yapped at me but I didn't stop to shush them, just powered right through the gate and into the house. I kicked off my shoes and went downstairs to the guest room.

I bumped into a shirtless and wordless William, who nodded at me before stepping into the bathroom. When I got to my room I took out my phone to charge it. On the screen was a notification telling me that Lee had accepted my friend request.

Part II

I REMOVED MY HEADPHONES AND SKIMMED MY HAIR WITH MY hand to give it life. My forehead felt clammy, so I wiped it down with my wrist. "What did you think?" I said into the microphone. I hadn't shown Reggie the script before we'd started recording, only described a loose outline of what I wanted to talk about today: the final time I'd seen Seth, less than a month before his death. As currently structured, the reflection—or at least a few parts of it, edited and reassembled as necessary—would introduce the fourth episode of what was currently referred to within my company as the Untitled Seth Project. Though we'd only completed the first episode, Reggie and I had outlined where we thought the remaining seven episodes needed to go, and I had continued writing what I hoped would be the insightful, devastating, and appropriately funny narration to accompany the litany of voices bringing Seth back to life.

We'd spent nearly a month shaping the pilot, and I'd memorized every narrative beat, every audio cue, every line reading, every audible inhale and exhale that Reggie had insisted on leaving in. Something too clean would reek of calculation, detachment, professionalism, he said, but the lightest touch of amateurism would invite the audience to trust my connection to Seth that much more. Currently, the podcast opened with a truncated snippet from an interview I'd conducted with Ruth, about the first time she met Seth: "Seth is wearing a Bikini Kill shirt, and he has this tote bag that says NO BLOOD FOR OIL on it, and he's just so serious as he explains why the Gay-Straight Alliance is important, why it's really where we can make a difference. He's not smiling. He's not laughing. He was so self-possessed, my God. And I just knew I'd made the right decision." That fed directly into a similar recollection from Anna, who'd signed up once Natalia had informed her about the project, which fed into a similar recollection from Joe K., who'd signed up once Anna had informed him about the project, and from there a series of other similar recollections from former classmates who'd also been informed through the grapevine, each testimony shorter and shorter until my voice—confident and collected and recognizably different due to Reggie's decision to frame it with a delicate arpeggiated keyboard sequence (a leitmotif for my narration, apparent in the following minutes)—entered the mix.

We all have a friend, I began, *who broadens our understanding of how the world can be.* From there I flowed toward my own first encounter with Seth, which flowed toward a general reflection on the nature of reflection, which flowed toward a series of complementary reflections from the voices we'd heard so far, now prefaced with their own introductions ("My name is Ruth McCluskey, and I met Seth Terry in the fall of my freshman year") and tightly edited by Reggie into a kind of Greek chorus singing the praises and impact of this extraordinary character, before my voice established some background. *It was 2002*, one piece of narration went, *and George W. Bush was president. Now, I know what you're thinking: "Jesus, 9/11 again?" But I'm not trying to dive into the geopolitical ramifications, the national climate of fear. I'm saying we were fourteen years old and didn't know a thing about anything. The world was insane, and we could barely grasp that insanity. So here's this guy who loved Harry Potter and graphic T-shirts just like the rest of us, but he's uncommonly put together. He's confident. He understands something about himself that the rest of us are trying to articulate for the first time, and at that age it's completely intoxicating to be around someone with that contagious energy. To be around someone who makes you feel like you're part of a world, even when you're so blinkered by being fourteen that nothing quite makes sense, much less 9/11.*

Holding this idea—that Seth was clearly special at that age—at the forefront of my mind, as though declaratively pinned by some heretical and insistent priest, had propelled me through the months of recording and editing and interviewing and rerecording and reediting and re-rerecording and reinterviewing and on and on and on. Seth's accidental overdose hadn't just been a tragedy, but a deprivation of someone real and true, someone worth summoning from the recesses of the not-so-recent past.

I'd accrued the glow of destiny in my pursuit of the truth, and the clarity of this purpose and my desire for more clarity occasionally startled me. Some nights I lay awake thinking, *Yes, fuck yes, this is happening, I am doing something vital and necessary and I am going to crack open the whole fucking case and lay this squarely at Lee's feet though I don't believe in carceral solutions, only moral solutions, and after realizing the depth of my commitment and insight and general understanding of how everything works, everyone will have no choice but to regard me as a semiprofound emotional savant.* In the morning, sober, I'd feel embarrassed, but upon opening the Notes app in my phone and reading the perplexingly cogent thoughts I'd dictated to myself ("What if the root of destruction is revelation?" "Life is just a sprawling, incoherent mass of cultures"), I'd think ". . . . . true though?"

After returning from Los Angeles, I'd started texting the classmates whose contacts had remained in my phone through all its upgrades and asking if they wanted to speak with me for a project I was working on—I was a writer, in case they hadn't heard. At first I was nervous about how people might respond, but their reactions broadly fell into two categories: those who didn't think about Seth at all (and barely seemed to remember that he'd died), and those who still did, it's funny that I should ask after all these years, but yes, of course, you didn't just forget someone like that.

Upon reaching out via text message and Facebook and Instagram and even LinkedIn in some cases, a network of long-gone friends and acquaintances and subacquaintances quickly came together. My company had insisted on collecting release forms before we could formally go on the record, but nobody had any compunction about giving me the right to do what I wanted with their testimony, because who else had a better idea? We'd make plans to talk on the phone or over a video call. They would begin nervously, as though they weren't quite sure what to say. As I logged their recollections, inevitably I would realize it had been so long since many of these people had been afforded the emotional space to talk about all this with someone else. Seth had died so long ago; who could care much about something like that, given every other available problem? But they did care, and they cared that I cared. I had questions, and I followed up on their answers, but slowly I started to submerge my personality as much as possible, serenely staring at my subject with the patience of a nun in order to draw out whatever it was they had to say.

It was now November, and word of mouth had gotten

around, Cooper told me he'd heard from Lucas who'd heard from Maya who'd heard from Susie who'd heard from someone else, she couldn't remember exactly who—a game of telephone passing along my interest in their perspective, for ulterior purposes nobody quite perceived in full because it was just a podcast-in-progress, for the time being. We'd talk, and I'd thank them for their time, but it was never the end; eventually they'd get back in touch with another new memory recalled after much concentration, presented for addition to the logs I was building up.

What did they remember? A lot.

- The time Seth spearheaded the Gay-Straight Alliance's first-ever Pride party, which drew all of twenty-two people to drink Sprite and listen to Kylie Minogue in the chemistry lab, until the security guards came by asking them to turn down the music, and Seth reacted so violently, accusing them of homophobia and hypocrisy—the band club made just as much noise after school and nobody ever accused *them* of being faggots, to which the security guard said *Calm down*, his cousin was gay, they'd just left the door open and the sound really was bleeding into the hallways, they could go outside and listen for themselves, and in the end it was no trouble at all. (Laura Connington)
- The time Seth had walked in on her and her unnamed boyfriend having sex in one of the reserve stairwells, not only had he not freaked out, or found a security guard, but he stood outside watching the hallway for intruders until they were finished (which only took another three minutes, sadly). Afterward, when they

were rushing to zip their clothes back up and head back to their lockers before lunch period was over, Seth revealed he was actually running an errand for his Spanish teacher. He'd taken the reserve stairwell to save time, and now he'd been gone nearly ten minutes and he'd probably be in trouble. And when she and her unnamed boyfriend expressed a combination of astonishment and wariness that he'd run interference for them at the expense of his own reputation he said not to worry, duty called, some things were more important than reputation, and if he wasn't getting laid someone else should be. (Lana Krugman)

- The time he'd signed up for the math team, attended exactly one meeting, and when the teacher sponsor said, "See you next week," at the end he replied, "Oh, thank you, but I don't think so," and never came back. (Graham Limbeck)
- The time during the spring dance when Seth planted one right on his lips, and when he pushed away and laughed it off, *ha-ha-ha, what's the deal*, Seth said he'd been standing by himself the whole night and if that didn't implore him to move his ass and ask a girl to dance, he'd keep on smooching him until he was embarrassed enough to go home, and while he'd ended up dancing with Rachel Watkins (his crush for months, though nothing came of it) the kiss stuck in his mind. It never came up again between him and Seth, but when he went off to college in California a couple of years later, he ended up "finding himself" (said with deeply exaggerated air quotes) and, you know, it was interesting, Seth didn't really have much to do with it, but he had something

to do with it, and this was something he continued to think about, the way you could have a little bit to do with anyone's life at the right moment. (John Rotter)

- The time they'd waited for hours at the Metro so they could be right at the stage for the Pixies reunion show, where to their surprise they weren't uniquely young, the crowd was filled with dozens of other teenagers alongside the gray-haired Gen Xers in their Yo La Tengo shirts, and Kim Deal had looked right at them when they'd screamed along to "Debaser" in unison with the sold-out crowd, what a memory that had been, in her top ten favorite shows of all-time, even though she didn't listen to the Pixies these days, and certainly not rock 'n' roll. (Anna Tillman)
- The time when he'd tried to pose with the African American Club during yearbook photos and Ms. Malone, the sponsor, had said yes, even if he wasn't a member they always wanted more people for the photograph, but was he . . . ? Wasn't he . . . ? "Gay?" he said drolly, to which she said no, *some other kind of brown*, and everyone started laughing, Ms. Malone meant well but sometimes it seemed like her brain was permanently wired in the seventies, she could barely get her head around a typical biracial, and throwing South America into the mix disrupted her machinery altogether. (Marissa Kenny)

Reggie and I had taken care to group these interviews by theme—emotion (HAPPY / SAD / ANGRY / CONTEMPLATIVE), identity (QUEER / BLACK / CHICAGOAN), historical (IRAQ WAR / GAY MARRIAGE / *BROKEBACK MOUNTAIN*), transgression (ALCOHOL / HEROIN / SEX)—so that we could easily contour the recorded material to sync with my narration. Because the point wasn't just that Seth had existed, since I had to concede formative figures like Seth existed at high schools all across America. The overarching story was the specific mystery of his death and the seedy world incubating that death, nestled at the center of his celebrated life, and my attempts to excavate the truth from these recollections. Reggie had warned against the pitfalls of wishy-washiness—the point of all this was actually not the friends we'd made along the way—and so we'd endeavored to locate a middle ground allowing me to contextualize why this particular death had mattered so much, even considering all the deaths at my high school.

I couldn't read Reggie's face as he gestured for me to leave the sound booth and join him at his computer. My company's initial podcasts had been recorded externally, but recently a studio had been installed inside an unused office, the walls lined with pink and orange padded foam for sound insulation, and the room partitioned in half with a plaster barricade. They had finished the setup by assembling a makeshift terminal from a standing desk and an array of computer monitors, and because the overhead lights were never turned on, the room looked like the Batcave. The one thing it lacked was seating—Reggie preferred to work upright for reasons I did not understand, but tried to embrace as I took my place at his side.

"So what did you think?" I repeated. Though we'd only worked together for a few months, I'd picked up enough to figure out that Reggie's lack of expression was not, on its own, an expression of judgment. Reggie took his time before speaking, and he hadn't been kidding about not wanting to give "the talent" an inflated sense of self. Working with him I sometimes felt like I was auditioning for this job, even though the entire thing was my idea. I didn't recognize how much I exerted myself in social situations until encountering someone who, in the parlance of the times, felt comfortable "giving us nothing"—not because he was dull, or boring, but because he hadn't placed the same pressures on himself to seem outgoing and interesting. We were just coworkers, after all.

On his computer screen, I could see the script I'd shared with him. "It's good," he said. "Thoughtful. Eloquent. Considered. Emotional. Literary, even. All the things you're going for."

This was another tic I'd picked up on: the deadpanned layering of increasingly exaggerated compliments, preceding the inevitable truth. We may have been coworkers, but I did want to be friends, inasmuch as two people paid to spend time with each other could be friends, and so I felt comfortable adopting a fake defensive stance to mask my actual defensive feelings. "Just break my heart already," I said.

"I'm not trying to fuck with you," he said. "It's good. It's thoughtful, like I said. I'm thinking, and I continue to think, and I presume our audience will do the same."

"And yet . . ." I swept my hand in front of me, as though I were rolling out a red carpet.

He smiled, a small victory. "And yet something's missing. You know what I'm talking about, right? You're smart, you get what's going on."

Now I smiled, grateful to have his approval even as it accompanied his disapproval. "I know what you're talking about, but it's better if you say it."

"All right, check this out." He hit a key, and the screen tabbed over to an episode-by-episode flowchart he'd created in an organizational program whose name I had forgotten immediately. "Right now we've got a great introduction"—the cursor hovered over a black box labeled EPISODE 1: INTRODUCTION—"and the makings of a mystery"—the cursor moved to another black box labeled EPISODE 2: THE MYSTERY // SECRET HEROIN RING—"and some nice historical background," he concluded, the cursor landing on a box labeled EPISODE 3: THE BUSH YEARS. "Even though we're still filling in the details, there's a real skeleton for this thing. I know we're waiting to talk to the parents. I know we're waiting to contact your old school. But all of that, it's coming together. The finished product is—it's not totally in sight, but I can imagine how one could see it, from where we are." He turned to me, and slowly nodded as if to say, *Not bad*. "I think this could work out really well, Jacob."

Warmed by the thought, I nodded back. "I'm beginning to feel that way too."

"The problem . . ." He cleared his throat, and hesitated. "Sorry, I realize this is a personal subject for you. I don't want to sound like J. Jonah Jameson screaming for more photos of Spider-Man."

"I would be shocked if you ever raised your voice," I said.

"All right, well—the problem is that it's really not enough to gesture at the mystery, the longer we keep working on this. What we have is thoughtful and considered and emotional, for sure. But there's another main character besides yourself and Seth, who right now is nowhere to be found, and that is going to be a real problem."

I absolutely knew what he was going to say, but I wanted him to say it, so that I might deny reality for just a few more seconds. "I think it's time we have a longer conversation about what to do if we can't talk to Lee."

NOBODY HAD AS MUCH TO SAY ABOUT LEE.

Toward the end of my interviews, I would slip in an aside about how I was looking to get up with some other people from Sayers, maybe Hector Aviles or Ben Porter or—casually as could be—Lee Finch, if anyone had heard from him. Sometimes, the mention of his name prompted unequivocal blankness. A couple of people asked if he was in that one band, and when I asked if they meant Milpool or Black Lodge they said "Yes?" They'd barely had any connection to him then, and certainly no connection to him now, and I'd wave them off by saying it wasn't a big deal, surely I could find out from someone else.

Occasionally, a story would trickle down. Laura Connington said she'd heard about Lee getting chased out of the funeral, and that someone had even pulled a knife (this was new data), but not much more. "Honestly," she said over the phone from Austin, where she'd been living for over a decade, "I was trying to move on from high school. Maybe that seems silly, but I had bigger things to worry about."

As for the heroin, I picked up a couple of allusions here and there, but if they knew anything serious they didn't want to go on the record right away, I could tell it was something they wanted to mull over. Chris Larkin, of all people, was the only one comfortable talking out loud about it. "That scene seemed wack as fuck," he said. "I was down to clown, but I was trying to take some shots and squeeze some titty. Staring at a wall for hours with the drowsy bad-time gang, no thanks. Hey, maybe I shouldn't say titty on this?"

Even over camera, his energy was unmistakably aggravating. "Don't worry about it," I said. "You were saying something about Lee and Ben and those guys, what they got up to?"

"I'm not surprised most people didn't know anything about it. They kept a tight leash on their shit. There was no internet. I definitely didn't know Seth was hanging out with them. I don't even think Lee approached me, it would've been Ben, and that was only because we did molly one time. I think they all had the sense it was not something to brag about. And, like, *duh*. I didn't want to know more about whatever was going on there. No shit he had something to do with Seth dying."

"Whoa," I said. "What do you know about that?"

"You're telling me right now, aren't you?" He winked, and I realized this was, in fact, true. "Don't worry about it, man. I'm happy to let you take the lead."

Yet Lee wasn't a phantom lingering indefinitely on the periphery. He was easily observed, right through my computer screen. After he'd accepted my request I'd meticulously trawled his Facebook profile for clues, compiling all available evidence of what he'd been up to into a digital folder now bulging with screenshots. His job history said he'd been employed at "Black Lodge" from 2007 to 2011, followed by a long stretch of nothing, and a recent string of bar gigs in Chicago. I logged his regular correspondence with the other members of Joy House between 2006 and 2016—shared links, references to plans, non sequitur riffing. "I was at work . . . hit my cell," Seth had written to him in the spring of 2007. Facebook now let you reply underneath a comment, but back then Lee would've just posted directly on Seth's profile—something else for me to look up, now that I had the time.

After Seth had died, Lee had shown no visible sign of personality change nor lapse in posting schedule. As far as I could see, he'd continued living his life. Within the last year, he'd posted statuses in support of abortion rights and Bernie Sanders, photos of new guitar pedals he was using, and links to assorted media (Julien Baker songs, Dennis Cooper novels, Gregg Araki films) he appeared to be enjoying. His updates had become less frequent, but that didn't necessarily signify anything. Nearly everyone I knew used Facebook less than they used to; beyond the partisan grievances about how the company had willfully swung the election and enabled a half dozen global genocides was the simple truth that the platform was antiquated.

One of his new posts—at the time, his first in over a month—had coincided with the night we'd become "friends." Drunk and overwhelmed in William's guest bedroom, I'd ended up resisting the urge to message him, conscious that I needed the right combination of words allowing him to open up to me. I also needed to sand off any antagonism or bitterness, anything that would allow him to intuit some prosecutorial intention on my behalf. The violent shock I'd felt during that first night with Kelsey, and the anger I'd sustained in the months since, also existed alongside a generative curiosity. My impression of Seth's life had been permanently flash frozen when he died. I thought about him over the years, but I had no reason to think I should think anything different; he remained as static as his Facebook page, posthumously transformed into a digital memorial. But now, everything had changed. I wanted Lee to feel bad, yes, but I also wanted to go over every detail of his relationship with Seth, to fill in what I didn't know. I wanted to know everything about the night he sold Seth the heroin that would accidentally kill him: what he was thinking, what he'd done before and after, even what he was wearing, compiling every minor and major detail. I wanted to be a detective, not someone consumed with grief, in order to unlock the end of Seth's life.

On my first day back from Los Angeles, Sadie, Reggie, and I had met in the office to properly discuss how to get going on the podcast. I'd transcribed a number of thoughts into a Google Doc, and Reggie had turned these thoughts into a rough structure, splitting the difference between my initial pitch and the company's interests. Sadie seemed enthusiastic about the project's potential, though she, too, was wary of the pitfalls of wishy-washiness. I also sensed a more general suspicion on her end, a doubt that I could pull it off, though this was difficult to confirm. "I don't want you drifting off into the stratosphere," she said. "You know, be realistic. We have some budget, but not all of the budget."

"A reasonable amount of budget. I get it." She asked me what my plan for involving Lee was, and I said I didn't know. "Part of me is nervous he'll go completely dark if he suspects I'm going to be an asshole about it. I think what I want to do is hit him up casually and plant the idea of his participation, before laying it on him more seriously in person. Not that I want to trick him, but . . . I guess we sort of have to trick him."

"I would not worry about that," she said, after a moment. "I mean, this is the job, it's what we're all paid for. Be a man about it." We both laughed at this last part, it was something I'd once told her about how she'd needed to break up with a bad boyfriend.

That night, I opened up Lee's Facebook and started a message. After several days thinking about what to say I suddenly thought, why not, it wasn't like there was a playbook for how to digitally approach someone you hadn't talked to in over a decade and ask them about their experience taking hard drugs in high school. "Hey man," I began. "I don't know if you remember me—I guess you did because you accepted my friend request—but it's been a while, I don't think I've seen you since Sayers. I'm working on a project about some of our classmates that I think you might have some unique insight into, if you'd be around to talk sometime. Let me know what you think, talk soon!"

Right away this sounded too chipper and false, as though I were making a sales pitch rather than sidling up in a very chill way. I deleted the text and gave it another shot. "Hey man, it's been a while. I'm working on a project about some of our classmates—I think it's going to be a podcast—and I was hoping to talk with you sometime. Let me know!"

There was something off about that, too, and I realized that I hadn't even explained why I was doing this. Who just worked on a podcast in their spare time? I deleted it and began again. "Hey Lee, it's been a while. I'm living in New York now and working as a journalist, and I'm making a podcast for my company about our high school. I was hoping to interview you about your experience, if you're around. Let me know!"

This was closer, but still eliding the main thing. Was it unethical to approach someone under neutral pretenses, before quizzing them about a very specific person and their very specific death? I didn't hump the rule book like some of my anal retentive peers, but I didn't want to be accused of playing gotcha. The problem with making journalistic inquiries over a digital platform was the permanence of your wording, the way every message had to be crafted for maximum ethical and legal solidity lest it be shared with the world and judged by public opinion.

But maybe I didn't need to explain everything over Facebook, as long as I wasn't explicitly lying. This is what journalists did and I was a journalist, technically, so I double-checked the message for typos and sent it. I knew he didn't update his page all that much, but it seemed possible he'd get back to me within a week or two.

Whenever I opened up my Facebook message to Lee, as I did multiple times a day for the next few months, a receipt had yet to pop up showing me that he'd seen it. Sadie and Reggie continued asking for updates, and I said I was working on it, I was coming up with angles, I hoped to have more for them soon. I thought I might go through his parents, but their number wasn't listed in the old Sayers student directories—Ruth had checked via her parents, who had kept them around. The actual phone book showed nothing. Google showed nothing. Kelsey had agreed to give me Ben's phone number provided I didn't reveal her involvement, so that I might try to get in touch with Lee that way. But when I called, the number was disconnected.

During that time I conducted my other interviews and recorded new voice-overs, and repeatedly went over the details I'd dredged from Lee's internet presence. He'd gotten fatter, yes, and he'd experimented with a beard, yes, and he worked in a bar and sometimes played music. All of this made him seem like any other former cool kid riding the slipstream of his glory days, transitioning to this next phase of his life without much to show for it. Skimming his page, as I did night after night, generated contradictory feelings of condescension and judgment and bitterness. That this was mostly projection occurred to me, though I couldn't help it; a default part of interfacing with people's lives on the internet was taking their constructed image at face value, filling in the blanks with your own assumptions and biases. But what else could you do? What did any of us know about one another, even in real life? In most cases, certainly not more than the impression anyone broadcast, which we sketched in during intimate moments at bars and restaurants and birthday parties. It was the same thing online. And since Lee remained out of touch, all I could do was wonder what he was like and how he'd been.

Finally, in October, I was in the office finishing up an overpriced salad when my phone buzzed. I checked it instinctively, expecting any of the usual notifications that might distract me throughout the day, but it was a Facebook message. "Sorry for the delay, I don't check this often," Lee had written. "Maybe you can tell me more."

When I saw he'd attached his phone number, my entire body jolted in my seat. Immediately, I got up to find an abandoned room in the office. As I held my breath, waiting for my call to go through, I became very aware my back was tense and my chest was tight. I hadn't suffered a panic attack since my return to New York, but all of that tension manifested instantaneously.

The phone picked up on the fifth ring, and a very sleepy, low voice answered. "Hello?"

"Hi, is this Lee?" I said too quickly.

A few, silent seconds went by. "Yeah," he said. "Who's this?"

"This is Jacob Goldberg—you messaged me about the podcast I'm putting together."

I tried to think about where he was. It was 2:00 p.m. in Chicago, and he sounded tired—maybe he'd slept in because he was shaking off a hangover, or maybe he just worked late. "Didn't I *just* message you?" he said.

"Yeah, ha-ha, sorry—I figured I'd call you right away so we moved faster this time." He said nothing, which I heard as an invitation to keep going. "So *yeah*, like I said . . . I'm working on a podcast about our high school. Specifically, it's about some of our classmates who've passed away. Caroline Blanchard, Jenny Collins, Josh Richardson . . . Seth Terry." I waited for a reaction that didn't come. "There's a couple of more people, obviously; we had a lot of dead classmates. But right now I'm just canvassing around, trying to get in touch with people to see if they're up for talking. Are you still there?"

"I heard you. I'm just, uh . . ." He cleared his throat and didn't elaborate.

"No, I get it, it seems a bit abstract. But it'll be about some other stuff, you know. Grief, memory, the emerging twenty-first century—that sort of thing. They make podcasts about everything, now; it's not just people talking about sports."

"I know," he said. "I have heard of podcasts."

"So you're in Chicago, right?" I said, attempting to get back on track. He didn't answer. "Sorry, this connection is *really* bad, I don't know if you heard me . . . you're in Chicago, right? I'd love to talk to you in person." Sadie, Reggie, and I had also discussed this; a face-to-face interview with Lee was the only way this could work, because he might abruptly cut the call if we spoke over the phone or computer. If he tried to back out in real life, at least I could talk about how he'd looked as he'd done it.

"I am," he said. "I'm pretty busy these days but I might have some time."

"What about next week?"

"Next week isn't good, I've got double shifts every night."

"Okay, what about the week after?"

"Maybe. I thought you were in New York?"

I forgot I'd included that in my message. "Yeah, but I've got a bit of a travel budget, I can get to Chicago no problem."

"I don't want to put you out," he said. *It's truly no problem*, I started to say, but he continued talking. "Look, I gotta run, I'm just completely wiped. Text me or something whenever you're in town, I'll try to make it work." Before I could say anything else, he hung up.

LEE AND I HAD COMMUNICATED ONE MORE TIME, A FEW WEEKS after our call, when I texted him saying I was about to be in Chicago. I wasn't, but thought he might bite; instead, he responded a day later saying he was battling the flu, and now wasn't a good time. I hadn't tried since.

After Reggie expressed his ongoing concerns, we agreed to formally hash it out with Sadie. I had very maturely committed to transparency even as I desperately wanted to say, "Just let me figure it out," the ongoing refuge of iconoclasts and slackers. We had 100 percent of one episode, and about 20 percent of three or four more episodes, and a smattering of outlines for the other episodes, and though none of this represented a monetizable product as far as our accountants might be concerned, to me it felt good enough to justify the incrementalist approach. Sadie seemed to be connecting with the material, especially one segment we'd recently played for her where I spelled out how my memories of Seth had been shaken up by this new information, and how carefully I'd been working to rebuild them into something whole. After it ended, she remained quiet. "I know exactly how that feels," she said, finally. "It's awful, to look back at someone you loved and think you might have understood them wrong this entire time. To think you might still be getting it wrong."

Now we sat in our office's main conference room, clustered at the far end of a table that stretched toward a whiteboard reading BUSINESS STRATEGIES and BUSINESS SOLUTIONS. Reggie and I had run through our progress thus far, and where we needed to be if this podcast was going to launch within the next six months. Lee, clearly, was the blind spot. A recorded confession was possibly too much to hope for, but we needed some form of real and sustained interaction to introduce some dramatic tension to the structure.

"Otherwise, we're in good shape," Reggie said. "I mean, it's a pretty big piece to miss, but . . ." He trailed off, before chuckling to himself. "It's going to get done or it isn't going to get done, is what I'm trying to say."

I watched Sadie take this in, her face difficult to read. "I have to say I'm getting nervous about it," she said. "We've committed a lot of time. If it falls through then we've just been paying you to catch up with some friends from high school, which . . ."

Reggie may have had a point, but hearing Sadie concur with that point and jump to the most dramatic conclusion wasn't inspiring. "Hold on," I said. "This is not going to fall through, seriously."

"There's only a small chance of it falling through," Reggie said.

"Look, I thought about this last night." Christmas was a few weeks away, and when my mother and I had gone over my travel plans, she mentioned she'd received a postcard from my high school advertising the annual winter reunion, where students from all graduating classes were invited to hang out before the holiday. "Lee will probably not be there, but I can canvass for more sources. Then I can hit him up when I'm in town, since it will be the most perfect and organic opportunity of all time. I'm crossing the country to see my mom and celebrate the birth of Christ. Who could be suspicious of that?"

Sadie squinted her eyes and clicked her tongue. "I'm onto you," she said.

"*Seriously* though. If he ghosts on me then, we can have another talk about what to do—but come on, this is the best possible option."

Sadie glanced at Reggie, and they exchanged a wordless nod. This was annoying—I liked Reggie, but he'd only been working at the company for six months. "It's not a question of belief in the material," she said. "I like the material. But I'm questioning the approach. I know we're being delicate here, but we're also talking about a guy, in Chicago. Just some guy, would you not agree?"

"Lee is definitely a guy, I would agree."

"Just a guy. So I understand the situation, but it's not really tenable to take months to get in touch with a key source, without any confirmation it'll work out. We can see how it goes over Christmas, but if it doesn't work out, then . . ."

"Then?" I said, and almost poked her in the shoulder before deciding that was a terrible idea.

This time she really did look at me like she was my older sister. "You're an adult, Jacob. I'm sure you can figure it out."

THE DRIVE FROM THE AIRPORT TO MY MOTHER'S HOUSE WAS well memorized because I flew home a few times a year—for her birthday in March, and a music festival in July, and sometimes Thanksgiving in November, and always Christmas in December, with occasional visits in between for special occasions like funerals or the renewal of my state ID. In the summer, I always had to shield my face with my hand as we curved along the highway into the heart of the city, the orange sunlight reflecting off the lake and through the passenger side. In the winter, the dark sky offset the taillights of the cars blazing a trail into the horizon, past the multicolored Christmas trees and Nativity scenes my mother delighted in pointing out. At this time of year I always savored the first step onto the curb where the newly deplaned waited to be picked up. The sudden reconciliation with the violently cold midwestern weather shocked my senses alive and allowed me to huddle in the warmth of the backseat, mindlessly catching up on my phone while my mother and her boyfriend, Harold, continued asking me questions and awaiting my apology when I revealed I was already barely paying attention, it wasn't personal, I just needed to look at this and that.

As my mother and I waited for Harold to pay the dinner check, I texted Ruth that I was headed to the Sayers reunion, if she happened to be free. She wrote back saying she was stuck in Washington, DC, due to inclement weather and wouldn't make it. Tell me how it is, she said. There was no one else to text, at least not anyone who might join me on such short notice, but I still felt the need for a witness, someone I could pull to the side and confide in whenever the need might arise. Back in high school, I had attended so many events where I clung to the walls and stared at the crowd until I'd transcribed everyone's faces and outfits, before returning home to feel uncreatively bad about myself. That had been over a decade ago, but nonetheless I'd downed two cocktails at dinner and made sure the vaporizer pen I'd brought back from Los Angeles was tucked into my pocket.

What struck me as I left my mother's car and approached my high school's entrance was how easily I could mentally rewind until I arrived at my first day of class, when I'd approached the entrance just as I was doing now, surrounded by dozens of other barely teenage children in backpacks figuring out where they were supposed to go. The first sight of the front doors, and the metal detectors just beyond, and the walls of red lockers just beyond that, didn't trigger some Proustian revelation of *Yes, my God, it had been like that, I was there and now I'm here, wow, wow, wow,* but constituted a seamless continuity between that first day nearly twenty years ago and right now. I had walked through those doors before, and now I was walking through again.

Shortly after stepping off the plane, I'd sent Lee a text I'd workshopped for weeks: Hey, I'm in town through New Year's, I'd love to talk if you're around. Sayers reunion maybe? He hadn't responded, which didn't surprise me. Invitations for these reunions had made their way to my mother's house over the years, and none of them had seemed even slightly interesting. We were all over twenty-one and could go to a bar instead of reconnecting in the old lunchroom. But right now I was hoping that, with some luck, someone I ran into might want to go on the record for the Seth project.

All this was on my mind as I approached the Sayers security desk and made eye contact with the guard, whose oval-shaped head and pitiful beard I instantly recognized. He hadn't aged all that much in the thirteen years since I'd graduated, but he'd looked like a poorly bearded egg back in high school too. At the eye doctor they made you read from descending lines of text using two different sets of lenses, which the ophthalmologist toggled between using a clicker, and I wanted a similar kind of portable viewer that would toggle between photos of people as you remembered them, and photos of people as you saw them now. A moment later I remembered I was a little buzzed, because that was basically just Facebook, and I was not going to friend my high school security guard.

I left my coat at a freestanding rack, and moved toward the locus of activity. One of several schedules pasted on the wall stated the reunion would begin with "opening remarks," which had been forty-five minutes ago, followed by "dinner," followed by "socialization," which was right now. To my disappointment there wasn't any alcohol, only a phalanx formation of water bottles, so I swerved away from the buffet—a partially emptied Chipotle station—to see if I recognized anyone. Not a single person stood out. In fact most everyone here seemed much younger, as if they'd only graduated a few years ago. Maybe I spotted my old gym teacher, but I'd need more alcohol for that conversation.

Intriguing environment . . . maybe wack . . . but will report back, I texted Ruth, who did not reply. I hadn't visited my high school since graduation, but I felt comfortable here, as though I could go anywhere I wanted and do anything I wanted within these walls. I was a fully grown adult, beyond the purview of egg-shaped security guards.

The common area led to a corridor of classrooms, and I started walking door to door, looking to see if any of my old teachers still worked here. The walls were papered over with posters for student organizations: the Gay-Straight Alliance, the literary magazine, a baking club, something called the Social Justice League. It even looked like the Libertarian Club, now rebranded as the Free Thinkers Institute, was up to its old bullshit. This inspired a surge of disdain but hopefully their classmates were mocking them the way we'd mocked our own libertarians, allowing the ecosystem to flourish as intended.

At the old choir room, I spotted my first familiar name: Mr. Kendall, a popular music teacher, remained employed, according to the placard on the door. I'd also taken chemistry and U.S. History on this floor, but those teachers had apparently moved on; I hadn't studied under the other names I recognized, which sapped any potential for a meaningful reunion. *Remember me?* I would've said. *You used to tell my friend to stop fucking around and start studying for his Latin test.* To which the Latin teacher would've said: No.

So I moved on. Sayers Prep was three stories high, centered around a pair of spiral stairwells installed next to each other in the middle of the building, each one explicitly designated for walking up or down. I walked slowly up what I remembered was the down staircase, feeling like a naughty child, before venturing into another vacant corridor of classrooms, where I took out my vaporizer. Since Los Angeles I'd resisted the urge to fully self-actualize as a "vape guy," feeling a small flare of embarrassment every time I publicly exhaled a plume of smoke from what looked like a miniature sex toy. But, and this was crucial enough to surpass that embarrassment several times over, the vape was odorless, and the THC concentrate—of which I'd bought several vials, enough to last awhile—was potent enough to instantly kick-start my high.

Right now I was sucking on something called Lightning Clap, which promised "an energizing high, perfect for social occasions and creative sessions." I certainly felt energized and social now, strolling through the hallways like I owned them, careful to exhale under the cowl of my shirt. It now felt absolutely necessary to traverse each and every nook of the school, retracing the routes I'd paced thousands of times as a student, just to say what's up. *Hello trigonometry room, how've you been?* I started giggling, it was so silly. Memory had its limits; it wasn't as if sitting in the seat where I'd passed a notebook back and forth with Ruth so that we could scribble inane messages to each other would suddenly activate the scene via holographic projector.

Then again, that's essentially what I was hoping for now, wasn't it? Strolling these hallways, vaping here and there, walking into this room and that room like an especially curious puppy. But I had a purpose, a grand one necessitating this experiment. I wasn't retreading just to retread; I needed to channel the collective memories of Seth and Lee and Ruth and myself and William and Kelsey and Natalia and Audrey and Anna and even Josh and Caroline and Jenny, regardless of whether my podcast no longer directly involved them, and crystallize all these lives as they'd existed back then. If saying hello to the trigonometry room could, in some small way, enable that, then it was worth my time. Historians spoke about the power of place; you needed to visit Buchenwald in order to understand Buchenwald, you needed to visit Hiroshima in order to understand Hiroshima, and I was visiting high school in order to understand high school. Each of us comprised an ocean of psychic sediment and detritus, dissolved into formless slurry. You couldn't holistically recall the past, only try to approach it from the present and account for all the factors that explained why the past wasn't even the past, not as you'd remembered it.

Boy howdy was I feeling clapped by lightning as I came to the end of a hallway and stopped at the English classroom where the drama club also met. The room was how I sort of remembered it: a big circle of chairs, sandwiched between a whiteboard and a small, portable stage. Along the walls were posters of previous student productions. The drama club had run three plays a year, as I recalled, and that was just too many renditions of *Guys and Dolls* to permanently commemorate every single one. But I did recognize a couple of posters from a distance. The gigantic, ornate fan that announced *Lady Windermere's Fan*, put on during my sophomore year. The Grecian scales of justice representing *Lysistrata*, put on . . . sometime. And what I clearly recognized as a full-frame photo of Seth, wearing a brown jacket and a beige cravat, underneath UNCLE VANYA, spelled out in big, block letters.

I approached the poster. Seth was wearing a pair of wire-frame glasses and holding a book. There weren't many details beyond "a play by Anton Chekhov" and "directed by Martin Stewart"; Seth's name wasn't even mentioned. But it did say that the play was staged during what would've been the spring of my junior year. I'd remembered this play as *The Cherry Orchard* when I was on my way to meet Hamilton, and I was a little humbled to realize I must've smudged the specifics of Seth's involvement altogether. The walk to Einstein's, the postscript with Anthony . . . surely that had happened, but we must have been talking about this play. What was *Uncle Vanya* even about, anyway?

At least it was still Chekhov though. I took a photo of the poster and, for a brief second, considered stealing it. Instead, I exited the drama room and turned toward a pair of double doors, expecting to find a different stairwell that would take me back downstairs. Instead, it opened up into an unexpectedly unfamiliar hallway. I ventured down the unfamiliar wing filled with blue lockers, not the red lockers in the regular part of the school, unfamiliar walls painted in black-and-white nebula patterns, not the uniform gray walls in the regular part of the school, unfamiliar classrooms with foreign layouts and unfamiliar undamaged desks and even flatscreen TVs mounted to the walls in some places. It was distractingly modern, like an Apple Store. Rather than continue exploring, I made a loop back to the main building. From this floor the windows at the back of the school offered a view of the elevated subway, and I stopped to watch the trains zooming by in the distance.

In the years since leaving Chicago I'd occasionally taken the train downtown, always gazing out of the window to check out the school as we passed it. The building had remained unchanged from that perspective, even as the new wing must've appeared at some point without me realizing it. It was literally so close and figuratively so far away. I had no desire to go back until suddenly I had, and now the space had transformed beyond my recollection into a building I only partially recognized and was struggling to connect to, in spite of what I thought it might tell me about the past, and the people from the past who I couldn't stop thinking about.

I turned around, intending to walk toward the staircases, when I spotted a blue bench facing the windows, airbrushed with what looked like a woman's head alongside some text: IN MEMORY OF CAROLINE BLANCHARD, 1987–2003. A black jacket hung off the side, covering up the left half of her face. I hadn't really thought about Caroline over the years; I don't know if we'd ever spoken directly for more than five seconds when she was alive. She was already dying; she wore a bandanna to cover her bald head and missed weeks of school at a time, and I hadn't known how to approach that. It seemed like the only thing I could talk about, if we talked, and the idea felt so unappetizing I'd stayed away altogether.

I had gravitated toward the members of the club who were not about to die, and in particular Seth. He'd made such an impression on me when we'd met at the literary magazine, and it seemed like a no-brainer to join the Gay-Straight Alliance in order to solidify our nascent friendship. Even then my friendships were self-selecting in a way that made me ignore the rest of the world, and I felt guilty that I couldn't remember anything about Caroline whatsoever, not the way she talked or even the way she looked, beyond recognizing her face on this bench. Everyone had mourned her death; at the schoolwide vigil, I lost track of how many were openly crying. Seth had been one of them, but I'd just watched from a remove. I didn't know how to console anyone, least of all myself.

I pulled the jacket off the bench and let it fall to the ground. Caroline's face, which was not familiar, smiled at me. I was ready to get out of here, and finally made my way toward the down staircase when someone called my name. I turned to see three women turning my way, who I recognized as . . . Olivia? Olivia! Along with . . . Molly, yes, Molly, and someone else from our class whose name I didn't remember, maybe Jessica or Emily. "I thought that was you," Olivia said. "I couldn't tell because of the glasses, but you still have great hair."

Olivia, Molly, and Jessica-Emily were all part of my graduating class, and like most people from my graduating class, I hadn't seen any of them since commencement. Suddenly, I felt no particular need to Uber back home so I could get stoned at my mother's house. After twenty minutes of loosely catching up about this and that we'd relocated to the library, which was completely empty, and where no one could observe us passing my vaporizer back and forth. Olivia asked me if I was seeing anyone, and how I was doing in general, before she somehow pivoted to talking about her daughter's Instagram.

"It barely shows me anything," she said. She leaned back against a bookcase and brushed a piece of lint off her sweater. "Everyone used to tell us not to put anything on Facebook that we wouldn't want to be judged by for the rest of our lives. That first semester at college I remember untagging so many photos where I was drinking a beer. But everything is temporary now.

She only posts to her Close Friends stories, which does not include her mother, and she won't even tell me what her TikTok handle is."

I knew she'd stayed together with Roger, an annoyingly suave guy from our year with a mustache and perfect hair, but the ease with which she talked about her *ten-year-old daughter* and her *ten-year-old daughter's Close Friends story* was sort of blowing my mind, since only a few of my New York friends were even in serious relationships. I tried not to let that on. "I don't want to be a jerk, but I don't know if it's good that children are on Instagram," I said.

"If you want to know something worse, she even teases Roger and me for being ancient, since we still update our Facebook pages every . . . God, I guess it's basically every week. Maybe we are ancient."

"Are you sure we can be in here?" Molly asked. Molly had been responsible, I remembered, one of those perfect students who seemed repressed and tortured from afar.

"Please, let me have some fun before I have to rush home," Olivia said. "I've got to relieve the babysitter, and Roger won't be back until at least eleven."

"Didn't he say ten?"

"It'll be eleven. Maybe later. It's his first night off in weeks, even though he said his friends were just going to watch the Bulls game. There's no way they'll stop after that." She didn't mind, she said, turning to me like we were having a private conversation. She understood he was still getting used to his adult responsibilities; he'd barely adjusted to the routine of waking up and driving to the suburbs and driving home and going to sleep and driving right back to the suburbs every day, except for weekends and holidays and vacations, when they remembered to take them.

They'd had a kid at the end of college, right? I nodded, as though she hadn't been talking about her daughter for the last ten minutes. But they'd broken up for a while after graduation, to see what else was out there. "It wasn't so bad," she said. "We coparented for a while, and I went on some dates, but it sort of felt like pretend. There was only one possible outcome, as I saw it. And sure enough, after four years of that he figured out he did want to be with his high school sweetheart and the mother of his child, actually."

"That's wild," I said, unclear of how I was supposed to respond to this sudden burst of transparency. Olivia and I had never been close, but I wanted to hear what anyone had to say about their chaotic situationship where a child was involved, obviously. "I thought you two had stayed together the whole time?" I had loosely followed Olivia's Facebook posts around the time their daughter was born, but hadn't registered the full story.

"No, no." She'd taken a leave of absence from college in order to give birth to their daughter, and in return he told her that he didn't think it was working out. "It was a shitty way to enter the real world," she said. She was twenty-one, and now she had to figure out the rest of her life with a child, but no degree or partner. "I read somewhere that women mature faster than men, which, duh. But they were talking about feelings, right? Not the stuff you have to go through in life. And that's what I was doing—changing diapers while Roger was hitting the town with the homies, playing *Madden* all night and acting like a dumbass."

None of this had explicitly registered with her; it was simply an obstacle to surmount, like she was competing on *Survivor.* She drafted plans to finish her degree, become a dental assistant, start her own physical therapy clinic—plans that inevitably sputtered out, given the realities of balancing all the demands on her time. "For a long time," she said, "it was really important for me to keep that energy going. I needed to believe that all this effort was going somewhere, that despite how my life was playing out, I could make something better of it just by giving more of a fuck. Do you know how that is?"

Lucky for her, she'd found an out. When Roger had surprised her by saying he wanted to get back together, they hammered out the details over a series of long conversations. It was a second courtship, but it was also a negotiation—a promise that he wouldn't run away. But he had changed. He took her hand and swore he was done playing *Madden* with the homies. With him he brought a well-paying suburban job where he did something with microprocessors, she wasn't exactly sure, but it didn't really matter to her except for the paycheck. "We're comfortable now, which doesn't totally feel real," she said. "After all that struggling, things have settled. Recently it hit me that I still might have some time left for myself." Maybe she'd go back to college, or try to get her real estate license.

"That's if we don't have another kid," she said, smiling, at which Molly and Jessica-Emily threw up their hands.

Olivia asked what I was up to now, and I hurried through a loose outline of the Seth project: dirtbags, drugs, death, mystery. "Did you guys ever hear about any of that?" Olivia shook her head no; Molly thought about it, then followed suit.

"Hector always had coke on him, I know he used to deal a little in class when nobody was looking," Jessica-Emily said. We all turned toward her to listen. "He'd always tease me about partying with him: *Jessie, baby, when are you going to walk on the wild side?*" (Jessica! Of course.) "But he was always kidding, honestly. He was kind of sweet. Our moms know each other from church so he never pushed too hard, I think he knew I was too straight and narrow to go along."

"That's cute," I said. "Those guys all seemed pretty rude at the time and not sensitive about stuff like that."

"You're a boy. Obviously they weren't going to be nice to you." I conceded this and asked if she knew what Hector was up to these days. She laughed and said that was like keeping track of the stray cats who live in the parking lot. "I haven't heard about him in years, not even from my mom. I think he's out of touch for good, you know?"

We were all quiet for the first time since we'd infiltrated the library. "But there's more to the project," I continued. "You know, it's about this milieu of death, and other stuff we were into then, maybe emo music . . ."

"I do think about that sometimes," Molly interrupted. "All of the kids from our year who've died. I was looking at an old yearbook before I came here and I found something really sweet that Jenny Collins wrote about how we might not talk too much in the future, but she'd always remember how helpful I'd been in class. And it's true, we didn't talk after graduation, but it really upset me when she passed."

"Jenny, yeah—I had a big crush on her, which is crazy to think about."

"That's an interesting idea," Olivia said. "Seth Terry . . . he was the guy with diabetes, right?"

I involuntarily cracked up at the idea this was any way to refer to someone. "No, he was not 'the guy with diabetes.' He was . . . the biracial gay kid the year above us, who once wore a skirt on Halloween."

"*Right.* I think we might have had an AP class together, I don't know." She appeared to really think about this. "To be honest I don't even think I'd heard he'd died. I'm sorry about that."

"I had," Molly said. "Facebook. But we didn't know each other, really."

"He was funny," Jessica offered. "And he was nice too. Funny and nice, I wish I could remember more. But that's more than you can say about a lot of people, honestly."

"I know what you mean," I said. "I've talked to Chris Larkin a couple times about this, remember him?" At this, they all groaned; Molly even booed. "Yeah, exactly. I was hoping to find more people to talk to tonight, but it's been a bust so far. I honestly was about to leave before you guys said hi, especially since there isn't any booze."

"Hmmm," Olivia said. She leaned away from the bookcase and looked at the door. "I think I saw Ms. Markson back there, maybe she'd be helpful." Ms. Markson was the gym teacher I'd avoided on my way in, a former skiing prodigy who'd injured herself out of Olympic contention and subsequently acquired a drinking problem that even a fourteen-year-old could pick up on.

"I don't think I can deal with Ms. Markson right now," I said.

"Rachel is here, obviously," Molly said.

"Rachel?"

"Yeah, Rachel Watkins. She's somewhere back there, or she was before we came here. She and Seth were pretty close. That's the only reason I remember he died. She was posting to his Facebook for a while, and it would always pop up in my feed." The collected expression I remembered from high school contorted into a slight smirk. "Damn, you haven't talked to Rachel yet?"

It came out like she was teasing me, but the implication stung. Had I really missed his *best friend* altogether? I tried to recall Rachel: white, brown hair . . . thick eyebrows, that was all I had before the image dissipated. But yes, she and Seth had been very close, I remembered that now. *Rachel Watkins, Rachel Watkins, Rachel Watkins*, I repeated to myself . . . Jesus Christ, of course. *Rachel Watkins.*

When I'd scrolled Seth's Facebook to see who'd left memorial comments over the years, she hadn't shown up and so I hadn't thought about her at all. But *what if*, I realized, she had just . . . deleted her Facebook? I absolutely needed to talk to Rachel for the podcast, if I was trying to get up with the people who'd known him best. I didn't remember her attending the funeral, but I didn't remember a lot from the funeral, and there was no way she'd missed it.

"Can you help me say hi?" I said. Molly nodded. We all stood up and I took my vaporizer back, following the women as they led me out of the library.

RACHEL WATKINS LIVED NEAR A DIM SUM RESTAURANT WHERE my family always convened for Chinese New Year's. When I was younger we had gathered at my grandmother's for the holiday, and I retained scant memories of lounging in her musty living room while she moved around the house, juggling a dozen different tasks as my mother and aunts tried to fit in where they could. After old age had crippled her mobility we started eating out for the meal and maintained the tradition after she died. But the neighborhood around the restaurant had changed, I was reminded as I left the train and walked toward Rachel's apartment. More white people had moved in, but also more young people in general, not all of whom were white, and thus the demographics had tilted away from the graying Oriental biddies from my youth, toward something I was still trying to put my finger on.

My cousins and I had created our own separate tradition of eating dim sum for Christmas dinner, once we'd broken off from the main family to smoke weed and play video games, and now we always called ahead after one year when we'd suffered through an unthinkable fifteen-minute wait just to be seated. "I can't believe all these crackers," my cousin Christina had hissed over and over again, sort of kidding but mostly not, until I reminded her that "crackers" was some of us, too, especially since we were all part Jewish, and most likely it was members of the tribe looking to score their dumpling fix on this gentile holiday. Besides, she lived in San Diego now and had grown up in the suburbs to begin with, so she really wasn't one to throw stones of authenticity at the glass house of gentrification. (A horrible metaphor, but we were ruinously stoned.)

Still, I understood her position. In the decade since I'd left Chicago, the city had changed enough that I had no idea what to do when I was here on my own. Its latest routines were obscured from me; I didn't know where to eat an unpretentious lunch or meet someone for an unpretentious drink. The old canard about not being able to go home again—that wasn't true, I was home at the moment, but all my claims of ownership felt like appropriation when I was actually here. It was much easier to trot out "I'm from Chicago" when I was hundreds of miles away, talking to people who had no idea what that meant beyond Barack Obama, Michael Jordan, or "crime."

And it wasn't just the city that had changed—an inevitability in every country and era, because cities were a locus of progress. The language for describing one's position and surroundings had warped as well. In the past, faced with the swell of palefaces standing in front of us at the dim sum parlor, my aunt might have remarked in a joking voice about how the place was becoming too *lofan*—a Chinese slang I always understood as "square white people"—and we all would've laughed, as would the family lofans. Now my cousin could come right out and cast her aspersions in our native dialect, not only because she was frustrated with the wait but because it was acceptable to distinguish between us and them, a sort of psychic back tax for all of the slights and discriminations she may have suffered throughout her life, of which our delayed dinner was just the latest.

Rachel, on the other hand, had stayed in Chicago her entire life. After attending college at DePaul, she'd ignored the teaching programs recruiting so many of her classmates to rescue the underrepresented youth of urban America and taken a job teaching seventh grade at the local public school. There was plenty of work to do at home, she said, as she stirred her coffee with a small spoon. We were sitting in her living room, a white-walled alcove filled with overflowing houseplants and bespoke artworks—a watercolor of Lake Michigan, a portrait of a small orange tabby I presumed was her own. "I moved to Edgewater after my first year teaching," she said. "The neighborhood was on the up, so rent was fairly cheap. Now it's hard to imagine wanting to live anywhere else."

Rachel had recognized me right away, after Molly had walked us over at the reunion. I'd played it cool as we made small talk, but my grand intentions were delayed when Ms. Markson ambled over and made a big show of reuniting with us, *It had been so long, oh my God, tell me what you're up to,* and I'd started nodding and smiling as though I cared even one infinitesimal iota until I managed to pull Rachel aside and tell her I was working on a podcast about Seth. She seemed curious, and said we could meet before New Year's since her class was on leave, but as we sat across from each other now I remembered I didn't know Rachel at all, and despite her friendliness there was always the possibility she could send me on my way the moment I said the phrase "secret heroin ring."

Her boyfriend was at work, so we had the place to ourselves. She'd greeted me with a tight smile that I worried indicated some regret about our appointment, before showing me into the apartment. But whatever trepidation I had about her enthusiasm dissipated the moment we sat down and I set up my recorder. "I have to apologize if I seem out of it," she said. "I was looking over some old photos before you came over, and I haven't completely recovered." Before I could finish apologizing, she waved her hand as if to say I shouldn't worry about it. "No, obviously it's going to happen if we're talking about Seth. I think about him all the time, but I don't *think about him*, you know. It's always a stray thought that catches somewhere. Some book he told me about, some movie we saw together."

"That must be easier to do without Facebook," I said.

It was partly why she'd deleted hers, and as she started talking, I hastily hit the "record" button. After Seth had died, she said, along with an apology for starting with a beginning that wasn't really the beginning, she had continued to post to his Facebook wall as though he were still alive and merely off in some foreign country without internet access. Short recaps of how her day had gone, nostalgic memories of some day they'd spent together, inside jokes that no one else could possibly parse from afar—stuff like that. She'd taken his death very hard, and a therapist had recommended she write to him in a journal. This seemed like an appropriate compromise, considering many of their friends were doing the same.

"I'd never had a best friend die before, and I certainly wasn't used to being told my best friend was dead every time I went online," she said. "But that's how the algorithm worked, not that I understood what 'the algorithm' meant back then. It would've been healthier if I'd just deleted my Facebook, but it was still a social hub for my normal life. I didn't want to lose the rest of my friends either."

"That was weird for me too." I also remembered logging on to Facebook not long after Seth had died and seeing right away that several friends of mine had left some form of condolences on his page. The idea that I might have learned about his death this way, had Ruth not called me, was chilling then.

It was chilling now, too, a reminder that our lives were overseen by hidden forces cataloging and shaping our perception of reality, something conspiracy theorists liked to attribute to the Illuminati or the Clintons, when it was just a cabal of well-compensated Silicon Valley engineers you could look up on LinkedIn.

"You want to hear the perverse thing? Sometimes I'd just sit on his wall and hit refresh every ten minutes, reading every new message that popped up." Rachel drank her coffee and laughed. "It was like I was addicted to feeling bad about his death. Or no: I was addicted to other people's feelings, as though absorbing them would legitimize my own. I didn't think twice about telling the whole world how profoundly upset I was. I can't tell you how many messages I left where I must've been sobbing as I wrote them—actually sobbing, I'm not exaggerating." She said this last part freely and confidently, and I recognized the smoothed-over tone of someone who'd processed a lot of their shit in therapy. "Did you ever do that? Hopefully without the sobbing."

"No, I think I was just too emotionally constipated." My grief was private; the idea of broadcasting it for everyone to see was deeply uncomfortable, even if I couldn't begrudge anyone their expression. When I'd come back from the funeral, and my friends in the dorms asked me why I was wearing a suit, I told them why but chose not to go into any detail about Seth or what he'd meant to me. They were separate halves of my life, requiring no intersection. That this was not a very healthy or honest form of processing had occurred to me eventually.

That wasn't the case for Rachel, who'd taken two weeks off from school, more than she'd need when her grandmother passed a few years later. But she wasn't so deep in her grief that she completely neglected herself, in the ongoing attempt to reconcile with the finality of his absence. "The therapist helped with that," she said, confirming my observation. "But also, his death didn't change anything for me. It didn't *literally* change anything, I mean. When my grandmother died, it took my dad and his sister six months to go through all her belongings and deal with the estate. But I had nothing like that with Seth—nothing to take care of, no will to settle, no belongings to comb through, no gym memberships to cancel or gift cards to redeem. His parents didn't want anything to do with me—they were completely ashamed about his death; after the funeral they pretended like they'd never had a son at all. He didn't have siblings I could latch on to. He was just gone. And that made it easier to continue living, in a way."

The years went on, she graduated school, vacationed abroad, dated men and women, went back to school and started teaching and notched so many life achievements that she chronicled in tedious detail on this public memorial to her dead friend, who by that point was a decade gone. It was routine for her, this declaration of catharsis. She'd stopped seeing her original therapist but continued posting to Seth's Facebook just as naturally as she checked her email or called her mom. There was no tradition dictating she adhere to these digital habits, no imperious grandmother saying, "This is the way you honor the dead." But as I might understand, she said, one didn't just stop using a website.

One day, she was clicking around his Facebook and came across a tab she'd never seen before, marked "See Friendship." The feature allowed you to look over your Facebook history with someone, revealing this aggregated collection of posts flowing in one direction from Rachel to Seth and Rachel to Seth and Rachel to Seth, repeated hundreds of times over the last decade. Her feelings, frozen in time, were astonishing to rediscover and brutal to revisit in their totality. She went back to Seth's Facebook wall, where she realized she was the only person still posting at all, and was struck by a sobering thought: *My friend has been dead for a very long time, and I am very different.*

The implications were obvious: She was fulfilling a need that no longer existed, her newer therapist said. She had new friends, a new boyfriend, an entire new life beyond the one she'd shared with Seth *in high school*, and meditating on that phrase, *in high school*, filled her with something she recognized as peace. Time had passed, and she'd come very far, she couldn't put it more profoundly than that, so in an impulsive mood she'd deactivated her account, sweeping all of those interactions into the digital dustbin. She felt some regret, she said, for how the deactivation also removed the dozens of photos of Seth she'd uploaded when he was still alive, and in the immediate wake of his death. But there were still other photos of him, and besides, like she said, it wasn't clear whether anyone was looking at his page besides her. After a few days, she stopped thinking about it entirely.

Not that she'd stopped thinking about Seth, of course. But now her thoughts were private, and she didn't need to expose herself in public. Furthermore, as an adult woman with adult woman priorities and goals, it wasn't straightforward for her to connect with the memory of a twenty-year-old man. More and more her contemporary experiences transcended what she and Seth had shared together, and she couldn't bring herself to gloss over the incongruities with platitudes like "He would've loved my boyfriend" (possible, not guaranteed, he never liked her taste in men), or "I wish he could see what I'm up to now" (wrangling tweens and not sleeping?). It was easy to declare they'd still be close today, but she'd had other best friends who'd drifted away over the years, best friends who'd been as close as Seth was and who today barely rated as acquaintances. In some ways, perhaps his death had merely served as a dramatic conclusion to a friendship that might have fizzled out on its own, had he lived.

"That's a hell of a way of looking at it," I said, surprised. I flicked my eyes at my recorder, to make sure it was still operating.

"It's my way of looking at it," she said. "Trust me, I've thought about it a lot. It was different at the end, you know, with everything that was going on with him."

I tried not to react. "With everything going on?"

"I mean, you were close with him, right? You're not just making a podcast about how much you miss him, and you know it wasn't a fucking ulcer." I shook my head to say, *No, that's not quite the case*, and asked her to say more.

DePaul was just a couple of blocks away from where Seth lived with his parents, so when she'd started college they continued to hang out all the time. He'd come to the dorms and meet her new friends; she'd walk over to his place and sit in his room like they'd always done, listening to CDs and talking about boys and every other dumb thing. He was disappointed about taking an extra year at high school when many of his friends were off to college, but was focused on the future. "It's just a few more months," he said, "before I get out of here for good." He was thinking about California, Oregon, Washington State—somewhere he wouldn't be targeted for being himself. This was 2005, she reminded me, when Bush was still president (I smiled, I couldn't help it, everything came back to George W. Bush in the end), and plenty of people who claimed they were for gay rights weren't really for gay rights, seeing it as a slogan meant to depress the possibility of actual change like the way you could say you supported the whales.

Her dorm friends loved him right away. Seth was so charismatic, it's easy to say that now—"Seth was so charismatic," like "Seth's hair was black" or "Seth lived in Lincoln Park"—but think about how many people you know who are actually charismatic, she said. Seth had the real stuff, a way of bending the light toward himself in any conversation. Even so, she couldn't always bring him around. It wasn't quite appropriate to invite him to a freshman mixer, or a dorm trip to Navy Pier, where she got to navigate the terrors of big, bad downtown Chicago for her new friends. He'd still visit in the dorms, and she'd still go to his house, but as freshman year wore on their conversations increasingly shifted to the phone and the internet, and she sometimes went weeks without seeing him in person. Seth didn't complain, he was busy with high school and knew better than to insinuate himself into a situation uninvited. But their relationship had changed, and neither of them could deny it.

"You know how that goes," she said, and I did. Plenty of my friendships had weakened during that first year at school, friendships I'd considered bronzed and polished to stand for all eternity, though they were sustained only by geographic convenience. Some of those friendships weren't even as solid as I thought they'd been, as I found out from Kelsey when she told me about Anthony's double-dealing. By the end of my sophomore year they'd sloughed off entirely, and in most cases weren't rekindled whatsoever in the following years, until I'd popped up in the past few months to ask them about Seth.

At the time, Rachel thought she and Seth were basically as close as they'd ever been. When the school year was over, they entered the summer on the same terms, defaulting to their old routines and rhythms. Seth wouldn't be attending college in the fall: he'd been accepted to some schools but the financial aid hadn't come through, and his parents wouldn't pay for him to pursue a degree they didn't approve of, which meant just about everything. He'd talked about theater, film, dramaturgy, English, anything in the arts; he'd even talked about teaching, but none of it mattered. As she remembered, they brought up the possibility of him joining the seminary.

It's like they want me to go fuck a kid so they'll never have to think of me again, he'd joked, a remarkably dark comment even given his taste for sarcasm. "You remember how caustic he could be?" Rachel asked.

"Definitely," I said. "In fact, we used to call each other slurs all the time. It was our way of forging biracial allyship, though I think I was more homophobic than he was racist? It was complicated, or maybe not."

She didn't even throw me a courtesy laugh, but kept talking. Despite his parents' obstructions, Seth had a plan: he would find a job and save enough money to attend community college the next fall, using that as a springboard to obtain a scholarship at a better school—again, ideally somewhere in California, Oregon, Washington State. It was all mapped out, and as she recounted this, I remembered him mapping some of it out for me. After a few weeks he started working at Panera as a cashier, though he insisted he was looking for something else. He hated the smell of bread, if I could believe that, one of the least objectionable smells there was.

But better work wasn't easy to find. He was too young for bartending, and temp agencies wanted older employees, and all the retail positions paid less than Panera, where at least he got thirty minutes for lunch. He took up smoking to justify the breaks. And soon enough, she said, his temporary job was just his job.

When her sophomore year started, it was a few months before they had the chance to hang out in earnest. "I didn't know what that means, when you stop seeing someone—even if there's a good reason," she said. And by then, something was off.

Nothing she could formally diagnose or question or side-eye. He had bags under his eyes, though he said that was just from the early mornings. He yawned a lot, though he said he was just tired. He took a half second longer to respond than usual, though again he said he was just tired. All of which was understandable except for the silences. Seth wasn't the type to wordlessly stare into the distance, impervious to your questions. He was a dreamer, but he was always tethered to his surroundings; she had never met anyone who was less distracted in the presence of other people.

But now he didn't seem interested in what she had to say, and when she asked how he'd been spending his time, he said something noncommittal about hanging out with a group of people from Sayers. People she'd never paid attention to, specifically Ben Porter and Hector Aviles and Lee Finch, who she remembered as deadbeats, not to date herself as a judgmental adult—*or a Karen!* she said, smiling—but they really seemed like deadbeats, she didn't have any other way to put it.

What are you doing with them, she asked, to which he said not much, hanging out, this and that, nothing much. Which was curious because he'd never failed to be specific with her, not about his family or his hopes for the future or even his sex life (because she might have been his only friend who really asked him about sex). But this evasion, that was notable.

"That's interesting," I interrupted. "I saw him throughout that year, and he honestly didn't seem any different. He acted like Seth, you know? Curious and funny and chatty and all of that, which is why it was such a shock when he died."

"Hmmm," she said. "A lot of things about him shocked me, at that point."

Here the timeline got murky, she couldn't exactly say when all of this had transpired beyond "the fall of 2006 into the spring of 2007," and in fact I should probably apply that to everything she'd said thus far. She'd always considered herself a reliable narrator, someone who was good at retaining names and dates and details. But it was breathtaking how much information disappeared when you didn't apply yourself to retaining it. The other day, for example, she'd forgotten Brad Pitt's name. Most people refused to accept any slippage of brain cells, the story they told was how it had happened, and over time she'd become convinced that people weren't even aware they were lying to themselves and everyone else. It wasn't as though anyone could prove otherwise.

"You must be dealing with this, right? Looking into the past so aggressively, it must surprise you how much everyone has misremembered. If not yourself."

I didn't want to linger on the porousness of my memory, so I decided to change the topic. "So when did you find out he was using?"

Rachel's face was completely still, but she turned her eyes toward the floor. "I never found out. Not officially."

"You didn't?"

"No, I mean, I *knew*, but he never told me, so it almost felt like it wasn't real. I learned from a friend of ours, Erica." I stretched my memory: Erica was the year below me, and was controversial for reportedly enjoying sex. "She'd been hooking up with one of those boys, but I might be wrong about that. Erica caught a lot of shit in high school for sleeping with guys, I'm sure you remember"—I tried to interject to say *of course not*, but she kept going—"and I think even when she was just trying to hang out, the reputation followed her around." She clicked her nails against her mug. "As you can imagine."

But anyway, it was Erica who'd called her up and asked if she'd heard from Seth these days. She'd seen him around at Hector's, and he didn't look like he was doing well. "To be honest," she said, pausing long enough that Rachel had asked if she was still there, "I think he's into something bad." That was what she called it: "something bad," the actual act obscured into a euphemism. Recalling it from the present, it was disturbing to consider how young they all were. Erica was a senior in high school, and even though her family wasn't rich they certainly weren't deadbeats; she'd just drifted into that crowd because she liked having sex and she liked taking drugs. Rachel couldn't fathom the act of courage it had taken to reach out to an outsider in order to figure out what was going on.

"Erica and I still catch up every now and then," Rachel said. "It's been a while, but she got married and moved out to the suburbs. It's funny, you'd meet her today and have no idea what she used to be into, especially since everybody has tattoos these days. I work with kids; I know how trauma sticks. Sometimes you can just tell it's going to be with them for a while until they figure it out. But what about when it's been figured out? What is everyone carrying around with them that's just a part of how they see the world now?"

"It's a good question," I said. "But what exactly did she tell you about Seth?"

It was enough for Rachel to get on the phone and insist they meet up as soon as possible. But Seth dithered, he said he was busy that weekend, then working a double shift the next week, and who could say what his schedule would look like after that? Pretty quickly she understood he was trying to justify not seeing her, and she didn't know how to respond. They'd never had any kind of rift before, not even when Rachel was dating her shithead high school boyfriend, Kyle, around whom

Seth was always conspicuously and uncharacteristically silent. (Not that Kyle ever noticed.) "Okay," she remembered saying, like a mother trying to plan a meal with her distant child, "but please let me know when you're free."

Two months later, she was wrapping up dinner with her friends at the local Thai restaurant when Seth texted her to see what she was up to. They'd texted in the intervening time, and she'd made delicate overtures about hanging out, all of which were gently rebuffed, and though she hadn't given up hope, the need to see him immediately had receded into the background. She sighed, and ran a hand through her hair. "I can't justify it," she said. "I knew something was wrong, I should've tried harder, but I didn't think . . ."

"It's okay," I said.

Yes, she said, which is why, enabled by the drinks she'd had at dinner and the promise of more drinks to come, she replied saying *not much*, she and her friends were about to party in the area, and if he was free he could join them. Had she been sober, she might have catalogued the various reasons why a house party wasn't the best place to see her best friend for the first time in months, in order to have a conversation about the shadow life of drug addiction he may or may not have been leading, according to the hearsay of their mutual friends. But she wasn't, so she thought nothing beyond *I hope my cell phone doesn't die before he gets here*.

Today she couldn't say how he'd looked when he showed up to the party an hour later, except that he'd looked like Seth. Normal, or at least normal enough that no red flags went off. "I'm so happy to see you," she told him, and it was true: after months of separation, his arrival in what appeared to be good form was unexpectedly reassuring, and all her worries temporarily abated.

"Same, same," he replied. They hugged longer than necessary, before withdrawing to fix themselves a couple of amateur cocktails with the house vodka. They started to catch up in a corner of the kitchen that hadn't been colonized by the party, and in her happy mood she felt confident enough to cut through the small talk.

"So tell me," she said, "why is everyone so worried about you?"

"'Everyone' is worried about me?" He looked amused, as though it were fun to be the subject of other people's conversations.

"Yeah, and I am too. We haven't seen each other for months, and meanwhile I'm hearing all sorts of gossip."

"What are they saying?"

She thought about saying exactly what she'd heard, but, in a split decision she'd later regret, decided to deflect. "All sorts of things, I don't know."

He laughed a typical Seth laugh, a giggle prompted by the self-evident absurdity of the situation. "That's crazy," he said. "I know I've been out of touch, but it's not that bad."

"Well, the last time I saw you, you looked like you hadn't slept in days."

"I probably hadn't," he said. "I've got to get the hell out of Panera, it's really eating me alive."

"You really do."

His face changed just slightly. "That's easy for you to say."

"Yeah," she said, drunk enough to forgo the delicate touch, "it's easy for me to say because you just said it." She poked him in the arm, and he jerked away. "And hey, it really sucks you waited so long to make plans. It's almost midnight now too."

"I've just been busy," he said after a pause. "I thought you'd want to see me no matter what time it was."

"I do. I always do. But it's almost midnight, and I am drunk."

"Then I guess I should catch up," he said, draining the rest of his drink.

It was, she said, the last uncomplicated time they spent together. In the months leading up to his death they still met for lunches, dinners, the type of hangs from the old days, which at that point meant just a year or two earlier, where they'd sit in a room for hours and talk about nothing in particular. But all of those occasions were overshadowed by the understanding that something was definitely wrong, beyond her initial instinct and Erica's vague intimations that something was potentially wrong, which for a short time—meaning, the three hours she spent with him at that party—seemed exaggerated, and not a big deal.

Seth was in great spirits, especially as they sluiced further into the free-flowing dynamic of best friends + alcohol. After catching up, they went back to her other friends and kept partying from there. At some point she lost track of him in the crowd, but she found him ensconced between a couple of men on a couch, passing around a joint and monologuing about the casting decisions in the latest Harry Potter movie.

She made him scooch over so she could take her place in the joint rotation and leapt into the conversation. But the moment she said something, Seth wrenched the dialogue toward one of the shaggy-haired bros, whose name was Derrick, about what he was wearing. It was just a Chicago Bulls T-shirt bearing cartoon renditions of one of the Michael Jordan championship teams, a shirt found in 93 percent of Chicagoland households, but Derrick answered seriously: he'd purchased the shirt from eBay, because he was a basketball fan and a '90s basketball fan in particular.

"That's fascinating," Seth said. "Rachel loves the Bulls too."

This was true, but considering she was born and raised in Chicago that really was not anything special, and she was about to say so until she realized Derrick had turned to her with an interested expression, and Derrick was quite handsome, and wasn't this just Seth pulling the strings again in a direction of his liking, now that they were all good and drunk and squished together on the couch.

"My favorite player is Scottie Pippen," Derrick said.

"Uh, mine too," Rachel said.

"I like Dennis Rodman, because he's a big ole freak." Seth shook his cup and frowned. "I believe I need a refill."

"We're almost out," someone with a Cubs hat—seriously, did nobody have a personality beyond sports—yelled from the kitchen.

"FUCK," someone else in a red tank top shouted, in the exact way that men in tank tops shout.

Seth stopped talking, and she still remembered the grain of this particular silence: he was deliberating, not waiting to speak. "The 7-Eleven is open all night," he said. "We could pick something up."

"Good idea," Cubs Hat said.

"I can pick up some cases," Seth said. "Anybody want to chip in?"

"Hold on." Derrick pulled a couple of bills out of his wallet and handed them over. Red Tank Top echoed him, as did several other men in the room.

"I'll come with," Cubs Hat said.

"It's not a big deal," Seth said.

"Yeah, but you'll need someone to help you carry everything."

"No worries, I brought a backpack with me and it's just a few blocks away. You should stay here and have a good time."

"I guess we still have some pot, don't we?"

"Your backpack can fit a case of beer?" Rachel said.

"It's a really big one," he said. "I left it by the front door."

"You sure you don't need any help?" Derrick asked.

"Yeah, why don't I come with you?" She made a move to get up.

"Absolutely not," Seth said, gently pushing her in the shoulder so she fell ass-first onto the couch. "Take a load off, I'll be back before you know it." He left the room before her passing suspicion could crystallize into a formal protestation, and then she was just sitting knee-to-knee with a boy who was paying her all of the attention in the world.

"So anyway," Derrick said, "Scottie Pippen."

That Seth did not return to the party, which they put together an hour later when they were definitively out of alcohol and he wasn't responding to texts or calls, was perhaps not so surprising, upon reflection the next morning. In the moment it was disorienting, especially when some of the men figured out she was the one who'd invited him and insisted on holding her accountable for the money they'd pooled, until Derrick intervened and said they needed to chill out, obviously she hadn't expected that to happen, and if he could let it go, since he'd chipped in more than anyone else, they could as well. The 7-Eleven was still open, and this time he would make the walk himself, and he'd even *walk faster* so the party could rage on. "You'll go with me, yeah?" he asked Rachel, and touched by his chivalry she did not refuse, nor did she refuse a couple of hours later when he asked if she wanted to come back to his place.

"Did you ever manage to get in touch with Seth?" I asked.

"I didn't have to," she said. The following day, after she'd walked back from Derrick's, Seth called her and started blabbing something about a friend who'd texted him saying he was in a tough spot at the exact moment he was walking to 7-Eleven, and in that exact moment he'd decided it was too complicated to call or text Rachel and explain why he had to bounce, but trust him, it was for a good cause, and also his phone had died just then so he couldn't have called or texted even if he wanted. He felt bad about it and would be happy to return the money if they wanted, though it would be tricky to track down everyone unless, by chance, she happened to have procured Derrick's number. During this mirror maze of excuses she cut him off to say it was totally fine, they had all assumed something like that, he shouldn't worry, and she was just glad nothing was particularly the matter.

There was a long pause on the other end. "Thank God," he said. "I knew you'd understand. Did you hop on that jock dick?" And then they'd just continued talking about whatever, as though nothing unusual had happened.

"So did you ask if he was using?" Immediately I remembered we'd already gone over this, but she appeared to think about it anew.

"No, and I never did. But I think he understood, because whenever we saw each other after that I wouldn't make any pointed comments or ask anything I knew he couldn't answer. And as long as I could do that, I could believe there was nothing particularly wrong. After a while, I convinced myself it was just a weird night. That's just something I'll have to sit with until I die, I imagine."

We stopped talking. I took a drink of my coffee, which by now had gone cool. "Do you remember the actual last time you saw him?" I said. *Oh yes*, she said. How could she forget? But she was getting sad thinking about it, and it might be better served for another day. I tried to press: "Are you sad because something sad happened?"

She smiled weakly, and looked at the floor. "It makes me

sad because nothing happened. Nothing at all. So I'd like to go back to the beginning—the real beginning. I think Seth deserves better than just the end, don't you think?"

WE KEPT TALKING UNTIL THE SUN WENT DOWN, PAUSING ONLY for the bathroom and so that I could replace the battery in my recorder. It wasn't even five o'clock by the time the sky inked out, but Rachel said we should wrap up soon, her boyfriend would be headed home from work and she needed to get started on dinner.

Our final topic was the funeral, which had been for her, as it was for me, completely overwhelming. I mentioned what Kelsey had told me about Lee being scared off by a group of Seth's friends, but Rachel said she'd only heard of it after the fact, at the bar where some people convened for a final toast.

"One of them was this guy Patrick . . . did you know him?" she said. "He was a year above Seth and me, so maybe two above you."

I vaguely recalled the concept of "Patrick" but could not connect his name to an actual person. "Patrick was . . ." She scrunched her face, and did not speak. "Patrick was a good guy. The type of person you could count on to make a scene when it was justified. We haven't talked in a long while but maybe he'd want to help out, I don't mind asking. It sounds very interesting, what you're putting together."

"That would be really helpful," I said. "I'm also planning to get in touch with his parents at some point. You haven't talked to them since the funeral, I take it?"

"I haven't," she said, after a pause. "I would definitely be very careful about that, whatever you do."

I told her not to worry, I understood. The afternoon had been extraordinarily helpful. I didn't know how much longer I'd be in Chicago but if she was potentially open to a follow-up chat, in addition to whatever she heard back from Patrick, that would be fantastic. I excused myself to use the bathroom one last time, and came back to her busing our coffee cups into the kitchen. When she walked back into the living room, she suddenly froze in place as though someone had leveled a spotlight on her. "I almost forgot," she said. "A lot of the photos I put on Facebook came from a hard copy." She adopted a fake-spooky voice. "In the days before digital."

"Yeah?"

"So when I was looking through those old papers, I came across some photos of the three of us."

I stopped fussing with my bag. "What do you mean?"

"Hold on, I'll find them." She left the room, and returned a second later holding a chunky leather-bound photo album. "It's funny, my mother gave this to me in high school and I never thought I'd put it to any use, but it's more or less the only way to hold on to these. Here, look at this." She flipped to a section of the album and pointed at the right-hand side of the page.

It was a photo of Seth and myself in a backyard I didn't recognize, lying on our backs in the grass, squinting at the camera with skeptical faces. Underneath it was a photo of us in the same position, except Rachel was hovering over us, and we'd adopted gigantic smiles I recognized as sarcastic. "That's why I remembered you right away at the reunion," she said. I couldn't believe she made the connection: in my mind I bore no resemblance to how I'd looked in high school, but in reality it was just a haircut and some weight gain. I thought of Rachel as one of those people I knew about but didn't actually know, but obviously I'd spent time with her because she'd been close with Seth, and I'd been close with Seth, and our closenesses would have eventually intersected.

I tried to place the day. I looked about fifteen or sixteen. I was wearing a red T-shirt with the Flash's lightning bolt logo on the chest. Seth was wearing one of his graphic T-shirts: two unicorns having sex. I didn't remember many of my friends who had backyards, or backyards where we hung out. Then it clicked: "Ruth's," I said out loud.

"That's right," Rachel said. She showed me the back of the photo, where she'd written "Labor Day at Ruth's 2004" in the upper-right-hand corner. She flipped through the album: Ruth was in some of the photos, as were Anthony, Susie, Natalia, Audrey, Kelsey, and plenty of others we'd been friends with, everyone making the slightly self-conscious poses of teenagers trying to pretend they were too cool for a photograph, even though we were excited to see how we'd been captured in one another's company. "I didn't put these on Facebook. I mean, duh, we didn't have Facebook then. But I'm sure I had them on my LiveJournal."

I tried to think of what had happened that afternoon and drew a blank. "Do you remember anything we did?"

"Ruth's dad grilled for us. Beyond that, nothing. It can't have been that memorable. I mean, I didn't even really remember it until I came across these photos. Look at you two," she said, pointing back at the photo of Seth and me resting on the grass. "Obviously, you were in your element."

Our ill-fitting shirts, our knowing smirks, our messy hair and casual demeanors—this was how I'd recalled Seth and myself, and the way we'd been together. Throughout the interviews, I'd only become further unmoored from my memories. Considering the enormity of what I hadn't known at the time, my warm recollections of years past felt explicitly delusional, a shallow fiction to make me feel better about how I'd lived my life. But looking at these photos of myself that I'd never seen before, from a day I couldn't remember, told me I hadn't forgotten everything. Some of it had taken hold in my memory because it was the truth, no matter what else was displaced.

"I think we were just being dicks," I said. "Can you send those photos to me?"

"Sure, I'll scan them. Maybe you could use them in the podcast? It could be an accompanying slideshow, or something nice like that."

I flipped through the photos again and visualized them blasted across my publication's website. "It is a nice idea. But it might also be too . . . sentimental for what I'm going for?"

"But is sentimentality so bad? I feel like you can't avoid that forever, with a project like this."

I wondered how to give her a gracious brush-off, until I had more time to decide for myself. "Maybe you're right. I'll keep them in mind, see how the vibe is shaking out. The project is about Seth but it's not just *about* Seth, if that makes sense. I want to make sure everything is calibrated just right."

Rachel withdrew her smile and stared at me with something I couldn't place. "What do you mean?"

"Obviously it's *about* him, and what happened to him, but it's also about Chicago, gay rights, 9/11 . . . you know, this kind of collective act of remembrance nestled within all these other ongoing historical inflection points. Also the druggy shit that was happening at Sayers, some people are beginning to go on the record about that, and I think that'll be a fairly big component when it comes together."

Before I could cleverly deflate how pretentious this sounded, a laugh I could only interpret as "rude" left her mouth. "Sorry," she said. "The more we talk about this, the more I feel like I'm helping out. But I also feel protective. I haven't felt that way in a long time, because what's been there to protect? What I said about Seth and me growing apart—that may have happened, in some other world. Then I think about all this going public, and wonder . . ." She stopped talking, and held her silence for a moment. "If it's not exactly about Seth then I wonder what the point is?"

No one had asked me this, throughout all my interviews. They hadn't seemed to think twice about the value of the podcast, possibly because projects like these, where normal people resuscitated their memories in service of solving some unsolved mystery or untangling some tangled emotion, now happened all the time. I'd understood that when I approached them, because I knew the allure of sharing what you had to say with the world. They might have talked about Seth with any old therapist, but it was a different type of validation to say it into a microphone—another form of those Facebook confessionals that Rachel, and so many others, had written down over the years.

But nobody I'd talked to had been closer to Seth than Rachel. I put my bag down, so it didn't look like I was trying to run out of the apartment. "No, don't apologize . . . Look, Seth meant a lot to me, I'm not just trying to turn his life into a podcast so I can get a raise. Projects like this can make a difference, because they can make other people think in a way that an article can't. That's part of why it's a podcast, so that I can include all of these other voices instead of just focusing on myself, and my own thoughts—find the thing in Seth that touched all of us, while also trying to find out why he died. The other stuff about drugs or 9/11 or whatever, that's an important sales hook . . . but I guess I'm just trying to do something he'd be proud of, if he were still alive. As a literary document, or something like that."

"That's very generous of you," she said quietly.

"But I know what I'm looking for, and I guess I'm hoping to make something that satisfies what other people might be looking for too—not just people who'd known Seth, but people who'd known anyone, anywhere. Because that's the necessary balance for this kind of emotional storytelling—attempting to elevate your own thoughts and feelings and experiences into something that matters to strangers, who can hopefully glimpse something of themselves in whatever it is you've got to say." I astonished myself with how natural this sounded, how I felt no need to joke, unlike my other miniature spiels about the goals of the podcast. It was the closest thing to the truth I'd said out loud.

I must have been expecting Rachel to visibly soften, or give her approval, which is why it surprised me when she did neither. "I suppose it's good to have some clarity there," she said.

"I promise I am going to do right by him," I continued. "I can't promise I won't get into some of the more sordid details, but I am not about to out my friend as . . . I don't know, some kind of depressed addict, or whatever. I'm not a moralist. I'm not judgmental. I know there's more going on than that. Something to take away from all this, I think."

Rachel looked back at the photo album, which had remained open this whole time, and shut it. I could feel her drifting away and didn't know what to say in order to reel her back. "I hope so," she said. "I really do. Because we can talk all day about his life, and what you think it meant, but it won't change the fact that he'll never be able to tell us himself."

MY ONLY FRIENDS IN TOWN WERE A TERTIARY MIX OF HIGH school acquaintances who'd stayed here after graduation, and college acquaintances who'd settled here after graduation. I'd texted Lee again—Just wanted to know if you're around!, like some perky HR representative—but he hadn't texted me back, and I'd resisted the urge to follow up again despite every nervous cell in my body shrieking, *Follow up, follow up, follow up!!!!!!*

"The vibes are . . . not great," I told William over the phone, as I maneuvered a slice of cold pizza toward my mouth. "You're lucky you left journalism. It's just a lot of sitting around, waiting for people to call you back, but then they never do."

"That's not just journalism," he said. "Sometimes, it's your own friends."

The comment hurt, but I saw his point. I'd blown our last few standing dates to catch up, on account of needing to conduct an interview or chase a lead for the podcast. Staying with him in Los Angeles had reanimated our intimacy, which meant he felt no need to disguise the tone of his voice. "Listen, I said I was sorry. It's been hectic here—and I've had to sort out some things in New York, now that I'm staying in Chicago a little longer. You know how hard it is to get an eighty-one-year-old landlord to make a spare key, so someone can come and water your plants?"

"The body breaks, and the body is fine," he said, quoting a song we used to love. "Of course I get it. But to be honest, the podcast chat is wearing me out. Should we just table the calls for six months from now, when you're hopefully a bit more settled down?"

"Suck my dick, ass man," I said, quoting a movie we used to love. "Come on, give me a break. It's just taking up a lot of my mental space." My effort was fermenting into obsession; it had been years since I'd committed myself to a long-term project, and my thoughts were progressively overrun with all of the work I needed to do, all of the people I needed to talk to, all of the connections to be drawn. I recognized this might be only so interesting to explain out loud but, hey, that's what friends were for. I'd listened to William blab about his work as a financial adviser, even when I couldn't follow everything he was saying.

The phone was quiet for a moment. "The difference there is I knew I was being a drag. And I'm sorry you were so bored by me talking about my life. What I'm describing here is a little more than boredom, I think."

"Yeah?" I swallowed the rest of my crust. "Hit me, dog."

"*Stop that*," he said. "I'm trying to have a serious conversation with you."

"Okay, I'm sorry. I'm glad to have a voice of reason on my side, seriously." I wasn't trying to be a dick, but William's attitude was perplexing; I felt like he was trying to give me a lecture about the merits of recycling. My sit-down with Rachel had already thrown me off my gait; I didn't need an actual friend to inject more doubt.

"You know . . . in high school, Seth sort of scared me," he

said. "I didn't find him as charming as everyone else. In retrospect, I can look back and go, *Okay, clearly that was a reaction to me being in the closet and him being so out there.* Clearly, I was put off by someone who seemed so comfortable with himself. And to his credit, he was always decent to me. He didn't throw it in my face. There was a lot of grace in that, and I appreciate that, I really do."

William did not often talk about this with me. We hadn't been close back then, but I'd never thought he had a bad time—he'd just had *time,* value-neutral and uneventful, bordered by the unspoken conclusions he'd yet to discover about himself. I had sympathy for that, but it seemed like a middle-of-the-road outcome. There were worse ways for things to have gone.

"But if Lee was wrapped up in that, I just have a bad feeling. Lee did not have that grace; he probably guessed I was in the closet, and he was an asshole about it. He was an unsettling guy, Jacob, and you're playing around with this for . . . what, exactly? Keeping your job is not your life's calling. And these are real people you're playing around with, real events that you're going to turn into some fucking . . . I don't know, something you're better than but other people aren't because they're so desperate for this cheap, unoriginal—"

"Whoa, hold on . . ."

"Sorry, but *emotionally unoriginal shit,* and you're going to serve it up because they're asking?"

I recognized the sincerity in William's voice and was touched that his conscience extended to my actions. Still, I was surprised by how forceful he was being, by how little he seemed to trust that I knew what I was doing. "I hear you, but you're giving me a lot of shit about something that I think is going to be a bit more thoughtful." I heard my own voice become stern, so that he could understand I wasn't being light. "It's not as simple as keeping my job, come on. I know you don't care about revisiting high school, but there's stuff here I'm tapping into that's not just about high school. It's something that benefits everyone, not just me."

While I waited for him to say something, I opened the fridge to see if there was more pizza. "Jacob, do you remember when my father died? Do you remember what you wrote to me?"

"Of course I remember," I said.

"Here's what I'm saying to you, now: Maybe this just sucks, and it's just going to keep sucking. Maybe you can't make anything good out of it. And if you try to struggle too hard to prove otherwise, you're going to run into a lot of trouble."

IN THE YEARS SINCE I'D MOVED AWAY FROM CHICAGO, MY MOTHER had begged me to sort through my teenage belongings—my action figures, my school notebooks, my school textbooks, my comic books, my board games, my DVDs, my ZIP drives and flash drives, my video game consoles and video game magazines, my CD bindles and CD burners, my books and books and books, I had so many books, how was that possible? I needed to file and collate and eventually dispense of this stuff, whether that meant selling it, lugging it back to New York, or throwing it in the trash. In response I hadn't touched any of it, always coming up with a semicharming excuse. But I had been in my twenties then, and I was in my thirties now, and I had nobody to see and nothing to do but wait around for Lee. With Harold's permission I poured a moderate glass of the nice whiskey I'd bought him at Christmas and holed up in my room.

My bedroom really was filled with so much shit, and the idea of becoming my own personal archaeologist was seductive now that I was looking at all this for the first time in years. A yearbook from junior year; a sheaf of school newspapers; the Sayers student directory from my junior year; a quarter-filled agenda covered in band names; a midyear progress report from my sophomore chemistry class, which informed me I was hovering just below the cutoff for an A. And that was just the stuff related to high school: underneath my computer desk, I discovered several pounds of magazines, and the patina of dust I wiped away from the cover of a now-defunct gaming publication touting the graphical innovations of the yet-unreleased PlayStation 2 confirmed the passage of time.

I went back to the kitchen to top off my whiskey and pulled a couple of trash bags out of the storage closet. In my room, I began mercilessly throwing away as much as I could, pausing only to briefly take note of what I was pitching into the bag. Goodbye G.I. Joe action figure, scavenged from a yard sale! Goodbye, tattered copy of *Superboy* #118, scavenged from a different yard sale! I was having a lovely time ambling down memory lane, conceding that my mother perhaps had a point. Not everything I owned was an essential document in the story of my life, as I'd joked about a few too many times in the past. Sometimes, it was just an issue of *Nintendo Power*. Into the bag it went, and soon I had filled up the bags I'd brought upstairs, requiring me to go back downstairs to get more bags and more whiskey, and before long I had seven brimming trash bags, which I lugged back downstairs to the front door.

I started rummaging through my closet to see what else could go. I'd worked on the Sayers newspaper for three years, and my preservationist tendencies had led me to save multiple copies of each issue, now congealed into a wadded brick of newsprint beneath my clothing hanger. Surely a single copy of each would suffice at this stage in my life. I separated these extra copies and tossed them into another trash bag, making sure to skim each issue just to remember what I'd wasted all my time on.

The paper was such an incestuous, small-time affair that most of the staffers' friends had shown up in there, at some point. For example I was somehow now looking at a micro-profile of Natalia, which thankfully I had not written, centered around something called the Good Luck Club. You see, Natalia had started a tradition where, every morning, she went around her circle of friends and told them "Good luck," aggressively shaking their hands like a Russian general standing on ceremony—and then those friends went around their friends and did the same. "'Good Luck Club' charms Sayers students," the headline read. Maybe thirty people had been involved in this semi-ironic twee ritual? Probably less? Not that I'd thought this was journalism at the time, but Jesus Christ.

The article included a photo of Natalia, done up in eyeliner and covered in arm bangles, staring at the camera with the apathetic yet probing expression that had minced my heartstrings. I took a picture with my phone, and texted it to her: Lmao, I wrote, hoping this phrasing would indicate I was feeling only the appropriate amount of nostalgic. I had enjoyed hanging out in Los Angeles, but I didn't think there was any chance we'd ever become regular text correspondents, nor did I want to insinuate I desired that . . . even though I sort of did desire that.

I'd continued to think about her, though we hadn't texted more than a couple of times since I'd flown back to New York. Catching feelings for Natalia, at this stage in life, was impractical and chaotic, but what if we just made out for forty-five minutes the next time we saw each other? It would be a way of closing the emotional loop we'd formed as teenagers and coming to terms with the people we'd ended up as . . . or something. Maybe it would just be making out. That still wasn't a bad idea; you didn't need a better reason. The rational part of me understood that reality was successive, and we moved on by necessity, and that idealizing the people you'd kissed without remembering any of the attendant messiness was for children and dating-show contestants. On the other hand, the degenerate part of me always wanted to kiss everyone I'd ever kissed, unless they were now a bigot. Maybe even if they were a bigot, why say no ahead of time?

It was past midnight in Chicago, but I figured she'd be awake in Los Angeles. I kept reading, taking note of the stories I'd written and the stories by others that had, in a humble way, re-created the social sphere of my high school. The micro-profile of Natalia might have been silly and self-serving, but something that affected thirty students in a school of eight hundred wasn't wholly irrelevant. I mean, why else had I written so many band profiles? Nobody cared about these bands except their friends, it wasn't like Milpool or anyone else had possessed real ability, something to vault them out of our local battle of the bands and into the pages of *Spin* or *Blender*, the magazines I'd desperately wanted to write for. (Though Lee had come close, I reminded myself.) But I'd written them because they were stories about the world around me, however self-contained it was.

That's what I was doing in my professional life, but my world had yet to fully open up the way I'd thought it would once I'd moved past high school and college and the early humiliations of adult life. I was still brushing up against the limitations of the space around me, as were my peers and the people aspiring to be my peers, the collective sum of our efforts to describe and probe and pathologize maxing out at the boundaries of our perception. Because everything was changing all of the time—

the universe expanded and contracted and blobbed into an omnidirectional mess resisting classification, despite what we might hope to convey in a nine-hundred-word or fifteen-hundred-word or even three-thousand-word piece. In some ways, these high school stories had laid the groundwork for the letdowns of my career, as the same flaws were observable here. I had believed that I could understand something just because I observed it, and those observations felt true to me.

That wasn't the case, as I'd learned the night I'd doubled over in my apartment, gripped by panic. It was partly why I'd committed to pursuing the podcast. I'd made my living by trying to map the world, as my insurance-approved therapist had pointed out. Instead of mercilessly diagramming the present or wishfully hunting out the future, it felt more centering to sort out the past, moving around easily recounted memories and formerly obscured memories into a mosaic capturing the full picture of what had actually happened, not just as I remembered it.

Now that I'd massively condensed the school newspapers, it seemed like a sensational idea to reconnect with my PlayStation 2. As I went to look for my *Guitar Hero* controller, I noticed a light-blue file folder bearing my mother's handwriting, next to the television: SAVE FOR JACOB.

Tucked in front was a copy of the newspaper obituary for my father, and right away I remembered what this must be. I'd amassed countless cards and letters and assorted clippings related to his death, and my organizational solution was to throw them all into the file folder I was looking at right now. I hadn't seen this since college, easily; most likely it had been buried in another corner of my room, and excavated by my mother as she was poking around to see what she could throw out without my permission.

I removed the obituary and started reading from the top. My father, Damien, had worked for the design team at the *Wednesday Journal*, a newspaper based in the suburbs, but he had also served as a kind of catch-all handyman, capable of building computers and writing ad copy and supplying cigarettes for anyone in need. He had suffered a heart attack while riding the train to work, and it had taken the hospital several hours to get in touch with my mother and myself. I remembered that the university chaplain had taken me to the hospital, and that we hardly talked during the long drive, since while they hadn't told me anything specific over the phone, I felt like I could surmise the likely event necessitating my sudden removal from class so that my school's spiritual counselor could personally accompany me to find out what exactly had happened to my father. I spent that long drive stockpiling my anticipation, thinking to myself, "*Well, heart disease does run in the family*," and "*Well, he could've stood to lose a little weight*," and several other reasonable and conscientious things I hoped would soften the inevitable blow, all of it rendered irrelevant the moment they brought us into the mortuary to identify his body and I realized he was actually dead, that I was experiencing an irreversible moment, that I had crossed over some invisible threshold into the *after* part of my life.

The obituary took up an entire page in the *Journal*, surrounded by photos taken around the office and personal photos provided by my mother. I appeared in two of them, first as a bowl-cutted boy holding on to his leg, and secondly as a gangly teenager pointing at him while wearing a colossal shit-eating smile. The obituary copy was lovingly written, summing up his entire life from birth to end, including several details I hadn't remembered until reading them now: a brief detour into his time working on a commune in his young adulthood;

a testimony from the *Journal*'s managing editor about how he'd modernized their computer system at the dawn of the nineties; a series of fond, if not slightly deprecating, quotes from my mother about how he had decided "to get a real job" after I was born, having come to the end of a noticeably protracted adolescence. I smiled reading this: I had never known my father as an adult, and reading evidence of how other adults had seen him was enlivening. I acutely remembered the feeling of standing at his memorial service, welcoming the coworkers I'd heard about but never met and realizing that their perspective was much different than mine, that they would honor him differently. I'm sure they'd all decamped to a bar afterward, whereas I'd returned home to sit totally alone in my room.

Thinking about it today, it was hard to believe I'd taken only a week off from school. Rachel had missed *two weeks* when Seth died, whereas I'd treated the death of a parent like a bad flu. The memorial service had happened, and then I'd helped my mother go through the initial documents related to his death, and then I'd returned to campus, all within seven days. Every night I fell asleep wondering what the future held, and how long I would remember the sound of my father's voice, and whether I would die of a surprise heart attack as well, before popping up in the morning to join my friends in the dining hall and talk about our upcoming lectures, an incongruence between mood and routine that left me unprecedentedly miserable. Nobody had really known how to talk to me, and I hadn't really known how to talk to anyone, so instead of attending therapy or crying or even getting into particularly depressing indie rock, I'd just resumed my usual habits as though nothing had changed. One night a friend had invited me over to get chaotically drunk on malt liquor and rap music, and just before we'd parted ways so that I could stumble back to my dorm and throw up into a trash can, he insisted on a final toast. "To Damien Goldberg," he proclaimed, "a man I never met, but whom we miss dearly." And I remember exactly what I'd thought, despite my violently drunk state: "Sure, that's nice."

Rachel Watkins had said you never knew what anyone was carrying around with them, how they'd folded those experiences into the way they interacted with the world. Anyone who saw me in the wake of my father's death would've assumed I was just another long-haired freshman in a Sonic Youth T-shirt, not someone constantly thinking, *Fuck, shit, life is misery, I'm a wreck, I am going to die at any moment and nothing can convince me otherwise.* I believed these thoughts were only valuable if I could find some eloquent or profound way to verbalize them, but every time I tried to express myself, it came out as doomed gibberish. I didn't know how to integrate my feelings into real life, how to communicate to people that something serious had happened to me, something I couldn't telegraph even when prompted by a celebratory, drunken toast. *It's just going to suck for a while*, I'd told William, and the bluntness of this observation really was the most accurate summary of my inner state. Hence I'd maintained my silence, turning over my thoughts in my head for months and years, until one day I realized I was no longer as sad as I'd used to be. It had only taken several years of solitary processing, no big deal.

I put the obituary back in the folder and looked at what else was stuffed in there. Lots and lots of cards, expressing thoughts singular (a note from a second cousin on how she'd dealt with the death of her father, whom I'd never met) and generic (a collection of signatures from my entire dorm floor, most of which were accompanied by a variation on "Sorry for your loss"). The program from the memorial service, and a copy of the lyrics for "I Shall Be Released," which a family friend had performed on a guitar. Envelopes containing letters, so many letters, written by hand and typed on the computer, from friends attempting to express their secondhand grief and offer whatever solidarity they could.

"Dear Jacob," began a letter from Aaron, a member of Milpool, "I don't know how to put this, but . . ." I read a few more lines before wincing and stuffing the letter back into the file folder; it was too uncomfortable to take in the feelings of a seventeen-year-old trying to make an eighteen-year-old feel better. It must have been a shock: if my father could die out of nowhere, then so could his. And so he'd attempted to work those feelings out as best he could, though there was nothing he could say that could mean anything to me in the moment.

I looked at a letter with no envelope, packed with tight, tiny print that I had to squint to decipher. "I feel like I can tell you anything, I think that's partly because you're older than me and have a different life. We don't have many of the same experiences, and it makes it easier to tell you about them. I know that you won't have any prejudgments on a situation, that you'll never make me feel bad or look down on me. And I wish I could do that for you, but I don't know what to say." I looked down to the bottom to see it was signed by Audrey, Audrey from Raytheon. Perhaps I'd been too uncharitable to her in Los Angeles, years removed from the closeness we'd once shared, a closeness I might never believe had existed were it not for the proof in front of me.

I flipped through a few more envelopes and their contents, most of which appeared to express the same sentiments, until I came across one bearing a postmark, indicating it had been mailed. The return address, and name, were Seth's.

I opened it up and pulled out a piece of stationery covered in loopy cursive on both sides. The paper was faux parchment, and burned around the edges. I smiled, tracing my fingers against his handiwork—of course Seth was melodramatic like that, seizing the chance to be a little cute about what most people had exclusively treated as a somber event. It was postmarked two weeks after the memorial service, and I remembered that during my freshman year, I'd given my dorm address to some of my friends so that they could write me letters if they wanted—an affectation, perhaps, but a nice ritual all the same. Even before social media took off we weren't exactly a pen-and-paper generation, so I didn't receive many, but Seth had written.

I started at the top, and began reading:

Dear Jacob,

First off, I want to say that I am so, so, so sorry I didn't come to the memorial service. I wanted to come, believe me, but if I can be honest with you—and part of why I treasure our friendship so much is because I can be honest with you—I haven't been in a good space at all, these days. That's a terribly selfish thing to say to someone who's just suffered a horrible tragedy, but on the morning of the memorial service, I was overwhelmed by my thoughts in a way I was not expecting. I wanted to be there for you, but I needed to be there for myself at the moment, and so I made this terribly selfish decision to stay at home. I hope you can forgive me. Ruth told me you spoke magnificently, and I wish I could've heard it. I know I'm always teasing you about your writing, but I have no doubt that you rose to the occasion.

As I sat down thinking about what to write, I thought about the last time we hung out, in the winter. Something that's stuck with me is how confidently you were talking about the future. You mentioned comic books you wanted to write, screenplays you wanted to develop, publications you wanted to pitch, internships you wanted to apply for, professionals you wanted to meet, and peers you wanted to befriend. I admit that a part of me thought you were laying it on thick, because that is an awful lot to intend for yourself, and meanwhile I've just been sitting on my ass at home. But I can't blame you. It must be so exciting to look at the world as this ocean of possibility; I confess I am just a bit jealous of your optimism, considering my own situation. But this optimism is why I think you, more than anyone I know, will be able to come through this with the proper perspective. I know I give off the impression that I am perpetually upbeat, but right now I am finding it very hard to be upbeat about the future, or anything. Then I think about you, and the way you're able to be hopeful against all odds—because, come on, wanting to write comic books is for babies, grow up—and I have no doubt you will reach the next step of this process, no matter how long it takes.

What that process entails, I'm not sure. My father is alive, and the loss I've experienced is a different kind—not the absence of an entire person, but the diminishing of potential. It's very hard for me to think that just a year ago, I could talk to you like someone who had an idea of what came next. That person feels very distant to me, and I wonder what happened to him. But you, you are the same, in a way that is not stagnant or dull—you are changing, of course, because you're in college and it would be kind of weird if you weren't changing, but that core spirit in you, that will carry you through this.

I don't want to make this letter about me, and how I feel, though I've done just that. I feel emo telling you this in a letter, like I'm some kind of Austen protagonist. I just want to say that I care about you very much, and I'm here for you, just as I know you're here for me. I think that very soon, we should meet up and talk about our lives. You know where to find me.

Love, Seth

I reread the letter two more times, trying to locate its contents within my memory. Seth hadn't been at the service, that was true, but I hadn't thought anything about it. Plenty of my friends hadn't come, they were out of town or busy with school or otherwise occupied, and I didn't hold it against them given the short notice. I would've read this letter and understood where he was coming from, without any animus or judgment.

Yet it was obvious now that Seth was trying to tell me something, something I hadn't noticed from within my own grief. I couldn't remember if I'd responded or seen him after; I must have, because I wouldn't have left him hanging, but I couldn't say for sure. If we had hung out we hadn't talked about any of that, as though things were normal. But it wasn't normal, and though he must have known this from looking at me, I did not know this from looking at him. And he must have made the decision not to say anything, even as he was desperate to share.

Something anxious and terrible roiled inside me as I suddenly wished, against all basic emotional logic or understanding of temporal reality, that I could peel back the years and return to the moment I'd received this letter, in order to properly respond. Before I could think anything else, my phone buzzed. It was Natalia, responding to the photo I'd sent her: Ha ha, very funny . . . what a loser I was. That was not how I would've described her, but it wasn't necessary to correct the record. Her next message was more surprising: I moved back to Chicago. Let's get a drink. Do you have any time next week?

All I have is time, I wrote back, pushing down these new thoughts and feelings. I could meet wherever she wanted.

IN LOS ANGELES, EVERYONE WAS ALWAYS AGITATING ABOUT HOW to better themselves, as though a new diet or jacket could radically transform their life. Natalia's job at the Broad, formally and informally, was rooted in saying *yes*—yes to that opening, yes to that launch, yes to that new outfit, yes to that drink and that drug and whatever else. But the longer she'd lived there, the more she'd been overcome with a powerful urge to refuse, abstain, *say no*. Slowly but surely she felt a deep need to recede from the expectations of her life, which increasingly felt shallow and unnecessary even if the parties were occasionally fun.

In Chicago, it was different. Instead of a coterie of tanned hangers-on and coked-out dilettantes, she had her mother, along with her father and her two sisters, both of whom were entering their final year of high school—a happy unit under the same roof, as it had been when we were teenagers. "Every morning my mother makes us breakfast, I go to work, and then I come home and watch a movie with my sisters. Nobody talks about something they think I need to know, or someone I need to meet. It's very, very nice." I asked what Anna had said, and she said Anna was a true friend, and true friends understood stuff like that. I asked what Audrey had said, and she said she did not care. I asked what she was doing for work now, and she said it did not matter.

She excused herself, as the bartender had signaled her over. Though the Inner Town Pub's clientele had gentrified in recent years, the bartender could still summon that old-school Chicago spirit and prepare a mug of chamomile to relieve a customer's congestion during cold season. Natalia had sounded terrible when I met her in the bar, but she waved off my suggestion we keep it short if she wasn't feeling well—a stuffy nose wasn't going to stop her from hanging out, come on. I had been to the Inner Town before, where the wood-paneled walls and fusillade of neon beer signs signaled it was still very much a dive, regardless of its clientele and surrounding neighborhood. But it had never felt like a bar I could claim as mine, something Natalia had done right away upon moving home, judging by the casual way she requested the bartender make this restorative brew.

Natalia was friendlier than I'd anticipated, despite her cold. She was dressed up as if we were going out when we were just getting a drink, my expectations far lower than her red leather jacket and delicately applied blue eyeshadow suggested. But we were rolling now, the vibe between us more convivial and casual than it had been in Los Angeles, where I had actively tried to impress her. Here we were just a couple of townies in their thirties, hoping to impress nobody.

I was surprised to learn that Natalia had just packed up shop and moved home. I'd pressed for more details—surely you didn't just peace out of a city when you missed your family and were sick of your job and friends and everything around you, but put like that, I suppose you did. The change of scenery had revived her manners: she'd asked far more questions than I'd prepared for, and at first I'd had to consciously rev up my social machinery to accommodate her. This friendliness seemed like a bit I wasn't yet in on, though it wasn't impossible that after all the years we'd known each other, and through all the hormonal tribulations, I'd become someone she was neutrally happy to see.

I was neutrally happy to see her, too, even as I was very neutrally thinking to myself, *I wonder if this person with whom I have a moderate amount of history will, at some point, wish to put their face on mine.* I'd filled her in on the status of my job, my family, my Brooklyn apartment, but she'd also asked about the podcast, and where it currently stood. "It stuck with me," she said. "That night at the hotel bar was perhaps the last interesting conversation I had in Los Angeles."

"Thank you," I said. "I have high hopes for how it's going, I guess? I still need to talk to Lee, but you know, fingers crossed."

"Has he been hard to get in touch with?"

"He's actually completely ignored all of my attempts to get together now that I'm in town, but I'll figure it out." I mock cackled, like a maniac who didn't give a fuck. "Or, you know, I won't."

Natalia took a long drink of her tea and cleared her throat. "It is weird to think about how many people at Sayers died when we were there. Maybe not weirder than a lot of things, I don't know, but weird for us. Like do you remember Caleb Fordham?" I shook my head no. "He was two years below me, maybe you never met him. He died my senior year, drag racing on Lakeshore Drive. We had this public vigil even though a lot of us thought he was an idiot. Not to speak ill of the dead, but . . . an idiot."

"That is funny," I said. "Yeah, that was the tricky part—initially I'd thought about focusing on some other dead people, but pretty quickly we figured out it was easier to narrow it to Seth." Part of that was my personal bias—I had always been much closer with Seth. But what had happened to him was also a better story, and I was trying to tell a story.

Was that a callous way to look at it? Perhaps, but I could only be honest about my own capacity for doing the work. Besides, I wasn't saying this in the actual work; of course I'd never admit that some of the dead classmates were less interesting to me and other people.

"You're saying that out loud right now," Natalia said, her face unconvinced.

"Sure, but it's just me and you. If I had to justify why I went in this direction I'd probably say something like 'We wanted to put all of our effort into fleshing out a single story as much as we could, rather than dilute the truth of anyone else's life.'"

"Jesus, now who's a hologram of a person?"

"I wouldn't say it exactly like that! I'm just talking, I don't know. I've had three drinks, give me a break." I mock-frowned, suddenly self-conscious that I was expressing all of my emotions in mock form.

"Uh-huh." She smiled, an expression I found unnerving, and coolly tousled her hair with her hand. "So what's next?"

"I guess I'm in Chicago until something shakes out. I was originally supposed to be here only through New Year's, but my boss told me to stick around and see what happens with Lee. Really, I'm just waiting for him. A lot of it is in place already . . . it's like, we start out with a portrait of this person, and reveal that something mysterious happened to him, so we work our way backward to figure out the truth—who did him dirty, what he meant to all of us, how it ended, how that ending teaches us something or other, blah-blah, razzle-dazzle. That's the gist of it, so far."

I was getting better at talking about this on the fly: Natalia hadn't lost interest, she leaned forward and nodded thoughtfully just as I might have, though I noticed her occasionally looking past me. "You had told me you wanted to speak with Ben Porter, right?" she asked, once I was done. "Ben from the Spit Lickers?"

I was touched that she'd remembered. "Why, do you have his phone number? Kelsey gave me one but it was out of date."

"I don't have his phone number," she said, arching slightly out of her chair, "but I think I see him in the back."

A minute later we were sitting with Ben and his coworker Rogelio, talking like this was completely normal. I was still trying to grasp the order of events. *That's him,* Natalia had insisted, and when I'd turned around I realized he did look familiar, though I didn't know what to do with that. Despite my protestations, she had stood up and walked over, affecting a big cheery disposition that had resulted in an invitation to join them in their corner of the bar. "I was *just saying* to Ben that I hadn't seen him in *forever,* probably not since *high school,* and it's such a coincidence to run into him here," Natalia said when I sat down, her voice bright and expressive.

"Yeah, it's wild," Ben said. "You went to Sayers too?"

Even if we hadn't interacted all that much, it was hard to believe he wouldn't remember me. Then again, why not? He'd graduated two years before me, and fifteen years had passed since then, and who knew how he'd nuked his brain cells in between. "I did," I said hesitantly. "I was a couple of years behind you. I was friends with Ruth McCluskey, William Smith, Kelsey Winters—did you ever hang out with any of them?"

"You went to high school with fucking Will Smith?" Rogelio said, astonished.

"Kelsey," Ben said, a hint of something materializing on his face. "Sure, I knew Kelsey. Not the other two. You still keep up with Kelsey? I hear she's doing well for herself."

"A bit. I saw her last year, she's in Los Angeles these days. Should I tell her you said hi?" I wasn't meaning to be provocative, it had simply come out.

His expression wilted, just barely. "Nah, that's fine. I'll pick up a new round. Old Style all right?"

"Of course," Natalia said, though she'd been drinking wine. Ben and Rogelio stood up and moved to the bar.

I pulled my chair toward Natalia. "What . . . are you doing," I whispered.

"You have to talk to him, right? Why not get his number?"

"I do need to talk to him, but . . ."

"But what?"

"There's better channels . . . I've been drinking . . ."

"Better channels like . . ."

"Okay, fine, but *I have been drinking.*"

"'I've been drinking.'" Her face was exceptionally rude right now. "It'll be okay. You don't need to say everything. Just be normal."

I tried to remember this after Ben and Rogelio came back with our beers, but it wasn't easy. In high school, Ben wore a leather jacket with spikes stuck on the back, he styled his hair in a mohawk, he sneered more than he smiled, he seemed like he truly did not give a fuck. I was fourteen when I'd first become aware of him, which meant he must have been sixteen at the time, and I tried to avoid him as much as possible. Despite the fact that nothing about any sixteen-year-old past or present could intimidate me at this point in my life, something about his demeanor put me on edge. He'd buzzed his mohawk and swapped his leather jacket for a jean jacket, and he'd been friendly enough to offer us drinks, but I traced a vestigial hardness behind his face, a wariness in the way he reacted to my presence. At the same time he was perfectly friendly to Natalia, who was laying it on thick; she wasn't quite flirting, but her personality was unrecognizably congenial. She was . . . smiling a lot? She was . . . laughing a lot? She touched me on the arm, at one point, and then touched Ben on the arm? Maybe she was flirting. As far as I knew Ben was still good-looking and Natalia hadn't said anything about a boyfriend. But how could she be flirting, given everything I'd told her about Ben? She was on my side, wasn't she? I was losing my grip; this was high school all over again.

"What do you think, Jacob?" she asked. I hadn't been paying attention at all.

"Uh . . ."

"I think you're right about Lightfoot," Ben said. "She's a total cunt." This was what we were talking about, really? His coarseness took me aback, and I glanced at Natalia, but she continued smiling.

I tried to recover. "To be honest, I don't know much about her."

"She's an asshole," Rogelio said. He was a stout man with a squashed nose and a bad haircut, and much older than Ben; I couldn't imagine what job made them coworkers. "I didn't vote for her."

"My dad isn't a fan either," Natalia said. "But I think that's because he's a racist."

"I don't blame him," Ben said. "When it comes to Lori Lightfoot, I'm as self-loathing as it gets." What was *happening* here? As they continued talking, I probed my memory for some trenchant observation I might throw in about her ability to govern from within the lingering infrastructure of the Daley machine, or something else I'd picked up from reading articles, but the moment never came. I remained on the sidelines, watching them jab back and forth. Somehow we'd warped to the past, and once again Natalia was a girl I didn't understand anything about, and once again Ben was a guy I was intimidated by, and once again Rogelio—well, I didn't know anything about Rogelio, but he filled the same role as any of Ben's tough-looking friends from back in the day. Suddenly, I was feeling the bad kind of drunk. I wanted to leave, but I also didn't want to leave Natalia there, and also I still wanted Ben's number. I wished there was a way I could just hit fast-forward on this evening, until we came to the end of the night and I got what I was looking for.

Natalia excused herself to use the bathroom. The three of us sat there, not saying anything, fondling our beer bottles and looking at the walls. Normally I would've broken the silence out of obligation but I was feeling petulant and distasteful, torn between what I needed from Ben and my desire to abandon the entire situation.

"Natalia the stallion," Ben said, interrupting my thoughts. Natalia was like five three; that was a ridiculous thing to call her. "Are you guys screwing?"

Finally, confirmation that I wasn't being unnecessarily judgmental. "Natalia and I dated in high school but we're just friends," I said. "For now." That last bit I tacked on without meaning to, though I sensed it was like expecting a screen door to block a hurricane.

"That's a shame."

"Why, are you interested?"

"Yeah, sure, why not? A hottie with a body from back in the day. We're talking, we're having a good time." Rogelio remained wordless and continued drinking his beer.

"Uh-huh," I said. "Well . . . that's great."

"That's what I'm hoping for." Natalia returned, and Ben made a show of welcoming her back by pulling out her seat and making a short bow. She laughed at this, even though it was something an asshole would do—the self-conscious song and dance meant to desaturate the chivalrous act into something humorous, when of course he was just trying to FUCK!

The conversation picked back up, once again centering the two of them as though Rogelio and I weren't here. From time to time I tried looking at him, to see if he wanted to splinter off into our own side channel, but he didn't seem to notice or care. "Yeah, I'm not a fan of Los Angeles," Ben was saying. "Every woman there is blonde or a comedian."

"Whoa, I don't think it's that bad," I interrupted. "There are some brunettes."

Natalia grinned, but continued talking to Ben. "Yeah, everyone was either anorexic or hopelessly addicted to Percocet. I always felt like an outsider."

"I can't imagine you feeling like an outsider," he said.

She laughed, and I traced something sly and interested in her eyes. "Well, life always gets you." He returned the look, and I felt the powerful secondhand embarrassment of lingering on the margins of an implicit sexual negotiation between two attractive people.

Now I really was annoyed, in spite of myself. It was so territorial, to hope that a girl I'd kissed more than a decade ago wouldn't accidentally fall for the charms of this idiot. It was far more respectable to behave as though nothing bothered me, as though I were a lovely blade of glass doing the watusi down a gentle current. But they kept laughing at each others' jokes, and the alcohol was not relaxing me, and before I knew it I was saying something that felt both very stupid and yet completely justifiable.

"Ben, you were friends with Seth Terry, right?" Natalia's frisky demeanor momentarily fractured, revealing something confused and uncertain, before she collected herself. Ben turned to me and nodded slowly, as if he'd needed a moment to think about it.

"I saw him around, yeah."

"Cool, I thought so. So listen, I'm working on this project—it's for my job, back in New York—that's about his life. You know, the people who mean a lot to us and the lives they lead, the impact they have on us in life and in death, that sort of thing, blah-blah. But also, specifically, the way he died, which as I understand was abrupt and surprising. I mean, people were using drugs like that, at our school? Crazy, right?" I heard my voice turning glib and sour and did not, in the moment, care that much. "I'd love to interview you for it, if you're around."

"Huh." His face didn't change despite my implication, as he appeared to consider this. "I'll think about it."

"I think you'd add something really unique. What's your number?" I took out my phone. "I'll shoot you a text, so I can follow up later. Maybe you can put me in touch with some of the other people I've been trying to talk with—that guy Hector, I'm sure you remember him, or Lee Finch."

Ben laughed a cocky, shitty laugh, and picked up his beer. "Yeah, I don't know if Lee is going to talk to you, man."

I flashed my most guileless face, like a puppy asking for an early dinner. "What do you mean?"

"Honestly, it sounds kind of gay." His bravado flinched for a moment, as he shot a look at Natalia. "Or, you know, lame."

I smiled very, very widely. "Now that is the kind of salty and authentic language I'm hoping to get into this project—a slice of real Chicago, just like in documentaries."

Ben smirked, and mouthed *ha-ha*. "I said I'll think about it. If I want to get in touch I can figure it out. I'm sure you've got a website or something." Rogelio laughed at this, the first noise he'd made in a while.

"Oh I definitely have a website, but it'll be so much easier—"

He abruptly slammed his bottle down, and my leg did something twitchy of its own accord. "We're having a good time, okay?"

"I'm only trying to—"

"Why don't you just back off for a bit? I'm sure your arts and crafts project will be fine."

"I know it'll be *fine* without him—that's what they pay me for, to make sure things are fine. I just think Lee can help me work some things out."

"Yeah, I bet he could."

"In particular, I've been wanting to ask about the funeral—I'm hearing a lot about how he got chased off by Patrick and his friends." I didn't know who else was involved; "and his friends" was the most I could muster, but I figured that Ben wasn't going to call my bluff.

Even in the dark of the bar, Ben's eyes were unmistakably wide. "*Patrick?* Man, fuck Patrick, I wouldn't listen to a thing that motherfucker . . ." He stopped talking, cutting off whatever it was he was about to say.

"Why, does Patrick have something to share?" My voice took on a more suggestive, smug tone. "Something you don't want me to know? Something you'd like to *confess*? You can talk to me, I promise. I do this for a living." I felt Natalia touch my arm, but I didn't look at her.

This appeared to startle him, but only for a second. "I don't have shit to say to you." He stood up and retrieved his parka from a hook on the wall. "Natalia, it's been cool, maybe I'll see you around. But you," he said to me, pointing his finger, "you need to get a fucking grip."

I thought about apologizing and trying to lower the temperature so that we could return to talking about how the mayor was a cunt or whatever other lovely thing Ben was itching to say, but then I said something else: "So, is that a no on getting your number?" Ben didn't react, only turned around and made for the door, followed by Rogelio. "I hope you change your mind!" I called out behind them, attracting the attention of a few other people in the bar. "It would be a valuable contribution to the endeavor! A much-needed perspective!"

When they were gone, I sat back down and finished the rest of my beer, as a reflex. My leg was shaking, but I held it underneath the table.

Natalia hadn't talked during this entire time, only observed. "What?" She kept looking at me as though there was a spot on my face. "What? I was cutting to the chase. What?"

"I think," she said, "it would shock you how much nothing I have to say about that."

I WOKE UP THE NEXT DAY WITH A DEBILITATING, LEADEN HANGover. The last song I'd listened to, before passing out, was Alice in Chains' "Man in the Box." After my breakfast sandwich kicked in, I decided to massage my mood by going for a bike ride. Before leaving, my phone buzzed with a text message. I heard back from Patrick, and he said he might be interested, Rachel had written. I've also been thinking, and I'd really like to hear how you use my interview, before you put it in the podcast. I'm having more and more concerns, and it would just make me feel better. Especially if you want to talk again. I didn't want to get into any of that, so I pushed it into the mental bin of "things to figure out . . . eventually."

It was a placid and chilly Chicago morning. The air was quiet, providing little resistance as I slowly wended through the neighborhood. My winter coat limited my mobility, but accumulating speed required no special effort. The streets were mostly empty, and I occupied the center of the lane, apathetic to who was coming or going as I traced long, lazy loops from side to side. After a while I reached the Buddhist temple near my mother's house, which sat next to a small rose garden. I circled the bushes for a couple of minutes as I tried not to feel too embarrassed about how I'd behaved the night before.

My interview subjects had mostly been uniformly welcoming, and the people who'd turned me down had been polite about it—they just didn't have much to offer. But Ben had explicitly rejected me, maybe because he had something to hide, but more literally because he thought the idea was stupid and I was being a dick about it. In the moment, I'd written him off as a jackass; twelve hours later, weary and partially sober and staring at some Buddhist scripture mounted outside the temple whose beauty and fragility reminded me I was a worm, I considered the opposite view.

Because so what if Ben had been up to some bullshit more than ten years ago? Maybe he didn't see the point in revisiting the past. My life in New York had allowed me to take for granted the idea that modernity shot us forward and made irrelevant the time-honored hierarchies dictating the way of things, the hierarchies that had suffocated our parents and pushed them toward ascendant divorce rates and alcoholism. My world carried a moral mandate for self-examination, and pursuing a rigorous accounting of how your life had unfolded. We pondered the grand questions, such as: Was it possible that other people had been the problem? Such as: Was it possible we had not just suffered, but were in the process of suffering, all of the time? Such as: Was it possible to put a name to this suffering, rather than wallow in a miasma of despair and misunderstanding like our fathers and their fathers before them? Such as: And through all this was it possible to not only revisit and learn from the past, but conclusively move forward?

It was just what you did—latch on to some unexamined dimension of your personal life and share it with everyone. *We tell ourselves stories in order to live*, Joan Didion had written, but the fact that she hadn't meant it positively had been lost in translation, especially in an era with reputations to build and raises to earn. I had moved quickly, but my bosses had encouraged that quickness, and it seemed like such a natural and appropriate thing to do that I hadn't thought otherwise. But Rachel had questioned my purpose and begun to distance herself; William had flat-out told me this was a bad idea; Ben had rebuffed me outright; now, lacking my main character, I was feeling very silly.

I really wasn't trying to out my friend as a depressed addict, though the fact that I had to confirm this to myself did not improve my confidence. Many people, some of whom I even knew, had used heroin, and other substances that transgressed my personal tolerance. I was trying to figure out why Seth had ended up in this place at an otherwise developmental stage of life, and why that maybe still mattered to me and the people who'd known him. I wasn't the only person who had been naïve about the drug use at Sayers, but others had offered subtle references—"All that was going on," they had called it, well accustomed to minimization and secrecy, just as Erica had done when she'd informed Rachel. Burying this deeper understanding of your environment was normal behavior, it happened all of the time. I thought I was giving people permission to put a belated name to what they'd experienced in the past. I hadn't considered whether it was better left to the past, regardless of my interest in unearthing it, or their interest in sharing.

I stopped biking, and pulled over to a nearby bench. Worried I'm hitting a dead end, I texted Ruth. William kind of made me wonder why I'm looking into all of this? And Rachel wants to back out, maybe? And that guy Ben basically told me to my face I was an idiot. Also I'm hungover. Lol idk whooooooo fuckin knows

I hadn't seen Ruth over Christmas; the inclement weather had delayed her flight again, and she'd decided to stay in Washington, DC. Her response time was not always ideal, even as I understood that "hanging out with your fiancé" was a stronger pull during the holidays than "texting with your ex-best-friend/boyfriend about high school," but now she replied immediately.

You're looking into it because we all deserve an answer, and nobody else has the time, she said. Those people are only speaking for themselves; the rest of us still want to know.

NATALIA AND I HADN'T TEXTED SINCE THAT NIGHT WITH BEN, and while I didn't think she was ignoring me, I didn't want to seem too needy by explicitly confirming it. In a rational world, I might simply apologize for being strange, state my intention to see her again, and Natalia would simply tell me what she was thinking. But we didn't live in a rational world; instead, we abided by dozens of overlapping dictums and mandates about how people supposedly thought and behaved, and how the best way to think and behave in return supposedly was, most of which aggregated into a portrait of emotional banality. In my heart, I was nervous about the possibility that Natalia didn't want to talk to me anymore, after I'd acted like an idiot. But I knew I absolutely could not let on that I felt that way, if I wanted her to talk to me again. While thinking this through forced me to admit how stupid it was, shutting the hell up seemed preferable to humiliating myself over text message, as I'd done all too often when we were teenagers.

Meanwhile, the people I'd interviewed about Seth were located firmly within that emotional register; it was difficult to imagine "going out" with someone I'd asked to ruminate on death for hours at a time. I was a journalist, and journalists did not fraternize with their subjects, even if the subjects also remembered those journalists from when they, too, were navigating the indignities of puberty. But Olivia, strangely, didn't sound like a bad idea. I'd enjoyed our conversation at the reunion, and that we hadn't been so close in high school was even more of an incentive to reach out. I didn't want to retrace old fault lines with former best friends, retreating to the comfort of "remember when" after it turned out we didn't have much to say to each other beyond "How about the Bulls?"

Obviously I grasped the irony of avoiding nostalgia given the nature of the untitled Seth project, which was itself partially rooted in nostalgia. The stories I'd heard were funny, or sad, or some combination of both, but many of them were also just stories, not particularly interesting on their own if you hadn't known Seth or the people involved. But almost invariably would come a moment in the conversation when, after the surface narrative had unfolded, the person I was talking to would lapse into reflection for just a moment, revealing something unintentionally profound.

"Give me an example," Olivia said, as our bartender slid over two more Żywiecs, a beer I didn't know how to pronounce. We were sitting at Alice's, my favorite bar in Chicago, because it was the only place where you could drink a gigantic unpronounceable Polish lager while watching a local screech their way through a Weeknd song at karaoke. We had made small talk for a few minutes, catching up on Roger and their daughter and my mother and time at home, before I swerved right into the podcast, because it was the only thing I thought or talked about these days.

All right, I said, for example, the story Marissa Kenny had told me, where Seth had pretended to pose with the African American Club despite not being a member, and Ms. Malone had questioned him about whether he was really Black. Afterward Marissa had started talking about colorism in the Black community, and how someone like Seth—whose skin she described with a variety of sensory adjectives like "cinnamon" and "dreamy"—had disrupted what she had previously envisioned as a fairly navigable spectrum, with Wesley Snipes on one end and Wentworth Miller on the other, because he seemed both somewhere in the middle and totally separate from that range of definitions, and thinking about it today, she realized that having to grapple with this, if not at that exact moment then at some point in the future when further contradictory examples had stacked up (for example, her college boyfriend, Jason, who was half Japanese and half Black), had in many ways dynamited her conception of race and identity and broadened her understanding of the diaspora, or rather, what the diaspora could be if it moved beyond petty delineations. That was what I was looking for, these small glimmers of how Seth had inspired some strain of thought or development of personality. All of which accentuated the whole heroin druggy mystery thing, in theory.

"I mean," Olivia said, "Ms. Malone was crazy as hell, I thought it was obvious he was just light-skinned."

"My point is that sometimes people just keep talking and surprise you with what they've thought about."

"I think I could've guessed that Marissa Kenny majored in African American Studies." We both laughed. "This place is a trip," she said, looking around the bar. The karaoke DJ, an ornery Polish man named Ivan, was now overseeing a steady stream of Top 40 and classic rock requests. Many of my friends gravitated toward private karaoke rooms, a safe space to get unmanageably drunk and dig into the underrated Mariah Carey B-sides, but the voyeuristic pleasure of watching strangers either embarrass themselves or be revealed as an *American Idol*–level talent was unsurpassable.

Olivia and Roger mostly went out in Humboldt Park, where

they lived. Their daughter, Nicole, who she now referred to as "Nicole" instead of "my daughter," as she had on the night of the reunion, was nearly old enough to look after herself; tonight, however, Roger was at home. Olivia had been preparing a casserole when I'd texted her asking if she wanted to go out, and after thinking about it for a moment, she gave him the oven instructions and said she'd be back in a few hours.

"Did he ask about me?"

"No," she said. We both laughed again. A woman stepped to the microphone, and the first notes of "Say My Name" started playing. "Hold on, I want to watch this." The singer made it through the opening chorus, but instead of matching the start-stop cadence of the verses, she took more of a stop-stop approach, falling behind each line and failing altogether when Beyoncé's vocals sped up. "This is just terrible."

"Are you going to put in a song?"

"Absolutely not," she said. She signaled the bartender for another two Żywiecs and took out her phone to send a text message, before placing it atop the bar. "Tell me about how this got started: You convinced your bosses to let you talk to your friends from high school, for work?" She said this innocently, and I tried not to read any negative implications.

I ran through a truncated version of the changes at my company, the initiatives pushing us toward conceptual innovation and medium experimentation and all the flashy buzzwords that had, apparently, guided us toward new streams of revenue, some of which might make their way into my bank account. "Podcasts take at least six months to come together, so the trick is to pick a project where you won't lose your stamina—something to really hold your interest, as well as your audience's," I said.

"Uh-huh," she said. "I don't know if I've ever listened to

a podcast." But she understood the interest in looking at the past, she said. Lately, she'd started thinking about the period when she got pregnant, in college, and how her life may have changed had she gone in a different direction.

"Like if you'd . . . ?" I stopped talking, as I wasn't quite sure how to ask someone I didn't know very well if they'd ever considered aborting their about-to-be-teenage daughter.

Thankfully, she picked up the hint. "Maybe for a single moment, but I *wanted* Roger. I *wanted* children together. And I thought, in some way, this was God's way of manifesting it." She became quiet and drank her beer.

"I don't regret anything," Olivia said, "and I don't know if I can put this into words. It's more like thinking about the decisions you made, and how they swung your life down whatever road. The small moments that end up deciding the larger moments. For example, if we'd never gone to Urbana—maybe we would've been more careful if we weren't drinking all of the time, surrounded by people who were doing the same. Or if Roger and I had broken up for real, because we were on and off for a while even before Nicole. But you know how people are at that age—they don't want to believe that anything less than what they want is possible." She paused. "Maybe your friend felt the same way."

"Seth?" I drummed my fingers on my beer and thought about this. I told her about the letter I'd found in my room, leaving out the part about how it made me feel. "He was clearly looking for something he wasn't getting, and this was his way of coping. Or so I think, anyway. I'm still trying to get in touch with Lee, from our year, who was selling to him. You remember Lee? I guess in my head all of the answers will snap into place once I get him on the record. But that's been tricky." She asked why, and I tried to sum it up. "I've done some important interviews while I've been here, but I'm getting kind of nervous. You know, ha-ha, no big deal, just the future of my employment hanging on a text back."

"Lee," she murmured. "I remember Lee. He was cute. I didn't hang out with those types of white boys, but he was cute. One time he helped me print something out in the library, actually. It was nothing special, but it always stuck with me for whatever reason, I can't say why." I didn't say anything to this, just considered my beer. "Why don't you just blow up his phone though? Smoke him out, if he's being a motherfucker."

"This is a fair point," I said. "But I'm worried if I come on too hard he'll just disappear forever."

"Yeah, but he's disappeared right now."

"This is also a fair point."

"So take out your phone right now and say something. You're just going to sit around and let him dictate what happens next?" She finished her beer and waved for two more. "You're *from New York*. You're working on a *podcast*." Her smile made it clear she was teasing me. "But seriously, why wait?"

Olivia was really racking up the fair points, and I did not have any counters. It did bother me, the way Lee had briefly popped up and teased his participation, only to ignore me once I'd made my way into town. It wasn't like he had ceased to exist—there were the Facebook posts, and Ben had alluded to their ongoing friendship, and he *worked in a bar*, I remembered, a bar where I could theoretically confront him in person, with my recorder in hand. I was used to hiding my feelings during the process of negotiating these journalistic asks, because not everybody wanted to talk to someone like me, and broadcasting any entitlement to someone's time was deeply off-putting. But I *was* entitled, I thought, given Lee's role in Seth's death. I was trying to close a loop, only Lee had grabbed one end of the rope and dragged it away to parts unknown. And that did irritate me, now that Olivia had pointed it out.

"Give me a second." I took out my phone, opened up my communication with Lee, and started typing. This time, I felt no ambiguity about what I wanted to say. Hey, I began, I've learned about some troubling things in Seth Terry's background that I think are very relevant to you, and I want to get your side of the story. If you don't want to talk to me, I'm still going to pursue the story, so I want to give you the opportunity to go on the record. I'm still in Chicago, so let me know if you have any time this week. I showed it to Olivia, who laughed and said she couldn't get *that* involved, she had no idea what was appropriate or not. But it seemed like the right thing, and so I sent it.

We sat with our drinks for a moment. A man with long hair was singing "L.A. Woman," a song I loved because of the way men with long hair incoherently brayed it at karaoke, as was happening right now. *L.A. woman Sunday afternoon!* The man growled, whipping his head around as he played air guitar with the microphone. Olivia's phone buzzed again, and she hesitated a second, as though it might be rude, before grabbing it.

"Roger?" I said.

"No," she said, after a beat. "Holy shit."

IN HIGH SCHOOL, OUR CHOIR TEACHER, MR. KENDALL, WAS NOT just beloved, but commonly considered to be the "fun" teacher. He made all sorts of inappropriate jokes about sex and drugs, and kept a handful of naughty tchotchkes on his desk—a fake rubber ass, a motorized statue of a Dutch boy pissing into a trash can. Once, he'd instructed us on how to tell if a woman had implants: by noticing, when she laid on her back, if her breasts fell or retained their shape. "Round means they're silicone through and through," he instructed, and all of us nodded as though we understood.

Mr. Kendall was young, he was funny, he had glamorous blond hair and a broad, handsome face like a cartoon prince. We considered ourselves privileged for bearing witness to his showmanship, when most of our teachers were grumpy humdrums who thought only to "teach" us. That we were thirteen and fourteen years old did not occur to us. When he told a joke about the taste of semen, no one raised their hand and said, "Hold on, we are children." It just didn't work that way.

So it was shocking, but also not that shocking, but also incredibly shocking in a way that made me cough beer, to learn in the bar that according to a *Chicago Tribune* story texted to Olivia, Mr. Kendall had been arrested for (she read from her phone) "having oral and anal sex with one student over a three-year period, showing pornography to that student and another student at his apartment, and sexually harassing multiple students at Sayers and at nearby Douglas Elementary school, where he previously taught." The allegations dated back to the mid-1990s and continued to the early 2010s, a stretch that covered our entire time at school. The lead photo in the story was his mug shot, and his facial hair was patchy and his eyes bleary, matching his ruddy skin tone.

"He was still teaching at Sayers," I said, somewhat dazed by what I was reading. "I looked inside the choir room at the reunion but no one was there."

Olivia's phone kept on buzzing, and she couldn't stop herself from responding. "Sorry," she said, "it's just—lots of people are texting me about this."

"Let's just be on our phones for a minute," I said. I pasted the story into a dozen texts, along with the comment ????????????

Within moments, Ruth responded Whoa followed by Kelsey responding Wow followed by William responding Jesus Christ, and so on, and the responses from other classmates kept rolling in along with their feedback: I had no idea, that makes sense; My God he looks busted as fuck in the mugshot; LOL shit; Ohhhhhh damn okay, I guess this explains the time he asked me if I had a nice cock . . . just kidding . . . unless???? I was touched by the instantaneous replies, the snowball effect of this story going around. I hadn't talked to many of these people since high school but now, following my inquiries for the Seth project, we were all in touch and circulating any relevant news. Then I remembered the circumstances. Nobody was totally ignorant about the strategies adults used to groom children, but it was wild to imagine they had been practiced on us by an actual adult in charge of our well-being, who had been covert enough to conduct his behavior for more than a decade before being caught.

I recalled one time, at the end of my freshman year, when I auditioned for Mr. Kendall in the choir room to see if I was a good fit for the advanced group. Mr. Kendall gestured for me to stand near his piano, which was also adorned with those naughty tchotchkes. He had me run through several vocal exercises, instructing me to go higher or lower depending on how I'd failed to hit the mark. At one point, and I remembered this as something he'd done dozens of times in the classroom, he placed his hand on my chest to guide my breathing, accurately pointing out that I was exhaling too quickly when trying to hit a particular note. There had been no hint of impropriety whatsoever. I was fourteen years old, but I'd also read some articles about the Catholic church; I knew how to tell if an adult was being inappropriate with me, and this wasn't the case at all.

The audition couldn't have taken more than twenty minutes, and then I went back to lunch.

"Yeah," Olivia said, when I finished. "He was probably thinking about fucking you." She tried not to laugh. "That's—that's really not funny at all, I'm sorry." She'd never taken choir, instead opting for band, and had more or less avoided Mr. Kendall altogether during her time at school. "I knew people liked him, but that was about it."

As I finished my beer, something else occurred to me. I opened up my thread with Rachel Watkins and remembered I hadn't responded to her last text. But I sent her the article and added Crazy shit.

She, too, immediately replied: I know what you're thinking, and let me just say that is a terrible idea. You're not thinking of putting it in the podcast, are you???? I replied Of course not and put my phone down before I could say something else. I didn't want to push; I wanted to trust her, if she was that serious. But who's to say Seth wouldn't have kept more secrets from Rachel? Who's to say he wouldn't have compartmentalized his lives in high school too? Oh, I was drunk again, I didn't know what the fuck I was talking about. Olivia, deep in her phone, wasn't paying attention to me at all.

"I think I've got to go," she said. "You know, we'd been talking about sending Nicole to Sayers. We thought it would be nice if she followed in our footsteps."

"Goddamn," I said. "Hey, maybe it would've been fine. The article didn't say if he swung both ways." She gave me a look like that was too dark to even joke about, and I flashed my hands in apology. After she paid her tab, we said nice things about what a time we'd had before she left to catch her car.

It was late, but I didn't want to go home. What are you up

to now? I'm at Alice's, come through, I texted Natalia. A moment later she said she was tired, there was no way. Booooo, I replied, to silence. Fuck it, I was flirting, my tab was still open, and I had nowhere to be.

My phone buzzed again. I picked it up, expecting another text from Rachel, or maybe Ruth, and ideally even Natalia. Instead, it was Lee. But unlike our previous correspondence, the sight of his name did not fill me with anxiety. When you put it like that I guess I don't have a choice, he'd written. How about tomorrow?

For a moment I wanted to reply aggressively, but I restrained myself and tried to remember the role I played, the sage information knower above such petty concerns. Friday would be better, I responded. After all this time, I wanted to make sure I was as prepared as prepared could be.

AS THE PODCAST HAD PROGRESSED, REGGIE AND I HAD CREATED a separate document comprising everything Lee-related—not just what we knew about his life, but how to slot the theoretically obtainable information about his role in Seth's death into the structure we'd created so far. Right now, his presence was teased at the end of the pilot, and there was some dedicated space to draw him out in the second episode, THE MYSTERY, before dropping more crumbs and revealing the full truth of his involvement at some point around the fourth.

I'd continued to add questions to the document, and Reggie had continued to organize them by approach and episode, in order to give me a better idea of how to stage the interview. "About that," he said now, with Sadie at his side in our office's conference room. "I took a look at what you added last night, and . . ."

"I know it looks crazy, but I was just trying to keep the momentum going." I'd stayed up late, vaping and typing out my thoughts, forgetting until the morning that Reggie had access to this logorrheic discharge of feelings and ideas. "Lee knows he was a handsome, charming guy who fucked a lot, do not let him get the drop on you" went one such observation, and I could see how this might seem incoherent. But Lee had to know he was a handsome guy who fucked a lot, because Ben was like that, and the two of them were still friends—and this was relevant, or, at the very least, potentially relevant.

I wanted to be ready, so that nothing he could say or do would throw me off. The uneasiness I'd felt with Ben, when all of my adult pretensions and protections had suddenly collapsed, would not repeat itself. I was charged up, I had a head of steam, I was ready to grab the tiger by his tail and swing him around my head like I was Hercules. Nothing could protect Lee at this point; the righteousness of my approach and the certainty of my judgment would be not unlike the Grand Inquisitor's from *The Brothers Karamazov*, if they'd ever read that. I had inflected my voice with jauntiness and mirth, so that Sadie and Reggie would know I was sort of kidding, even as the root idea of what I wanted from Lee remained inviolably true.

To my great relief, they smiled. "I don't think you're remembering that book quite right," Sadie said. "But I'll hope for the best. Where are you meeting?"

Lee said he lived in Pilsen, but I'd asked if he would come to the La Colombe near my mother's house. I imagined this would allow me to control the playing field—to remind Lee that this conversation was taking place on my terms, not his. We'd spent months trying to pin him down, and it was almost hard to believe how everything had turned in a couple of days. But this was why we'd prepared during all those months, so that I could seize the opportunity once presented. All I had to do now was follow through.

Sadie nodded at all this, and for the first time in a while I felt she was not unconsciously displeased with what I had to say. "Nice. Just remember you're in charge."

After Sadie excused herself from the call, Reggie and I went over my game plan. Lee and I would talk about this and that, like how he and Seth had met and the exact nature of their relationship, and eventually I'd walk through the concept, or a version of the concept ("It's a podcast about Seth's life and death") before mentioning the more prurient part, which was the connection to drugs, and while I didn't want to be presumptuous I'd heard this and that about what Lee had been involved with. To be clear, I'd emphasize, we were still just speaking informally at this point, and it wasn't my intention to make him air all his dirty laundry for an audience of thousands (though that was, ultimately, my intention). And if he was extra nervous, we'd consulted with lawyers who'd informed us that the statute of limitations for prosecuting drug distribution had long since passed.

This was more about the court of public opinion. Surely he knew how people talked about him and what he'd been up to. His honesty was required to properly honor our friend, and if he was interested in making amends for the life he'd lived back then, then maybe he'd want to help me out. I'd pushed him, sure, but since he was meeting me he must've felt some responsibility to Seth. Why else would he bother coming to Lincoln Park? I repeated all this to myself, so that I might instinctively default to a primary objective if our conversation ran aground. More than any other interview I'd conducted, my conversation with Lee had a purpose. It needed to go somewhere, or else none of this would matter.

Before I left, I double- and triple-checked every possible item I might need: recorder, recorder stand, spare batteries, notebook, primary pen, secondary pen, release form. I changed outfits twice, settling on a light-blue button-down over black jeans, and the jacket I'd brought back from Los Angeles. I wanted to look tasteful, intelligent, professional; I did not want Lee to think we were friends or contemporaries. The pressure to perform was doing weird things to my body. I couldn't stop using the bathroom or wondering if I needed to use the bathroom again. As the clock ticked closer to our meet time, I focused on memorizing the questions I'd written out in my notebook, so that I could concentrate on reading Lee's face.

Even though I lived five minutes away, I was somehow the second to arrive. When I came into the coffee shop, Lee stood up to greet me. He was wearing a camouflage jacket, and the long sideburns from his profile photo were now mildly refined. He basically looked like he did in high school, plus some wear and tear—slightly ebbing hairline, pockmarked skin, the faintest sign of gray in his beard stubble. I felt nothing as we shook hands, and he appraised me with skepticism. "I almost didn't recognize you," he said. "The glasses, your hair. But who else could you be?"

"I'm getting that a lot these days," I said. His handshake was solid, but not stiff, and as I caught myself thinking this I hoped I wasn't focusing on the wrong details. "You look about the same, from what I remember."

"Oh, that's nice of you. But I'm fat as shit, I can't kid myself." He smiled, and I could not stop from smiling back. I pointed to the table he was sitting at, and said I'd put my stuff down before getting us some coffee, if he was interested. "Yeah, I'd love a cold brew. But should we stay here?" He waved his hand around the coffee shop, which was mostly full. "All this noise, that can't be good for your recorder."

"I thought we'd start out here, but if it gets too crazy we can go somewhere else."

"No, trust me, I've worked in studios, you'll be fucked. You lived nearby, right? I assume you're just staying at home."

Ten minutes later, Lee was surveying my mother's living room with curiosity, looking at the walls and ceilings as though he were appraising it for a sale. We'd brought our drinks with us, so I pulled out my recorder again, along with a notebook, and set it up on the coffee table as he talked. "Your place is really nice. I always heard about it. It's crazy to finally see it in person."

"Yeah?" I tried to sound very casual as I fiddled with my settings and attempted to forget how swiftly this situation had pivoted. I didn't mind that Lee was standing in my mother's home; I did mind that he might break a vase if he wasn't happy with my questions.

"Yeah, when we'd go to the open mic shows." Around the corner was a musical instrument store that staged a monthly open mic. All of our school's bands played there, and it drew a cross-section of Chicago Public School students flirting with punk rock and performance art. Afterward, my friends and I would decamp to my house, and drink 7-Eleven Slurpees while talking about the girls we hadn't talked to.

It was something I hadn't thought about in years, and I was impressed that Lee had quickly put it together. "That's funny, that anybody was paying attention to where I lived."

He picked up one of the many framed family photos lying around the living room and immediately put it down. "You know what kids are like. Sometimes we'd finish up and want to go party somewhere, and someone might say something like 'If only we were friends with Jacob Goldberg, we could just go to his place.' But we weren't, and so we didn't."

I laughed without meaning to. "My parents were always upstairs, so I don't think we would've had much luck anyway. We were dorks with soda pop and Flamin' Hot Cheetos. It is impossible to stress how much we did not party."

Lee sat down on the couch, across from the recorder. He took off his jacket, revealing a tattoo of a grim reaper on his right bicep. "We weren't partying *too* hard back then. It was just alcohol and a light amount of meth, it was no big deal." I tried not to look at him like he had to be kidding me, and I confirmed the recorder's red light was on. "That is a joke, for the record." He leaned down to speak into the microphone. "*We did some meth, no big deal, he cracked, in a funny way.* We weren't actually doing meth, then. I want that clear in your podcast, whatever it is."

He looked up at me and snapped his fingers. "Which reminds me: What is your podcast, by the way? All you said was it's about our dead classmates. I didn't know Caroline Blanchard. I didn't know Jenny Collins. But I did know Seth. And here I am, in Lincoln Park, ready to be of service. 'Or else,' I think your text implied."

His tone—lilting, playful, subtly insinuating—was throwing me off, and I tried not to show it. *Lee knows he was a handsome, charming guy who fucked a lot, do not let him get the drop on you*, I reminded myself. "Sorry about that, but it was very important to get in touch with you. The podcast has gone through a few iterations since we first talked, but the gist of it is that I'm looking into the life and death of Seth Terry, who I was close with, as well as about half the people at our school. He died at an age when most of us—not all of us, but most of us—didn't have much experience with death, and in talking to people I've learned that he was as important to them as he was to me. I'm trying to interrogate that importance against the backdrop of, you know, the Bush years, while also trying to understand more about what was happening in our school at the time."

Lee crossed his legs and balanced his elbow on his thigh. "What was happening in our school at the time?"

"You joked about meth, but as I understand there were a number of students who were into hard drugs. I've heard that played into the circumstances of his death, so I'm trying to interrogate"—I mentally flinched, I really had to stop using that word—"that environment as well."

If he felt a way about anything I'd said, he didn't show it. "The circumstances of his death," he repeated. "Okay. So what do you want from me?"

"First, I need you to take a look at this." I took out the release form, along with a pen. A part of me wondered if he'd walk out, but he barely looked at it before signing. "All right, so I thought we'd start at the beginning, and you could tell me your first memory of Seth."

"Why not?" He turned in the direction of my recorder, and slightly bent his head toward the microphone. "My first memory of Seth . . . it must've been freshman year. I was sitting on one of the benches under the staircase at school and sketching in my notebook when I heard someone say over my shoulder, 'Boy, isn't that interesting?' I looked up and it was Seth. You know, I was a jerk then, so I probably said something like: 'What's it to you, dickhead?' But he just laughed, and said, 'Don't get upset, baby. I was just admiring the view.' That made me laugh, so I guess we started talking."

"You weren't put off by that?"

"No, of course not. I mean, yeah, I dropped a *faggot* or two when I was a teenager, but he was just being funny."

I made a brief note in my notebook: *Surprisingly not a bigot, did say "faggot" out loud*. "Did you talk a lot after that?"

"Like did we become friends? Yeah, definitely. He was cool. I went over to his house once or twice, but his parents always gave me the eye, so I figured it was better if we went elsewhere. Usually we'd sit in a group out on the soccer field, before one of the security guards yelled at us to get moving. You didn't hang with those people, but you know who I'm talking about, right?"

"Remind me?"

He rattled off the names I was expecting, the names I'd heard throughout my interviews: "Erica, Hector, Ben,

Dominic . . ." If Ben had told him what had happened at Inner Town, he didn't betray anything. "They were the homies. They were good for a good time, if you know what I mean." I asked him to explain. "You know, we got up to some fun. Not right away, but later on. Sometimes Seth joined in, sometimes he didn't. Mostly he didn't. He walked the straight and narrow, he didn't want any of that. At first, at least." I asked him to explain that too. "A lot happens in a few years. I think he became more open minded after he graduated. You maybe know about my trouble at school"—I nodded, and made a mental note to return to the subject—"but Seth, he kept in touch afterward. He was nice like that. So I guess we kept on hanging out, and you know . . ." His momentum broke off, and he leaned back into the couch.

"And you know what?" I said.

"I don't know," Lee said, after a pause. He fluffed his hair with his hand. "I know he had a tough time at home. I know he wanted to be in college. He wasn't dating anyone, and I don't even know if he was sleeping with anyone. I remember we talked about that. I think he was lonely. I think he felt like he didn't have a lot of people who could understand everything that was going on with him. And that was surprising, because for a long time it didn't seem like we were that close, but when he said this I realized we were. Or you know, as close as kids can be at that age. We weren't *kids*, but . . . it's how I see us now. And so obviously I was missing something."

I remembered how Rachel had said something like this too—how she'd never sensed any problems, because to her, their relationship was as good as ever. For all of the mental thruways I'd traversed, and all the angles I'd mapped out, I hadn't considered that Lee and Seth might have actually been friends. "But it shouldn't have been so surprising," he continued. "I mean, who feels understood at that age? Shit, I'm just figuring out how to talk about some of this stuff for the first time."

I pressed on. "So how did he deal with his feelings?"

"Like any of us did. It was college." He laughed, exposing a couple of discolored molars. "We weren't in college, I don't know what the fuck I'm talking about. What can I say? We were all trying to get out of ourselves for a moment. It did bum him out that he wasn't in college, I remember us talking about this."

"What did you talk about?"

"We talked about you, actually." I attempted not to be visibly thrown off by this, but Lee smiled, just a little bit. "Not to exaggerate—you weren't the only one. His friend Rachel, he talked about her too. I think it was hard for him to visit you guys at college and see what he was missing out on. No shit he did not want to be working at Panera instead of studying the classics, or whatever you did."

"To push back on that, I don't think he ever visited me at Northwestern."

"Well, why do you think that was? At least DePaul was just close to where he lived, and he could get out of there quick if he needed to. That train ride from Evanston is a long time to feel like a loser."

This detour had interrupted my momentum, and I looked over my notes for the next subject. "How did you learn he'd died?"

His eyes did not move at all, but he massaged his knuckles with his thumb. "Text message. Or maybe Ben called me, I'm not sure."

"And when did you learn how he'd actually died?"

Now his eyes crinkled, though he continued looking at me. "What do you mean by that?"

"I was told that it was something with his stomach, but it was a few years before it came out that it was something else."

"Uh-huh," he said. "I didn't know something else had come out."

"And I learned . . ." I felt my voice get soft. This was the moment, the actual moment we'd been working toward for months, and I needed to say everything exactly right. "I did learn what happened, which frankly blew me away. Maybe this is just naïve, but . . . we were all so young, like you said. You look at someone and you think you know what's going on with them but it's just not true at all. And okay, this is what happens in books and movies and TV shows and magazine articles, but this was real life. It was our lives." He didn't react, and in spite of my training I found myself continuing to talk. "I had no idea Seth was the type of person who could accidentally overdose, is what I mean. I had no idea anyone I knew was using drugs like that. Even today, I don't know anyone using drugs like that."

Lee's expression was strange, like he was working through something in his head. He muttered something I couldn't make out. "Say that again?"

"You're lucky," he said.

I tried to read his face, which remained opaque. "I guess I'm just trying to get a sense of who knew what—what the news was like for different people, at the time." Lee's silence in response to my verbosity was becoming a ritual, one we kept repeating. "I mean, I lived fifteen minutes from him, I saw him all the time, but I can't really remember a lot of the time we spent together. I saw him less than a month before he died, but I don't know what it was like for him at the end."

The only sound was the slow rattle of the cars driving by, outside the window. "And you think I do?" he finally said.

"I think you do," I repeated. "Don't you?"

I became aware that we were both sitting very still and looking right at each other. Lee was my age, but already he had crow's feet around his eyes, smashed blood vessels in his nose. There was still the old trace of handsomeness in his face, an inlaid charm made soggy by years of misuse but not destroyed altogether. He was probably a favorite at the bar where he worked, already a character despite his youth, someone you could knock back a few with and trade tales about your wild days. He'd been through the wringer, but who hadn't? Who didn't have a story to tell, after everything they'd been through?

"Yeah," he said, his voice low. "Yeah, I do." I waited for him to say more, the levels on my recorder flashing up and down even as neither of us spoke. I sensed we might already be at the pivotal part of the interview, where Lee would open up the way I'd hoped for. All I needed to do was wait for the answer.

Again he muttered something I couldn't hear, and I craned my head to hear better. "What was that?"

"Accidental overdose, is what you said."

"That's what I heard," I said. "I mean, I never learned it from the family or anything. But that's what happened, wasn't it?"

Lee was leaning back entirely into my mother's couch, his right leg crossed over his knee. He finished the rest of his coffee and looked at me with amusement or sympathy, I couldn't tell which, before shaking his head. "Hey, do you mind if we turn the recorder off?"

"I don't know if that's the best idea," I said.

"I would really like it if the recorder was off, so I can talk to you like an adult. And frankly, I'm not stupid enough to incriminate myself on a podcast, despite what you might think."

"We actually spoke to a lawyer about this, and it turns—"

"I have a theory," he said, cutting me off, "that the only

reason I'm here is because I decided to come, because for all your digging you don't really have much of anything."

"So you think I'm full of shit, is what you're saying?"

"No, I don't think you're full of shit. I think you mean well, and you've figured out some things. You obviously figured out I was selling to him, which, congratulations." He clapped in a very sarcastic way. "But it's not close enough, and so what's the fucking point?" His face had shed any hint of jocularity or charm as he stared right at me. I tried not to look away, and for a moment we sat there, looking at each other, not talking.

"Okay," I said. I turned my recorder off but didn't put it away. "I'll let you say your piece, but I reserve the right to turn this back on at any moment. And"—I grabbed my bag, and fussed around for my notebook and pen—"I'm sorry, but I'm keeping this right here, just to write anything down."

He looked over to make sure the red light was shut off before he continued talking. "I mean, think about it. You said you saw him less than a month before he died. Did he strike you as someone who was slipping? Someone who was fucking up? He seemed like Seth, right?"

"He did, but there were a lot of things he wasn't telling me."

"All right, fair enough. But I was seeing him a lot then. We were using together—a couple times a week, probably." He waited to see if I reacted. "We did drugs together, because that's the type of drug users we were, in case you didn't know about the different types of drug users. We weren't trying to be by ourselves. Seth was fucked up, but not that fucked up—fucked up like anyone else, and looking for something to make it better."

"And this was your answer?" I heard the judgment lacing my voice and almost winced.

"Sure. When you're that age, heroin doesn't seem so bad. That sounds insane, I know, but it's just the truth. It wasn't like he was a heavy, hard-core user. It wasn't like he was scavenging bottles from a dumpster to pay for the next fix."

"How do you know he wasn't using that much?"

Lee gave me a look like *Come on*. "Because he wasn't buying from anyone else. And this may surprise you," he said with a sudden grin, "but I did know some real hard-core users in those days. People who were really down the rabbit hole. Nobody who'd ever sit in a house like this. Seth, trust me, was not on that level."

The presumption in his voice was irritating me, and I couldn't resist the pithy instinct. "Come on, a house like this? You're not exactly from the wrong side of the tracks, from what I remember. And neither was Seth."

"Maybe not. But I was doing some walking around at the time, and Seth was hanging out with me, wasn't he? It was a different world—I was buying drugs."

"'Was' buying drugs, you said?"

"Sure, I'm what they call aspirationally sober. I'll have a beer. I'll puff a joint, if someone's offering. The hard stuff, I've been out on that for a long time."

"See, this is all why I wanted to talk to you," I said. "I've heard some gossip here and there, and it just seems crazy to me. You were in a band that was getting some attention, but you were also selling drugs to your friends, and maybe it was a bad batch, so one of them died."

"I don't know what my band has to do with anything. And I wasn't really a dealer. I just bought the drugs myself and gave them to my friends in exchange for money. And, sorry, 'bad batch'? Where did you get that from?"

"You didn't have some iffy shit? Pardon my terminology? That's not what killed him?"

"No way, man. I was using the same stuff, and I'm still here. I don't know how that got around."

I tried to move past it: "Whatever it was, you were the intermediary, and you were in this band, and everything just . . . petered out. Seth was this person who meant so much to so many people, but was kind of idling while waiting for the next step, and then the person who is"—I paused, choosing my words very carefully—"closest to his actual death is also dealing with these expectations. I mean, I used to write for those kinds of blogs, I know what it's like when a career is coming your way and then suddenly it doesn't. That's what the podcast is about, trying to grasp the weight of expectations. And I'm hoping you'll be a real part of it."

He coughed a couple of times and covered his mouth. "That sounds fucking ridiculous, sorry."

"But it's a chance to tell your side of the story, with all this gossip going around."

"People have been gossiping for a very long time, Jacob," he said, as though he were explaining Santa to a child. "I have a little experience with gossip."

"Okay, but it wouldn't hurt. And look, whether you're in or out, I'm going to go forward with this thing. I'm in too deep to slow down."

"I see," he said. Lee was silent, and I could not guess what he was thinking. "If you want to know what I think, I was always pretty convinced he overdosed on purpose."

I tried not to roll my eyes at this pivot. "Come on, give me a break."

He shrugged, like there was nothing he could do about it. "It's just the impression I got. I remember this one time we were sitting at Joy House, and he asked me if I'd ever thought about offing myself. When I said obviously, we both cracked up."

"Let me get this straight," I said, but he kept talking.

"I knew we were just fucking around. You can make jokes like that when you're young. I would've stopped selling to him if I thought he was seriously considering it. I wasn't some monster trying to take advantage of his friend, or whatever you're thinking."

"I know you were trying to sell at his funeral," I said.

"Yeah?" His posture stiffened. "Who told you that?"

"It doesn't matter."

"Yeah, all right, I was trying to sell at his funeral. At that point of my life, I will admit I was not big into reflection. What was done was done, and I was still myself, so why stress? So yeah, I got a little high, and I sold a little heroin at my good friend's funeral, and I got kicked out because of it. But there's a difference between being a dick and being a monster."

"What are you talking about, what's done was done? Like it was something that just happened? You're telling me you think he . . ." I struggled to finish the sentence; my face was getting hot. "When you put the gun in his hand. Or the needle, whatever." I didn't want to seem angry, but the spirit was catching me; I couldn't believe how blasé he was.

Something about the way I looked must have registered with him, because Lee became very serious. "I'm not trying to . . ." He pursed his lips, and reached into his pocket. "I want you to look at something, okay?" He tapped his phone screen a few times and pulled up what I saw was Facebook. "It's funny—I didn't remember this until you insisted on talking. But all this stuff gets preserved in your account, and I looked at it for the first time . . . well, since it happened."

The screen showed his private messages with Seth, beginning

with the summer before his death. "What, you want me to read all this?" I said.

"You can do whatever you want, I'm just saying it might be of interest." He held his phone out to me. I'd been so irritated that I hadn't realized what was being offered and took it before he could change his mind.

JULY 16, 2007

SETH TERRY: thanks for talking last night

SETH TERRY: I was a little embarrassed thinking about it today but it really helped

LEE FINCH: Bro yes

LEE FINCH: Like I totally get it

SETH TERRY: I know but i'm still saying it

SETH TERRY: I don't take it for granted

SETH TERRY: sometimes it's hard to know if anyone really cares

LEE FINCH: You fuckin' emo fag

LEE FINCH: Jk

LEE FINCH: You're my emo fag

SETH TERRY: LOL

SETH TERRY: I will interpret that as an "I love you," you . . . hetero

SETH TERRY: that doesn't work does it

JULY 29, 2007

SETH TERRY: you around tomorrow?

LEE FINCH: Yeah all night, come through

AUGUST 3, 2007

SETH TERRY: you around tomorrow?

AUGUST 4, 2007

LEE FINCH: Didn't see this

LEE FINCH: Just text me next time, it's faster

SETH TERRY: don't worry about it

AUGUST 16, 2007

SETH TERRY: that was so stupid

LEE FINCH: Hahahaha

LEE FINCH: What the fuck is her problem

SETH TERRY: I don't KNOW

SETH TERRY: it's like

SETH TERRY: don't snort something if you don't know what it is

LEE FINCH: Thank God we are licensed medical professionals

LEE FINCH: Look at me NOW, mom

SETH TERRY: hahaha

AUGUST 29, 2007

SETH TERRY: I HATE my job sometimes

SETH TERRY: I hate EVERYTHING sometimes!

LEE FINCH: That's why I play entry level buzz band rock

SETH TERRY: oh shut up

SETH TERRY: you're not entry level

SETH TERRY: you're like

SETH TERRY: what comes after entry level?

LEE FINCH: Better be MONEY!!!!!

SETH TERRY: hahaha

SEPTEMBER 4, 2007

LEE FINCH: You around 2 clown tomorrow

SETH TERRY: maybe

SETH TERRY: feeling a little under lately

LEE FINCH: All good just hit me

SEPTEMBER 9, 2007

LEE FINCH: You alright

LEE FINCH: We were all like "Where's Seth"

SETH TERRY: sorry, still feeling under the weather

SETH TERRY: i'll be over tomorrow for sure

LEE FINCH: All good man just checking on you

LEE FINCH: Feel better, can't wait to hang

SETH TERRY: <3

SEPTEMBER 13, 2007

LEE FINCH: Hey are you there

LEE FINCH: ????

LEE FINCH: Text me when you're up

I handed Lee's phone back to him, unclear what this was supposed to prove. "I don't see anything in there about suicide," I said.

Lee violently massaged his left temple; it looked like he was attempting to scrape his skin off through sheer force. "Are you dense? Nobody who's serious about it says 'it's suicide time' over fucking Facebook. That's why we'd joked about it."

"But you're saying he changed his mind, a few months later."

"Yeah, I'm saying he changed his mind a few months later. Come on, don't be naïve. Do you know what that's like, to be caught in a bad cycle? Of course you don't." I wanted to challenge this, but held back. "I'd thought about it; I just didn't have the courage to follow through. So all I did was make my dark little jokes, like I was the coolest motherfucker who didn't give a fuck about shit. But Seth wasn't afraid of anything, even death. And he did not want to be alive anymore, is what I realized when he no longer was."

Lee's head was bowed toward his feet, ignoring my attempt at eye contact, and I felt my momentum flagging in the face of his logic. "What burns me is that . . . in meetings they tell you to apologize to everyone you ever wronged. And I accept that I wronged Seth, I do. I could've told him to be more careful, or think about why he was doing heroin in the first place. I could've not sold to him, obviously. But let's not kid ourselves. He's not listening from the afterlife. He's not looking down from heaven, waiting to absolve me. That's just how it is. So I've got to make amends with myself."

The room felt completely sapped of energy. Whatever it was I needed to say right now, I couldn't summon it as we continued sitting there. My eyes started to drift toward the ceiling, which I'd looked at one million times in my life, and which now offered respite from whatever was happening right now. I forced myself to regain eye contact with Lee, who had trained his gaze on a spot outside the window. Through all my interviews, I'd understood the value of shutting up, in order to draw something out from the person you were talking to. But now I was just quiet, and Lee didn't have anything else to say, not right now.

Another minute went by in total silence. "Look, I'm sorry if that hurts to hear, but it's the truth," he said suddenly. He turned back, and by the look on his face he really did feel sorry for me. "I don't think he wanted anyone to know. He didn't leave a note. He didn't send any emails. He just did it, and that was that."

I snapped back to the room. "I'm not sure I believe you, is the problem."

"You can believe whatever you want," he said. "I'm just telling you how I see it. I thought that's why you wanted to talk so bad?"

I didn't know what to say to that. I didn't know what to think about it either, and once more we sat there for what seemed like hours, not talking. "I will say," he said, breaking the impasse, "that it's a relief to talk about this stuff out loud. You didn't have to go about it this way, but still."

I was just trying to, I started to say, but he raised his hand to cut me off and took his phone out again. I watched him as he tapped on the screen. "You have somewhere you need to be?"

"I've got nowhere to be. Nowhere at all." He put his phone away and went back to looking out of the window.

"So," I said, "can I turn my recorder back on?"

He turned back and gave me a once-over as though he were really looking at me for the first time all day. "If you want to keep talking, if you think it matters," he said. "But don't ask me to repeat anything I just said. If anyone is going to tell the world that Seth Terry killed himself, it won't be me."

LEE AND I ONLY STOPPED TALKING WHEN MY MOTHER AND HARold came home in the late afternoon and asked for an introduction. "We went to high school together, I'm talking to him for a project I'm working on," I said. When my mother said she didn't remember him, he played it cool and said we traveled in different circles back then. Everyone shook hands, and they went upstairs to the bedroom.

I attempted to resume the conversation, but the knowledge that my mother and her boyfriend were upstairs made me wary of talking loudly, or frankly. Lee sensed it too. When I told him that perhaps I was being crazy but this reminded me of high school, attempting to conceal whatever I was getting up to from my parents regardless of how innocent it was, he laughed and said he'd thought the same thing. It was probably a good idea to get going, as his shift started in a few hours.

I asked if he was working on anything creative these days—music, perhaps? He said he was enrolled in a writing class and had sketched the beginning of what might be a memoir, according to his teacher. I asked what it was about, and he laughed. "Drugs, so far. But it's more than that. How would you say it? 'A multidimensional narrative.' Yeah, it's got so many fucking dimensions." He laughed again. "I'm being an asshole. Old habits, sorry."

We walked downstairs and I led him outside, unlocking the gate so he could leave. Another idea for the podcast had come to me during our conversation, one that still required his participation. But the idea of asking him felt silly in a way I couldn't shake, as I'd watched him put on his jacket and put on his shoes and make sure he had all of his belongings. Eventually, I decided to say nothing at all.

"I hope this works out for you," he said, in front of the house. We shook hands, and I watched him walk down the block before turning toward the train, disappearing out of my sight.

I went back inside. My mother and Harold had come downstairs to start on dinner, but I told her I wasn't feeling well and went up to my room.

My mother had never replaced the twin-size mattress I'd slept on through high school, and I had never minded because the worn springs and thin fabric were nurturing and familiar in a way that no space-age bedding technology could ever surpass. But right now I wished I could sprawl my arms and legs without touching air. My thoughts felt uncomfortable, oppressive. It was difficult to believe what Lee had said about Seth. He was depressed, I knew that, but . . . that didn't . . . I mean, obviously he could've killed himself; just because I'd dismissed it initially didn't mean I couldn't have overlooked something. That had happened all through the reporting process; I'd constantly moved ahead from one set of presumptions, only to double back when some other, more enlightening piece of information revealed itself.

It kept boomeranging back into my mind, impossible to push out of sight. The suicide, by itself, was believable; people killed themselves all of the time, for reasons nobody exactly understood. But accepting Lee's story would've also meant accepting he'd been a better friend, at the end, because he had been there for Seth when so many of us were not. It was much harder to embrace that, even if it may have been the truth.

When I'd started throwing out the contents of my bedroom, I'd kept a lot of the material related to Sayers—it might have been extraneous, but I wouldn't know that for sure until I was done with the podcast. I returned to one of those errant piles of crap and pulled out the student directory I'd held on to.

During one of my interviews with Ruth, she mentioned that she'd been fixating on Seth's parents. It was funny, getting older and remembering all the parents you'd spent hours with as a child or teenager, but whom you'd never see again, and who would forever remember you as a young person even as you grew into an adult. It was strange to think that after Seth had died, his parents had just kept on living in the same house, in the same city.

"I mean, they were only fifteen minutes away from your mom's," she'd said. We were speaking over video, and I remembered the earnestness in her eyes as she declared this, as though it were a groundbreaking observation. "Your mom probably saw them at the grocery store." My mom had never met Seth's parents, but the point was true. Ruth said she'd used these student phone books to recall their names, so she could see what they were up to. Seth's father she couldn't find anything about. But Seth's mom was on the board of a private school in Chicago, which blew her mind. "It's a Catholic school, go figure. But isn't that crazy? That she's responsible for other kids despite driving her son into an early death?" This didn't feel totally fair, even if I didn't have the sunniest view of his parents, though I hadn't objected.

The phone book reminded me that Seth's mother's name was Sonya, and his father's name was Richard. I could recall talking with them at Seth's house—his father standing in the doorway, his mother standing in the kitchen—but the specifics of those conversations were long gone. It was dark outside, but it wasn't late; if they still lived in the neighborhood, as Ruth had guessed, they might be sitting down to dinner.

The phone rang three times before it was picked up. "Hello?" a woman's voice, bright and slightly accented, said.

"Hi, is this Sonya Terry?" I asked.

"Yes, this is her. May I ask who's calling?"

"My name is Jacob Goldberg, I don't know if you remember me—we met a few times, years ago." I paused and waited for a response. "I was good friends with your son, back in high school. I've been thinking about him lately, and I wanted to ask you some questions, if you wouldn't mind talking to me."

I could hear her breathing on the other end, followed by a muffled conversation just out of earshot. "Yes, Jacob, I remember you," she said a moment later. "You were very polite. How are your parents doing?"

Reggie and I had written out a script for how to approach them, but I was going off instinct. "My father actually passed away some time ago, but my mother is doing very well, thank you."

Her silence was broken by a microwave beeping at the end of its timer. "I'm . . . very sorry to hear about your father. How can I help you?"

"I'm a journalist now . . . I'm working on a project . . . it's about high school, and the way we remember things, but it's mostly about Seth. In particular, it's about the way he died, and what was going on with him, and . . . that's the idea, I guess."

"Hold on a second." I thought I heard her hand cover up the receiver. "You're looking into how my son died? Why?"

"It's something that felt unbelievably weighty at the time,

in a way I never really processed. But after learning more about what happened, it felt like something worth revisiting—a way of closing the loop, I suppose, especially with the people involved. I presume you and your husband know a little more, and maybe you've wanted to know a little more than that. I was hoping to help."

I heard more muffled conversation in the background, more shuffling. I felt tremendous unease as I waited for her to start talking again. "That is very kind of you," she said. "It is meaningful, to know that people still think about my son. Before I say anything, my question is—"

"I'm sorry," a male voice interrupted, gruff and clear. "Thank you for calling, but we're not interested." Before I could say anything else, the line went dead.

ON MONDAY, SADIE INVITED ME TO VIDEO CHAT WITH HER AND Reggie. It had snowed the night before, and the light reflected brilliantly off the undisturbed whiteness coating the rooftops outside my window. I hadn't found the time to shower, and I was aware I must have appeared especially haggard, unshaven, lightly crusted over with the remnants of coffee and breakfast.

I had never said anything along the lines of "I think my friend maybe killed himself" out loud to anyone, ever, in my life, and I was surprised by the freeness with which Sadie and Reggie emoted upon hearing me say it. "God, Jacob," Sadie said, when I was done summarizing what Lee had told me, and my concerns about the direction of the podcast. "It might be easier if you send the tape to Reggie, so we can see what we have?"

Sadie and I had worked together for a couple of years, during which we'd texted each other aggressively detailed descriptions of our hangovers, and innumerable screenshots of bad dating profiles. There was an inherent closeness cultivated by these working dynamics; she was my boss, and I was her employee, and she often reminded me of that, but we'd talked too much to pretend the relationship was strictly professional. I did actually know she, unlike Reggie, was my friend, which made the thought of categorically disappointing her all the more terrifying. "Ah," I managed to say, "I got most of our conversation on tape, but for that part . . . the recorder was turned off for that part."

Reggie turned his head and smiled, while Sadie looked truly scandalized. I did not realize people's jaws dropped, but there was her mouth, slacked open in surprise. "Sorry, but—back up a second, you talked about everything but the thing we needed? How did that happen?"

"Lee knew what was going on from the moment we sat down," I said. "If I hadn't shut off the recorder right then, he probably would've walked out."

"Then you should've let him walk out. Come on, this is as basic as it gets."

"It just didn't feel right," I said. "We were talking about other stuff, and it was going well, and I didn't want to scare him off. He was happy to talk about *everything* else, actually, but on this he was pretty clear. I thought it was a good trade-off." Sadie made a disapproving grunt and tapped her keyboard. Reggie motioned at her screen, at something I couldn't see. "What are you two looking at?"

"We'd mapped out some other possibilities, if Lee suddenly backed out. I know you said you were pretty sure it wouldn't fall through, but here we are."

"Hey, it's not like—"

"For the last several months you've been focused solely on this project that, I think we can agree, is fairly personal to you. It's not the type of thing we can pass to someone else."

I tried not to laugh, considering the circumstances of this conversation. "That might be interesting but no, I agree."

"But now we're missing the drama that makes this a real narrative, and not just some stuff you've been looking into. You understand the position that puts me in. The position that puts *you* in, frankly."

"Well, I did have this other idea that came up during the end of our interview." Maybe if I said it out loud, it would appear reasonable and actionable. "What Lee and I discussed—Seth, and his memories of Seth, and his memories of Seth at the end, all of that could take precedence. The appeal of the oral history was to summon a collective memory while pursuing the investigation, but it could be narrowed to a more specific perspective, the more I think about it. You know, I'm at the center of this thing. So maybe that might be me and Lee, using each other to better understand what was happening with our friend before he died."

"That could be good," she said. "Do you think he'd agree to that?"

Unfortunately, it still felt silly. I sighed and shook my head. "Honestly, it felt like he probably wouldn't have, which is why I didn't ask."

Sadie pinched the bridge of her nose and flicked her eyes toward Reggie, who remained silent. "We're going in circles here. Okay, so what about the original plan? I'm not sure if I see the problem with continuing in that direction. We don't explicitly need Lee's participation, is what Reggie and I talked about. There are ways to work around his absence and gesture at his involvement—especially with the bit of tape you have."

"I think the problem there is that it just wouldn't be true if we did that," I said.

"I mean . . ." Sadie's expression was as serious as I'd ever seen her. "It's still a really gripping story. Does it matter if it isn't totally true?" My face must have thrown her off because I watched her attempt to backtrack. "It's true enough, is what I'm saying, and I think that's obvious if you try to look at it without being precious. Lee sold him the heroin, and that's what killed Seth—that part hasn't changed. You have enough material to lead listeners in that direction. And then they can decide for themselves. It's not just about your feelings."

When Natalia had told me about her time in Los Angeles, I had identified with the pressure of saying yes. Too many jobs were built on that pressure, and the accompanying belief that you didn't have to directly coerce people into going along, only cultivate and sustain an environment where this expectation fermented naturally, until inevitably there was no other choice. I had said yes to many things over the years, never doubting their necessity; it was simply something I had to do in order to get where I was going, wherever that was.

But I had said no, too, guided by an innate instinct I couldn't solely rationalize as "gut," because that implied the unknowable, when in reality I knew the exact nature of my refusal. Sadie was pushing for something that didn't make sense, and looking at her I felt pity—for her, for me, for all of us at our moderately respected website, and what we'd forced ourselves to extract from our lives.

"I just feel like . . . it doesn't work," I said, trying to dial it back. "Sorry, I'm trying to be helpful, but . . . You didn't want me to be wishy-washy, right? And that's all I'm feeling right now. But look, when I get back to New York, I'll start brainstorming another concept. Maybe we can even revisit this in a little while, see if Lee ever changes his mind. I won't waste your time the next time."

Sadie may have cared about me, but right now she looked completely exhausted. "I'll talk to Karl, and see what he thinks," she said. "Jacob, I love you, but frankly—right now, I don't think 'the next time' is up to you."

THE BLOCK LOOKED LIKE A WAR ZONE, MISS DOLORES SAID. She'd been sitting in her living room, watching the latest episode of *Jeopardy!*, when all of a sudden there was a rumble followed by what sounded like a car collision. When the fire department arrived and made their way through the dust, it turned out that the facade of my building's top floor had simply peeled off and made straight for the ground. Now she and her husband were staying with their daughter in Bed-Stuy, awaiting the insurance company's verdict. That shouldn't be a problem, because the accident was purely an act of God, she emphasized. Nobody was at fault.

"I don't understand," I said. I envisioned my bedroom with the ceiling ripped off, all of my belongings exposed to the rain.

"That's the good news," she explained. The structural integrity of the room was preserved; it was only all of the bricks outlining my window that had fallen down. It was lucky that I wasn't at home, she said. And if it wasn't too much of a hassle, I might consider staying wherever I was until everything got sorted out.

The sum of all this, I told Ruth, was that my stay in Chicago was now indefinitely extended, because I didn't have the funds to put myself up in a New York hotel and I did not want to crash on a friend's couch. My mother and Harold had flown to Costa Rica for their annual winter vacation and didn't mind if I stuck around by myself. So now it was just me, in my mother's house, alone, sleeping in my teenage bedroom, doing absolutely nothing at all.

Ruth offered her condolences about my apartment, and my latent dread that my adult bedroom would just fall out of the sky. "But you can't deny it's a good opportunity to reset and think about what comes next," she said. "It sounds like your boss is really unhappy about this thing."

"That's understating it," I said. "I told her I might need to remain in Chicago a while longer and she said there was no rush. So now I'm back to writing about albums, for now. I don't think anyone is paying much attention."

Ruth asked me to sum up where I was at the moment. I took a second to formally locate my feelings. It was hard to say—I was disappointed, and even angry, about the retroactively visible boundaries of my relationship with Seth. He had tried to let me in, and I hadn't noticed, and after that he hadn't tried again. I'd returned to this as I wondered how Lee, of all people, had known what he was thinking toward the end—not myself, not Kelsey, not even Rachel Watkins. We were close, and even if we weren't the closest and even if I was depressed about my father and even if I was like every other oblivious teenager who needs the obvious declared and lit up in neon in order for something to take hold, he should've known he could count on me. But maybe it was something in my affectation, or my demeanor, or my general everything that held him at a distance. That was hard to grapple with, in the present, as I couldn't remember exactly how I'd been at that age. I could only accept that it hadn't been enough.

"I meant more with the investigation," she said. "You haven't really said much about what happened with Lee. What do you mean he knew what Seth was thinking at the end?"

"Oh," I said, somewhat embarrassed I'd misinterpreted her question. I hadn't even realized that I'd skipped ahead in our conversation to the dilemma I was facing about my future employment, without spelling out exactly why I was at a crossroads.

She didn't react at all as I told her about Lee's theory that Seth had killed himself. When her silence persisted, I checked in to see if the connection had dropped. "I'm here," she said. "I'm just processing." We didn't talk for a moment, and I switched the phone to speaker so that I could grab another beer.

A minute later, Ruth asked if I was still there. "To be honest," she said, "it doesn't surprise me." I asked if she could explain, because I was having a hard time with that part. "Obviously it's surprising, but it's not a new thought. Didn't you wonder about that over the years?"

"Maybe for a moment, but not really," I said.

"That does surprise me. There's only so many mysterious ways one can die."

I took the phone off speaker and put it back to my ear. "It just didn't seem possible. Seth was . . . I don't know, Seth seemed happy at the end. We were seeing each other here and there. Enough to pick up on whatever was going on with him. So it never occurred to me." I believed it was something to do with his stomach, I believed in the family's right to privacy, and the sum total of this belief was the firm knowledge, today, that I was a complete idiot.

"I don't think it was as simple as him being happy or not," she said. Ruth hadn't grown up anything like Seth—her parents supported her, she was white, her attraction to the same sex had lasted exactly for the duration of her time at Mount Holyoke. But she understood something about the crushing burden one could feel to make something of yourself, she said, because that's what other people expected of you. In moments when she felt like quitting her shit-ass corporate job and telling Donald they needed to move to the woods or Argentina or wherever, she realized she didn't really have that much mobility. Sure, she could uproot her entire life, but it would uproot how everyone else saw her. That was something she wasn't ready for, even if the cost was her own happiness. And that was the sobering thought, in the end: Life could slowly condition you for disappointment, and melancholy, and a general abdication of everything that had once defined you, and you could only swallow it. "Or find another way out, like Seth did."

Hearing this took me aback, because throughout our friendship I'd always considered Ruth's brand of cynicism to be a defense mechanism, the way everyone was a little cynical—not something she'd consciously thought through and accepted. "That's crazy, because I've never felt that way," I said. Wasn't life just doing what you wanted? Within reason, of course, because we were bound by our responsibilities to others. But we were in control of ourselves, and those responsibilities couldn't—or rather, shouldn't—prevent us from seizing that control and pursuing our desires.

The sharpness of Ruth's cackle forced me to hold the phone away from my ear, as the sound filled up the room. "I'm happy it's that easy for you," she said. "But, you know, sometimes it's harder."

IT WAS STILL EARLY WHEN WE GOT OFF THE PHONE, SO I DEcided to heed Ruth's belief in me and do what I wanted. This time, Natalia didn't turn down my invitation to hang out by citing the hour or the fact that it was a weeknight. Forty-five minutes later she was sitting on my mom's couch, just as we'd done in high school, only now we had wine.

The night with Ben hadn't come up. I had run through a truncated version of my discussion with Sadie, and the possibility of losing my job; I folded in Lee's theory about Seth's suicide, prompting a suspiciously understanding nod. "Don't tell me you'd worked this out for yourself," I said. She hadn't thought about it, she said, but it made sense now that I said it. That it *made sense* is partly why I was at a loss for what I should do about this podcast, which felt distant and unnecessary, but was still tied to my employment and career and future in New York, even, because what else did I have to do there besides work? Especially now that my apartment was fucked.

"You need a more existential view," Natalia told me, on the couch. I'd put the television on mute, just to have something on, and Guy Fieri was currently expressing joy over a hamburger. "You know, work sucks. You do it or you don't, until you die." She'd been born in Ukraine, she reminded me, in a dirt-poor village filled with alcoholics who beat their wives and mistresses. A literal fucking wolf had bitten her in the leg when she was a child, leaving a scar I could still see as she bunched up her pant leg, revealing a faint divot running alongside her ankle. But she was here now. Life was about surviving, until you could make sense of it. Sometimes you didn't even make sense of it. You just kept going until you were dead too.

I made a face and tried not to look too closely at her ankle. "I know about the unknowable," I said. "I *have* been to a few funerals in my life." To this expertly delivered point she only shrugged and drank her wine.

Natalia was wearing a white cable-knit sweater over black jeans, and was nestled in the corner of the couch. I was sitting next to her, not too close but not that far apart either. I didn't know what we were doing, exactly; we were friends, but neither of us were dating anyone, and both of us were living at home. I was conscious of looking at her too much, because I understood looking sometimes implied something that wasn't always the case, but after a few glasses of wine I accepted that I was too weary to think about the ramifications.

We weren't talking. I refilled our glasses. The light from the living-room lamp cast attractive shadows over her face, and I got a very stupid idea that I justified by thinking: we're both in our thirties.

"Hey," I said, very boldly.

She looked at me blankly. "Hello."

"I was thinking . . ." I adjusted myself on the couch, so I was sitting straight up. "We've been spending some time together."

"Uh-huh . . ."

"And . . . look, I realize bringing this up is a cliché on several different levels, but I keep thinking about what it would be like if we gave it another shot."

Natalia smiled like she absolutely understood where this was going, her expression holding steady like a record needle following a groove. "I see . . . What do you mean by 'it'?"

"I don't know, I just know that I like spending time with you, and I keep wondering why we haven't made out already."

She laughed, which I tried to take as a good sign, and changed her position so she was facing me. "Jacob," she said, suddenly very serious. "You are . . . not unpleasant to hang out with. But come on, even if you're being moody about it you're still going back to New York."

"I am, eventually. I'm not saying we should date from long distance or anything. But . . . we should definitely make out, I think."

She laughed again, though not unkindly. "I think," she said, gently patting my shoulder like a coach giving a pep talk, "that some doors are closed forever, and with good reason."

I nodded and tried not to feel too embarrassed for putting myself out there. Looking at her again I got another goofy idea and put my hand on her ankle, near the scar. "Okay, but did I ever tell you about how potatoes are a perfect expression of love?"

She rolled her eyes so intensely I thought she might have hurt herself, and swatted me away. "Don't be ridiculous." I laughed, and we went on drinking the wine and bullshitting until she said she had to wake up early the next day and should probably call an Uber.

As she pulled on her jacket, she asked how long I was staying in town. I had no clue, I said. I didn't know how long it would take to resuscitate an apartment in a state of semicollapse, and so it was looking like I'd be in Chicago for at least another week—maybe longer. "I don't know, it's kind of nice. I don't know anybody here, not really. My mom is out of town. I can just sit in my room, looking over the old school newspapers and playing *Guitar Hero*. Fully regress into some pathetic teenage memory, fuck it."

We went downstairs, and I put on my shoes so I could walk her outside. "You know," she said, before I opened the door, "not that it should change your mind, but I keep thinking about what Seth would've said about all this."

Now I couldn't help myself: "Oh, so you admit you've thought about what I'm up to?"

She *tsk*ed dismissively. "Anyway, my thinking stalls out when I remember it was fifteen years ago that we were friends. Soon it'll be twenty, and then thirty, and then eventually, in the summation of everything we've ever done and everyone we've ever known, Seth will rate as this very small figure. If you want to look at it like that."

I looked at her like she needed to give me a break. "Well . . . I feel better already."

"But what I do know is that you two were close. Maybe not as close as you could've been. Maybe not as close as you wanted. But that is clear, in my memory: 'Jacob and Seth were friends, Jacob and Seth were friends.' It's so fixed in my mind. It matters, you know? Whatever he didn't tell you, it wasn't because he didn't care, I know that much. And"—I took my hand off the door, surprised by this burst of disclosure—"oh, God." She laughed, somewhat wildly. "I can't even say it, I feel like a moron."

Her hand made its way from her side to my face, startling me. "He would've understood, okay? Whatever you do, he would've understood. Even if you end up doing the wrong thing. But I don't think that'll happen." She kept it in place for a beat, before she slapped me—not hard, but not gently either. I stepped back, stunned by whatever that meant. "And if you ever try to kiss me again, I'll fucking kill you."

After collecting myself I nodded and opened the door. When I unlocked the gate, she gave me a very long, very close hug. "Text me before you go back to New York?" I said I would, and watched as she disappeared into the car, before pulling off into the night.

WHEN I WENT BACK INSIDE, I FORAGED MORE OF HAROLD'S Christmas whiskey and retreated upstairs to my bedroom. The house was silent, except for the soft *whoosh* of the elevated train rolling past my window. The recurring rumble and noise had kept me up when we'd first moved here, but I'd slowly grown used to it and sometimes didn't remember there was a train at all. Only when I opened the blinds and saw the lights rush by did I realize there was something out there. Even now it still surprised me to see the train, as if there wouldn't be another train five minutes after that, and another train five minutes after that.

I thought about what Natalia had said. Maybe I'd moved too quickly in my meeting; maybe there was still a way to go forward with the podcast, like Sadie had suggested. I didn't know everything about Seth, but I knew enough to say what he'd been like, at least to me, and what I wanted from my pursuit of the truth. Kelsey, Joy House, Rachel, Natalia, Chicago, the bit of Lee that he was willing to share—possibly there was a story here, from the work I'd done so far. And if I included the voices of everyone else who'd known him, too, it might fill out into a complete picture. It wasn't a murder mystery, but it was something—something that other people could understand, even if they hadn't known Seth, in order to understand something about themselves. He could be a symbol next to all the other symbols, a stand-in for something greater and deeper about the way life worked. It mattered how he'd seen himself, but it also mattered how other people had seen him, too, and what he'd meant to them. And maybe we could even fold in the theory about his suicide in order to spark a larger conversation about, I don't know, suicide.

As I cycled through these considerations I felt mildly ashamed how quickly I'd laid it out, as though I were making a pros and cons list about an apartment listing. What Rachel and William had said echoed back to me—the idea that I might only be exploiting Seth by dredging all this up for the public. After all the people I'd talked to, I knew a little more about where Seth was at the end of his life. But those final moments—more than that, his final feelings and final thoughts in the days leading up to his last one—remained unexplained. And in searching for the answer, all I'd found were the limitations of my ability to understand, and the depths of how unsatisfied I felt.

I took a deep breath and tried not to spiral. Once again the emotional valences and logistical permutations of the project sprawled infinitely in my mind; I could perceive every angle, and every angle splitting off from those angles, like a river thick with tributaries. But rather than filling me with unresolvable panic, these myriad interpretations receded toward something resembling zen. It almost shocked me, this feeling, but I held it in and tried to understand it as something that might be true.

In New York, Reggie had requested that the company send me a USB microphone, so that I could continue refining my narration when I worked at home. Since we'd last recorded, I'd shown him drafts of potential scripts for upcoming episodes, but he'd insisted that talking out loud was the only way to arrive at the proper combination of words, the one that would sound just right when our listeners hit play.

"Think about all the people you've interviewed," he'd said. "They're not reading off a script. They're just talking." I was the writer, but this wasn't writing, and through my ongoing refinements he'd pushed me to break down that barrier of literary pretension and come closer to speaking my truth, whatever that might be. I often didn't know why people talked about the concept of "my truth," as though this existed separately from "the truth," a concept that I hoped might bond all sorts of people, not just the ones who seemed predisposed to agree with me. But it was all I had to offer at this point.

I'd brought the microphone with me to Chicago but hadn't touched it, as I'd been too wrapped up in my interviews. Now I retrieved it from my luggage and plugged it into my laptop. I was struck by the need to say something, something I couldn't put into writing but that might emerge if I allowed myself to talk as though I were being interviewed myself, without any consideration for how it might slot into the narrative I'd created.

I opened the recording software he'd instructed me to use and checked the audio levels to make sure everything was functioning. In a different window, I opened up a selection of the recordings Reggie had edited from the interviews I'd conducted. Immediately I closed out these edited versions and loaded up the raw audio—the sprawling material encompassing the hours and hours I'd spent talking about Seth with the people in his life.

I'd provided my notes and given direction in the studio, but I hadn't listened to these unedited recordings since the moment I'd handed them in. I remembered what everyone had to say, but I wanted to hear it again, before I decided to join them.

Transcripts from Untitled Seth Project (canceled)

"HUMOR IS IMPORTANT IN A PERSON; SOMETIMES I THINK IT'S the only thing. I should rephrase: It's okay to not be funny, I suppose, but to be the type of person who can't even register humor—that's a nightmare. Or at least it's my nightmare. Did you know there are some people who don't understand irony? I don't mean people who aren't ironic—that's completely fine. But there are people who don't even know that irony exists. You try to be droll, or clever, or two-faced, and they think you're talking literally. For example my barber, Steven. He does amazing things with his scissors. But last time I saw him, I had to wait an extra hour, and when he apologized I said something like *It's not a big deal, I can just pay my rent check tomorrow.* And he was really worried, like he'd actually gotten me in trouble. Obviously I was just saying words. I pay my rent online, anyway. But that's the type of thing most people can't recognize, at all. Do you know what I'm saying? Maybe you don't.

"One time Seth and I went to Hot Topic together. We tried on a lot of belts. White belts, studded belts, studded white belts. We looked so good. We looked so *fashionable.* I mean, we looked horrible. Objectively, we did not look good in the belts. We knew we did not look good in the belts, but still we kept trying them on, because it wasn't like we were hurting anyone. Maybe the clerk. You know, I do feel bad about the clerk. She had to put a lot of belts back on the rack, and she did not seem happy about it. But so what, I've worked retail. Shit happens.

"Okay, so maybe we were jerks. But we weren't callous. We weren't ignorant to the hassle of putting back several belts. We were trying to have a good time. We weren't attracted to each other, and we weren't old enough to go to bars, and we weren't old enough to do a lot of things. Still, we could try on silly clothes for an hour. We had a problem, and then we adapted. Life's hard when you're fifteen years old and gay in 2002, even if you live in Chicago. But you deal. I think I got that from Seth. I know I didn't get that from high school. I mean, do you remember [*five-minute ramble about Mr. Henderson the calculus teacher, unusable*]? Yuck, yuck, yuck. Anyway, what were we talking about? Is any of that good?"

—Kevin Randle, speaking at the Lincoln Park La Colombe

"Up at Evanston Township they had a Russia Club with these really neat shirts, all red, the hammer and sickle on the front, and on the back, text that said THE PARTY IS OVER. We thought that was so funny. We didn't go to ETHS, but we'd hang out with kids from ETHS, and whenever we saw one of those shirts we'd just fall over laughing. So what could we do? We bought shirts from the Russia Club, even though we didn't go to ETHS. We wore them happily for, I don't know, a couple of months. I don't have it anymore. I don't know what happened to it. I think my mom threw it out. I definitely didn't take it with me to college. Anyway, during this time Seth decides he wants to start a Russia Club at Sayers. Did you ever start a club at Sayers? You didn't? You had to get a teacher sponsor first, and then fill out an application. But we couldn't get a teacher sponsor. In fact, every teacher said we were crazy. Even the friendly ones, they said it was suicide.

"And, God, do you remember Ms. Krystal? The one who dated that baseball player? [*Laughs.*] Yeah, you remember. She taught European History so we figured we might as well ask. I guess we didn't know how much of a Republican she was. She started *yelling at us*, I swear to God. It came out of nowhere. Well, we'd just asked her to sponsor the Communist Club, I guess. Yeah, that's what we were calling it. No, I don't know why we changed the title. Maybe to be funny. Anyway, she starts threatening to get us suspended, and she'll call our parents, and do we have any idea about what happened in Vietnam and so forth.

"Now, at the time I didn't really have any political beliefs. I was . . . fifteen years old. I know that's privilege talking, in other countries you have to be with it by the time you're out of diapers, but I just wasn't. But Seth, he just starts reaming her out about how she doesn't understand what she teaches, how she's generalizing an entire country, several countries in fact, she hasn't even read Marx or Engels or Lenin. Now, has Seth read Marx or Engels or Lenin? No. And Ms. Krystal was an asshole, but she had studied this stuff, even if she drew the wrong conclusion. But she doesn't know he hasn't read Marx or Engels or Lenin, so what happens is they start debating, right there in her office: Ms. Krystal, who doesn't know anything, and Seth, who definitely doesn't know anything. Just two forces, butting heads over something unresolvable. Long story short, the club never happened, and Ms. Krystal never said hi to me in the hallways again. But I think about that: the insistence that you're right, even when you're wrong, because you're probably right. It takes a lot of courage, I'll tell you that. I don't know if I have it but I hope to."

—Kelsey Winters, Skyping from Los Angeles

"Rachel told me what was going on, and where she thinks you're going with all of this, but she didn't tell me not to speak with you. She let me make my own decision, which I appreciate, because I understand the importance of correcting the record. Of speaking for yourself. And the truth is that I'm not a confrontational guy, honestly. I can count the number of times I've been in a fight on one hand. It's not a good experience for me. My teeth start chattering, my armpits start sweating, everything seems to exist in this awful state where the wrong move could lead to serious, serious trouble. My father is a lawyer, and growing up, he made me intimately aware of how intent did not matter, how an accident could happen and all of a sudden your life is changed forever.

"It's not with tremendous pride that I think about the funeral. I don't want to make it out to be some gigantic heroic act. I know how word gets around, how it's gotten around. It's easy to sit here and say that I was protecting Seth's honor, but that didn't appeal to me at all. The truth is, I was furious. We were already weeping and holding hands and thinking about our friend, when someone said a situation was developing. And it surprised me that it was Lee—I mean, I liked Lee. [*Unintelligible.*] Well, it's true. I hadn't talked to him since I graduated, so it was a little devastating to hear that not only was Lee involved, but he was involved in something *right now*. But pretty quickly that devastation turned to what I can only describe as pure, incandescent rage.

"I have an open enough mind about what addiction forces you to do. My younger brother struggles with opioids, and I don't think he's in the clear. But there's a line. And we can debate where that line is, but for me, it's as simple as: don't sell drugs at the funeral of the person who died from the drugs you sold him. So we're standing there, waiting to meet his parents in the condolence line, and humming with anger about where this is going to go. I say 'we,' and I'm talking about David, Jay, Bobby P., Samson. We all loved Seth. We looked at him like a brother, someone we wanted to protect. We were all worked up about Lee and ready to do something about it. And Bobby P.—Bobby was nuts. We don't talk so much these days, it's a different story.

"But, yes, it was Bobby who waited until we were outside and made a beeline for Lee, who was smoking a cigarette. Shoves him right in the chest and tells him to get the fuck out of there. And Lee was not a wilting flower—he was not the type of guy to bow his head and say, *You're right, how inappropriate.* He told Bobby to go fuck himself and shoves him back. By now I can tell a situation is unfolding. I'm beginning to sweat, my eyes are going fuzzy. But it's necessary, I know that, so I go to back up Bobby, who is now talking bullshit with Lee and the rest of his friends, a true bunch of degenerates about whom I have nothing nice to say.

"It's a blur, what happens. It was years ago and I wasn't in the right state to remember much now of everything as it was happening. I just remember a lot of shouting. A lot of gesturing. I didn't know what was going to happen. I wasn't going to stomp out someone at my friend's funeral, even if I was worked up. But I do remember that something changed when Lee realized I was yelling at him. Like I said, we got along. He didn't say anything about it but I could see it in his eyes—a dimming of the self-preserving instinct. He got quiet, even as he was still yelling. And he continued to yell at us as he backed off, *but he was backing off.* It was his choice, I do remember that. Of course Bobby does make it out to seem like we stomped him out of the parking lot, but that's just mythmaking. It didn't make me feel good to think about. It wasn't a fun story to tell at the bar and show off how brave we were. Except that's exactly what Bobby did, which is how the better story spreads, I suppose.

"Like I said, it's not something I think about with tremendous pride. I think of us as little boys, frankly, each on a different side of an uncrossable barrier, making threats that weren't going to go anywhere. And I don't think Seth would've been proud of me either. I think he would've said the entire situation was ridiculous, and that we should all calm down. The line for him was much different, I know that, and that's something I'm still thinking about today."

—Patrick Wagner, Skyping from Boston

"I've had a lot of time to reflect. You see people come and go—at first they announce themselves with wonderful fanfare, and by the end they're backing out of the room, hat in hand, trying not to get your attention. Most people don't want to admit when their time with you is over. It's easier to let it fade, to cast everything into the realm of 'remember when' and 'wasn't that a great time' when all of a sudden it's ten years later and you can no longer recall if someone's father is dead or alive. I've had that conversation before, where someone asks me how my mother is doing and I remind them she died seven years ago, not a short time but not all that long either. But it's difficult to think about the scale we're currently operating on. You're, what, thirty-one? I'm thirty-three years old. That's nothing. *That's nothing.* The majority of life experiences that might happen to us have yet to happen. We're so bereft of real perspective, everything feels so immediate and consequential, when in reality the bulk of it will average out to nothing. Nothing at all. I look at arguments I had a year ago and feel completely alienated from their substance, I can't understand how I ever cared. I look at people I dated and it's amazing I ever felt any kind of affection for them. I exist in a perpetual state of surprise that anything has happened whatsoever. You can quote me on that.

"Now it's possible I take too long of a view on things. I've been criticized for my stagnancy. Yes, I smoke pot. Yes, I drink alcohol. I've taken ketamine. I've taken ecstasy. I've taken mushrooms, acid, you name it. One thing I come back to is that people like Seth, their deaths serve as a fixed point in time. All this growth, all this change, all this reflection that people talk about—it's a bunch of shit. People don't change over time. They exist before and after events. That's it. And death is one of those events, it pulls people across some threshold, and they can't go back.

"Imagine a series of doors, lined up in front of each other. Some doors are separated by a few feet; some doors are separated by a few miles. In between each door is another version of you, one who's yet to cross the next threshold. Now imagine that you're using a telescope to look through those open doors. Perhaps a telescope isn't the right metaphor. Maybe the doors aren't the right metaphor either. I'm sorry, I'm not making any sense. I did smoke some pot before we started. My point is when I think about Seth, I don't think about Seth. I think about myself. In particular I think about myself at twenty years old, which is about sixteen doors ago. Who do I see? I'm not sure, because he's very far away, but I know he's looking back."

—Ian Tremaine, Skyping from his apartment in Berlin

"It's difficult for me to be nostalgic, or sentimental, or sweet about the past. I don't turn over rocks, expecting to find treasure. I look at rocks and go, *These are rocks.* Of course it has something to do with my upbringing. I'm not oblivious to myself. It's very difficult to think about the past when the present is so present. I don't think I was able to calm down until high school, and by that point I was already mean. And in America, meanness is a shield. Nobody tries to mess with a scowling girl in black eyeliner who doesn't talk.

"[*Unintelligible.*] Why did I let you ask me out, then? You asked very nicely, and you were cute. It wasn't a problem that you obviously had no idea what you were doing, not at first. But eventually I just wanted to go out with someone who had it figured out. That we were teenagers, and this was not likely to find in an American high school, did not factor in my thinking. It led to some poor dating decisions when I was in college, though I don't need to tell you about that. The point is that nobody had anything figured out, back then. Not even a mean girl in black eyeliner from Ukraine, raised by alcoholics and hooligans.

"And I really don't think Seth had anything figured out. That's your mistake, I think: you look at him and see someone who was showing you a different side to the world, someone who was funny and clever and kind to a degree that our other classmates weren't. And maybe he was, but he was also a teenager. I adored him, but I always saw that side: nervous, unsure, not particularly sophisticated.

"Yet I don't think he was posturing about that. He was honest about it, at least with me. Maybe because I was mean, maybe because he sensed I wasn't easy to impress. With you, he could be this magical older brother who understood the way of things. With me, he could admit he wasn't always up to it. And that honesty was impressive, it was. I don't know if it was intentional, but he didn't try to cover it up. Eventually he did, from the sound of things, but that's how I'd like to remember him: as himself, the good and bad, the certain and uncertain."

—Natalia Ramazanoff, Skyping from
her apartment in Chicago

"At first it's fun to be a man from nowhere, a man without a past. Clint Eastwood crossed with Wolverine and Cloud Strife. When I was younger, I loved the power to walk into a room and be 'the fun guy,' who makes the night come together. Even then, I had the ability to see how uncomfortable other people were, how they thought before they acted, how they'd hover and linger before picking their moment. I never had that issue. I just did what I wanted, more or less. It's what brought Ben and Lee and myself together—we had this edge to us, you couldn't tell us how to behave. It felt like we'd discovered some secret about life, a way to be that nobody else had figured out yet. Certainly not the other students at Sayers, who we thought were losers.

"No, Seth and I were never particularly close. He and Lee were friends. He and I were friendly, but we never spent time one-on-one. I think he figured I didn't need him around, that I wasn't looking for some kind of perspective that only wise Seth could provide, and that wasn't incorrect. Whatever he had to say, I probably wouldn't have listened. It's not that his death didn't affect me, I'm not a sociopath, but he wasn't the first person I knew who'd died. Not the first friend, even, and not the first friend to die from drugs. It was sad, but not unprecedented. It didn't make me want to clean up my act. And besides, I didn't use all that much—I didn't have a problem, or so I thought.

"It's partly why I left Chicago without telling anyone—I

just had the feeling that if something was going to change, it wouldn't be here, where I knew too many people. I know everyone's doing well, everyone who's still around. Lee figured himself out. Erica got married. I'm sorry to hear you didn't hit it off with Ben, but he's not a bad guy. Still, I couldn't be in that environment. People become too familiar. Places become claustrophobic. A clean break can make you feel clean. That's what convinced me to leave, I think. Seth and I weren't close, but I know he wanted something else for himself, and he never got it. And the denial of that—the idea that you could run out of time before you got to where you needed to be—just seemed so overwhelming, something I needed to avoid for myself.

"It's harsh to say, but I never wanted to be the inspiration for someone else getting their shit together. I wanted my own life, not just a passing mention in someone else's. So I try not to take what I have for granted, and I'm happy to talk with you now, even if I'm not sure I understand where any of this is going."

—Hector Aviles, Skyping from Houston

"I'm not ashamed of my past. It's not something I want to explain to my daughter, necessarily, but I'm not ashamed. What I'd tell her is that sometimes you're young, and you're looking for fun, and you have a confidence that allows you to think about yourself and your needs as disposable. It doesn't seem to hurt, if you get hurt. You're resilient and flexible, you like to party and you don't give a fuck, maybe you've been burned but you're flying high. You feel as I imagine how robots feel, cold and hard and fast and sleek, and you're fueled by something more powerful than a nuclear reactor.

"I've thought about this a lot, obviously. Something good has to come from giving five hundred unsatisfying blow jobs.

I'm exaggerating, of course. What you learn is how other people are comfortable treating you—not *how* they treat you, but the calculations they make in whether or not to acknowledge you as a total person. It's a light in the eyes, you can see it dim at the moment Todd is about to ask if you want to go to his bedroom and see his record collection. That's what kept me going, I think—this feeling that I had the power, even if everyone else saw me as powerless, even if every joke about the town bicycle and pump was applied to me. Other girls were even meaner, as you can imagine, and I remember how I'd think to myself: *I could drain your boyfriend dry, do you want to test me?* I saw it as an act of grace, that I had such restraint. You're very arrogant when you're young. In the end, a blow job is a blow job.

"Seth wasn't like that. He wasn't the only person who was nice to me—my life wasn't unhappy, it was just sort of cheap. But Seth was authentic, he showed concern. I think I brushed him off initially because he was so . . . friendly, you know, sometimes you can't gauge if that's real or an act. But I'd see him around Joy House, and it didn't look like when he was doing well, and when we talked he seemed so exhausted, so tired—yet he always asked after me, he always paid attention. I have this memory of us lying on the couch, when he must have been strung out, and I must've been stoned myself, and he was just mapping out how I should go to community college and transfer to a bigger university in a few years. He'd stop talking for long stretches, but he'd always come back to the conversation. Sometimes we'd talk about books. One time we picked up food and he just spent the entire walk asking me about my mother.

"It's what was on his mind, as we were wasting our time with people who didn't care about anything at all. He didn't talk about himself like he had a way out, a path to something different—but he made me think it was possible for me. It's hard to find people who care that much, people who aren't just being fake-nice or fake-curious. I don't know how much it counts for, in a world like ours, but I haven't forgotten about it, and I don't think I ever will."

—Erica Pickering, Skyping from Downers Grove

"It's a terrible thing, telling your students one of their classmates died. You remember Caroline Blanchard. That was an awful day. Most young people can't wrap their heads around the idea of finality. The cliché is that everyone young is filled with fire and brio and not much sense, and I understand the risks of generalization, the nuances that exist from person to person, but by and large—in my experience, that is—I've found it to be true. Young people can be geniuses, but they're often just very silly.

"Don't disagree with me. I'm too old to be disagreed with. I've done nothing with my life besides teaching and parenting and if I want to have an opinion about what's essentially the overlap, I can. It's not easy, shepherding that emotion. You want to say: Look, this happens. Life is finite. Death is real. Cherish what you have. Platitudes, yes. But helpful platitudes. I've never understood why people look down on platitudes. Sure, they're not original, and they gloss over quite a lot. But they become platitudes because they ring of truth, more often than not. Such as live, laugh, love—absurd language, risible in most contexts, likely to make anyone with a college degree roll their eyes. *But that's what a good life is.* Living, laughing, loving—who could disagree? A young person could, that's who. They'd say something about cynicism, clarity, the need for looking at the world as it is, not as you want it to be. I don't disagree. We have to approach reality and interrogate it when we can.

"But also: we have to accept that interrogation most often leads to nothing. You do the right thing because it's the right thing, but right, wrong—all of it ends up in the same place. I'm not saying nothing matters. Everything matters. The young people have it right, on this. But learning how to live with the fact that everything matters, and yet there's very little you can do to wrap your arms around the everything—that takes a lifetime. Still, you try, and you try to help other people along.

"When we learned that Seth died, it was a very sad day. He was beloved by the students, yes, but also the teachers. Why isn't there a bench dedicated to him, like there is for Caroline Blanchard? I'll tell you why: because he wasn't going to be the last student to die, and you can't have a school covered with benches. That's where all this goes, all this memorialization, all of this processing, all of this reflection and grief and maturity and coming to terms: benches, benches, benches. Hallways filled with benches. It's untenable. It doesn't work. So you say a prayer and hope for the best. I'm sorry that's another platitude."

—Martin Stewart, speaking at Jake's Bar

"He was unhappy. He didn't feel good about his life. He wanted something to take him away, and that something happened to be drugs. It happens all of the time. It happened to me. Look, my parents paid attention to me. My mom is a professor. My dad worked for a union. They had good jobs. I had a good upbringing. I didn't want for anything. I went out on my own because it happened to be the way the wind was blowing that day. I remember one time, in therapy, they asked me why I used. They wanted me to go deep into myself and find the reason why I was content to waste my life away. But I wasn't content, is the thing. And I didn't have to go that deep to figure it out.

"You know, everything is so hectic these days. Even before the internet. There are so many pressures, so many things to do, a checklist for this and that and everything in between. On drugs, the small amount of time we have to do any of those things can last forever. You can live inside of a moment for years, literally. Now, you don't end up doing any of those things. It saps your productivity too. You feel bad; like I said, I wasn't content. But you lose the feeling that you've wasted your time. I don't know if that makes sense. Of course, you've wasted your time. Whole years have gone by. But you didn't notice it at all. Off drugs, you notice the time you've missed, and you still might not be content. Does that make sense?

"Things weren't going great for him. Yes, he had a place to live. Yes, he didn't think his parents hated him, and that counts for something. But that sense of being stuck in the mud—it's bad, man. It nibbles you from the inside. People disappear into that mud for years at a time. Life eats them up, and that's the end for them. You're lucky. You do things with your life. You make use of your time. But it's not always so easy. For a long time, I didn't want to live. And now I do. There's lots of reasons why, but the biggest reason is that time passed, for real—not drug time, but actual time. And not everyone gets that chance.

"I feel bad about selling to him. I do. But, and I believe this is true, if it wasn't me it would have been someone else. And I thought . . . I mean . . . [*long pause*] I thought that if it came from me, if we did it together, it would be better. I didn't think about what was really hurting him. Now, I think about it a lot. Not all the time. I can't handle all of the time. But a lot. There's no law that covers it. I can't ask for penance. I'm not religious. But it gnaws on me, it does, and now that I'm where I am, I hope that I can do better. The sad thing, if

I'm being honest, is that his death didn't make me change. I didn't change for years after that. But it's something I regret. You can put that in your podcast, I don't care who gets mad at me. I don't talk to almost anyone from the old days, anyway. And I don't need to talk to anyone from the old days either. I'm trying to focus on my life now. Please put that in too. I'm trying to focus on my life now."

—Lee Finch, speaking at Jacob Goldberg's house

"My last living memory of Seth wasn't anything special. It really wasn't. After a few weeks of phone tag, we'd finally linked up to split a joint and catch the second *Harold and Kumar* before it left theaters. We were broke, and neither of us drove, so we walked all the way from my mom's house to the Bucktown AMC where second-run movies were five dollars every Tuesday. God, I still don't drive, how pathetic is that? But it's nice to walk. It was nice then, and it's nice now. We printed out the directions on MapQuest, and I remember how the sky slowly shaded into darkness, traversing this path we never observed on foot. That part of the city didn't feel like Chicago, up close. The cars sped up, the sidewalk felt like a desert, and whenever we came across somebody they didn't look our way. It felt like Los Angeles, almost. Even Phoenix, where I've been before. Well, not New York. The point is it could've been anywhere, almost, and the only thing that made it familiar was us.

"At the movie theater we split a large popcorn, and an extra-large Dr Pepper. Afterward, we played *Time Crisis 2* in the lobby, which that movie theater used to have. We probably beat a few levels, because I was great at that game. Seth was terrible, but you can carry someone through that. [*Pause.*] I can talk more about this stuff, the details that people want to hear in these types of projects. The re-creation of a scene, as though specificity is enough to pull a stranger across time and space. But it's what happens after that I'm really trying to recall, if I can recall it. We must've talked about going to the Golden Nugget, which was this shitty little all-night diner where you could sit for hours with a plate of cold hash browns. I don't know if they're still open, but I hope they are. But you know, we were broke. We'd split a popcorn and a soda. So we must've decided against it when we remembered we were both out of money. I would've been headed home, because of my summertime work-study job in Evanston, which took an hour to get to on the train. It's sad to think about how much of my life I've spent on trains. [*Laughs.*]

"This is coming back to me now. I remember asking Seth if he was headed in the same direction as me, but even though he also had an early start, he said he had to stay out. 'There's some people I have to see,' he tells me. I don't ask about who he wants to meet at this hour. It's 2007, and I'm nineteen, and it's August. I could've stayed up until dawn, if I wanted, because when you go to sleep, you give up on wringing every last bit of life out of the night. I don't stay up as much as I used to, but I remember that feeling—the belief that even if you're just by yourself, in your room, doing nothing at all, something might happen. It's how I feel right now. But I did have to go to bed back then, because I was tired from the walk and the pot and the movie theater. So I hugged him goodbye and made idle chitchat about hanging out soon. I watched the back of his head walk down Fullerton until I couldn't see it anymore, before turning toward the bus I needed to catch to make it home.

"I know what happens next, because I've looked this up. A couple of weeks later, Seth writes on my Facebook page saying that he's sorry he hasn't been responding to my texts, stuff has been busy for him, but maybe we can hang out later in the week. I didn't respond, at least not there. Thinking about it right now, I can't remember if I texted him, though I hope I didn't ignore him altogether. I wouldn't have left a friend hanging, I don't think, my etiquette was better than that. And if he didn't reply to my text, I would've kept texting him, confident that I'd eventually break through. But I can't say for sure. Either way, we didn't manage to get together before I go back to school. A few weeks later, I receive the phone call telling me he's died.

"I'm trying to remember the last thing he said to me, the exact last thing. [*Long pause.*] It's not coming to me. You know, I can probably make something up—reconstitute the general stuff we talked about and the way we felt about each other into dialogue our friends would believe if I lovingly recalled it at the end of a drunken night. 'Seth looks at me and he says, "I'm glad to have a friend like you, Jacob."' The thing is that we did say shit like that to each other. We were open about our feelings. But I don't know if we said it then. More accurately I can trace the gleam in his eyes and bounce of his hair as he turned to pass the joint or repeat himself as we exited the underpass on our way to the theater. The shape of his body, disappearing into the shadows on his way to the bus. In fact it might be the thing I can recall exactly: the way he looked, the way he laughed and smiled, the general texture of his voice despite its lack of mooring to any particular interaction. Even after concentrating on Seth, rummaging through all my archives to find our photos together, scouring my old journals to see where he popped up, revisiting our LiveJournal interactions and our Facebook interactions and somehow our fucking Xanga interactions, digging deep into the mulch to uncover something profound, something that would surely be revealed if I found a way to access it.

"But that's just not the case. I want it to be the case, but it's not. All that is gone, along with Seth himself, which . . . I can accept it in the abstract but it horrifies me, if I think about it too much. It makes me very sad, I can say that out loud. He's slipping away, Seth. With every year, he's slipping away. Maybe he's already gone. I can't think about that. All that time we spent together, dissolving into something that might never have existed, if I wasn't here to remember it had. And I can't even remember it all that well.

"[*Long pause.*] I wish we could talk right now, is how I feel. That's all I want, is to talk to my friend. That's the truth of all this, past the elevator pitch of what I'm trying to accomplish, past the sales pitches, past the neat and tidy emotional prompts that might render his life legible for strangers. I don't care about anything else. I wish he was here to help me understand, because without him I can't. I'll never know. And I have to accept that. I know I can accept it, eventually. I just have to believe he's out there, somewhere on his own, somewhere I can't see, even if I know I'll never find him."

—Jacob Goldberg, speaking at his house

Acknowledgments

SEE FRIENDSHIP WAS WRITTEN ON MORNINGS, NIGHTS, AND weekends—through employment and unemployment, in between assignments and occasionally on vacations, on lots of coffee and sometimes, unfortunately, after vaping. I'm eternally grateful to my agent, Kirby Kim, at Janklow & Nesbit for working with me closely on the manuscript, to Eloy Bleifuss at Neon for all his valuable insight and effort, and to my editor, Sophia Kaufman, at Harper Perennial for taking it all the way home.

I could not have afforded to write this novel were it not for my regular work, and the people who kept me steadily employed, among whom I must mention: Nitsuh Abebe, Caryn Ganz, Jane Kim, Kevin Lozano, Amy Phillips, Joshua Topolsky, Ben Williams.

My friends were an invaluable resource in both the writing, and the nonwriting that went into the writing: Meher Ahmad, Blair Beusman, Katie Bloom, Emmy Blotnick, Claire Denton-Spalding, Sam Donsky, Aaron Edwards, Leah Finnegan, Peter K. Jackson, Eleanor Kagan, Jeremy D. Larson, Shelby Lorman, Drew Millard, Lauren Oyler, Brittany Patch, Puja Patel, Amy Rose Spiegel, Tyler Trykowski, and Erin Vanderhoof. Late in the game, Peter Mendelsund provided some priceless advice and perspective. Special thanks to Matthew Richardson and

Daniel Kolitz, my true ride-or-die writing comrades, who read multiple drafts and commiserated on many more late-night texts.

The unconditional love and support of my family—in particular, my mother, Mary Gordon; her partner, Don McDougall; my cousin Mariel Fechik; and my uncle, Jim Gordon—meant everything throughout this process.

And nothing would have been possible without my wife, Jen Vafidis, who was the first person to suggest I might be writing a novel, and read countless drafts with a keen and encouraging eye. I owe her everything, and more.

About the Author

JEREMY GORDON's writing has appeared in the *New York Times*, *The Atlantic*, *The Nation*, *Pitchfork*, *GQ*, and *The Outline*. He was born in Chicago and lives in Brooklyn with his wife, Jen. *See Friendship* is his first novel.